THE DRAMATIC DEAD

To Ava! Enjoy Victor.

BRYAN NOWAK

CHAPTER 1
IN THE VIRGINIAN DUSK

Two figures worked on a mangled and lifeless corpse in the Virginian dusk. Dark liquid oozed out from its broken body, forming a muddy slurry at their feet. The once-fierce creature had given its life violently the day before. The pair of workers had the thankless task of cleaning up the earthly remains.

The nearly two-meter cadaver was too long and heavy to move inside a nearby building's protective embrace. They worked feverishly to pull enough from the large frame to allow them to drag it the rest of the way.

They labored in a forgotten industrial area, past the suburban landscape, row houses, and what many considered the 'bad' part of town. The desolate landscape was filled with post-industrial refuse, which had succumbed to the ravages of urban decay. Their headquarters, of sorts, stood halfway up the rise of a hill dotted only with gnarled trees and crabgrass. Its silhouette painted as desolate a picture as the world surrounding it.

The early day sun had been beating down on them as they took to their task. However, the weather changed rapidly in this part of the country, and clouds now blocked their tormentor. Sustained winds blew with staunch determination. In the distance, lightning struck the ground. The heavens would open up soon and drown the inhabitants of this small corner of the world.

Oblivious to the brewing storm, the pair continued their labor.

One of the two, a strong-looking man in overalls, struggled to remove pieces. He stood at almost six feet tall, topped with a shock of

3

dirty brown hair, which he occasionally shaved bald due to his thinning hairline. His face sported a short, well-trimmed beard. He painted an imposing figure against the early evening sky.

The second person, a young woman, had a thin frame and hair held together in a ponytail, which poked out from the back of a baseball hat. She took the items from the man, carefully examined them, and placed them carefully into a waiting wheelbarrow.

Pulling a knife from his belt, he cut something out of the body, which sprayed fluid everywhere. The extracted organ was gently, almost reverently, handed to the young woman who treated it with a similar amount of respect. It was dreadful work, but the utmost care needed to be taken as the process unfolded.

From out of the nearby building, a third person walked slowly toward them. He was skinnier than the other man and stood slightly smaller. His hair was light brown and his face clean-shaven. His walk suggested he was in no hurry. Or maybe he hesitated to look upon the crude autopsy taking place. He tentatively stopped a few paces away, watching them delicately sever sinew and ligament until salvageable parts were free.

The messy work was always done outside to keep the dirt and grime to a minimum once they transferred the unfortunate victim to the building. The shorter man wanted the most valuable larger pieces torn off for now. "Sad, isn't it?" His voice cracked just a little as thunder broke in the distance.

"Sure is, Dirk. What'd you say happened?" the taller man asked.

"From what I heard, it was a front-end collision. Someone not paying attention. Poor thing didn't deserve this." Dirk shook his head.

The bearded man, Keith, gently pulled another piece from the wreckage. Sinews, of a sort, still held it in place. Using his knife, he sliced through them. A few persistently remained, but they were no match for Keith, whose skill at this work was unparalleled. "This is in good shape. We can use this." He handed the piece to Dirk.

Dirk kicked a little dirt toward the stilled remains on the ground. "Oh yeah, it looks nice." He placed the item in the barrow with the rest of them.

Keith picked up a larger organ from the torso and examined it with the eye of a jeweler appreciating an old piece of jewelry. "Don't worry, baby, we are going to put you back together, good as new." With over twenty-five years in the business, Keith was the best of the best. If he said a part could be reused, then it could.

"Hey, guys, watch the fluids leaking out. I don't want this shi— I mean, stuff everywhere."

Keith raised an eyebrow at his friend. He hated Dirk's swearing as much as Dirk despised Keith's admonishment.

The young woman, no more than sixteen years old, untangled two pieces of metal hopelessly intertwined. "I have to go. Mom wants me home soon."

"Alright, thanks for hanging out with us today. I suppose you want to be paid too, huh?" Dirk said.

"That would be superb," she said. The girl pulled off a bandana she had used to keep her long hair out of her eyes.

"What if I refuse?" Dirk said with an upturned eyebrow.

"Well then, I'll have to tell Grandma."

"Oh, sure, play the niece card. Why don't you get cleaned up, and I'll find you some cash. Cash is still good, right?" Dirk said.

"Are you kidding me? Cash? How old are you exactly?"

"Go get cleaned up, kiddo, before I decide to pay you in knuckle sandwiches."

"Nice, Uncle Dirk, now you think I'm like five." She hugged him and walked off toward the building. "You really need to get a cash app though. I can show you how. Seriously, modernity won't kill you."

Dirk watched her as she made her way back to the shop. Claire was his sister's only daughter. She grew up seeing him as a father figure, and the two were almost inseparable. For most of the summer, she worked at his repair shop. She was the closest thing he had to a child and was coming along well as a motorcycle mechanic in her own right.

"Sad to see these Indian Classics after a wreck. Good thing they called us to scoop it up." Keith pulled another piece out. "A lot of the structure will have to be scrapped. I'll save what I can though. Forks can be straightened, and we can fix the frame."

"Thankfully the rider survived." Dirk turned from the wrecked motorcycle. Keith was the best motorcycle mechanic in the state, possibly the country. Inside the building, Dirk closed the door behind him and switched on the night light for the shop. A neon sign sprang to life above the big bay doors reading, "Dirk Bentley's Motorcycl Repa r." It had once spelled the name of the business correctly until someone came along and shot out two of the letters of the sign.

Reaching into his desk, Dirk brought out five ten-dollar bills. Fifty bucks was about the going rate for his niece. She was worth double the price to him, but if he paid her more, his sister would tell him he was spoiling her. She was his right-hand girl at the shop, quickly learning to do everything from handle customer payments to turning a wrench on the shop floor.

From hanging around the shop as a baby, she developed a fascination with the tools and the loud motorcycles. Dirty brown hair, a family trait, which bleached blonde in the summer, framed her late-summer dark tan. Dirk had told her, more than once, that she was the spitting image of her mother.

He flipped on the television and collapsed into the large desk chair to finish up the day's bookkeeping. Parts needed to be ordered, and invoices had to be prepared. Owning a motorcycle repair shop was a never-ending stream of paperwork.

The newscaster on the screen filled the quiet in the office as he worked. "The series of murders targeting young women from the local high school have police baffled. Running short on clues, the police are asking anyone with information to please call …"

Keith came in from the shower room in the back of the shop, looking like a completely different person than when he went in. "You know, Dirk, something should probably be done about this," he said, pointing to the television report.

In addition to running Caral city's only independent motorcycle repair shop, Dirk was also a private investigator. When he was a teenager, he had romanticized notions of solving cases on the back of his Harley. Dirk had grown up listening to an old radio show called *Yours Truly, Johnny Dollar*, about a suave insurance investigator who always got the bad guy. After exhausting the entire run of the radio program, he knew he wanted nothing more than to be a private investigator.

When his dream of thrilling cases and beautiful clients didn't come to fruition, he'd fallen back on his skills as a cycle mechanic, turning his investigative work into a side gig. His skills in tracking down suspects started, albeit unintentionally, making the police look bad. With the help of a friend in the department, he had brokered a peaceful, if not occasionally contentious, existence with the police. He gave the police a lead and let them make a collar, as it did not interfere with him meeting his client's goals and his payday.

"I've been keeping my eye on it, but no one has asked for our help. Each of the murders looks like a ritual killing, possibly a serial killer. Four bodies, all drained of blood. None of them appear to have been violated in any way. It seems, I don't know … antiseptic. This new one makes five. Bad stuff going on here, lad."

Keith, in addition to being a good motorcycle mechanic, worked as a part-time investigator, was a part-time Methodist pastor, and served as adjunct faculty at the community college. He also wrote a regionally syndicated religion column for the local newspapers. "Well, I've gotta be off. Services tonight, you know. You're going to be there, right?" Keith said as he combed his hair in the dirty mirror hanging from the wall.

"And miss your scintillating sermons? Never," Dirk said.

Keith was dressed in a black pair of polyester pants with a black cotton button-down shirt, complete with a well-worn pair of black leather loafers. An expert at the quick shower, he was in and out in two minutes. He turned toward Dirk again, putting in his clerical collar. Striking his best fundamentalist preacher pose, he shouted, "Let us save this brother Dirk! Let us exorcise his demons!" For flavor, he threw in an Elvis Presley hip swing.

"You're so odd, Keith. Oh, I'm sorry, Honorable Right Reverend Pastor-Brother Keith," Dirk laughed. "I'll be along soon enough. I should probably shower and change."

"El Gran Pastor is a fine title. Feel free to use it. See you there." Keith walked out the door to his truck.

Keith and Dirk had been friends since the first time their parents let them play together at the park. As kids, they would break into industrial buildings as a tag team and fought over the same girls. They were as thick as pea soup as kids and even thicker as adults.

Keith was one of those people who would never be satisfied with a single paying job. His broad range of experience made him an excellent associate investigator, since he knew how to speak on a wide variety of topics to almost anyone. His skills as a pastor had come in handy on more than one occasion during an investigation.

Dirk stretched in his chair, arching his back and shaking out his shoulders before hunching down over the pile of paperwork. Try as he might, the papers held little interest.

The television report and Keith's cajoling had put murder on his mind. The killings seemed like they were part of a pattern, but the pattern was unclear, and there was nothing specific about it to indicate a solid motive. Each girl was about the same basic age and had similar physical characteristics. One victim was African-American, several Hispanic, and the rest were Caucasian of varying ancestry. Dirk was certain the girls weren't being chosen based on their looks.

The bodies were found in well-trafficked areas, as if the killer wanted to be sure they'd be found after he'd killed them. As if taunting the police with his cleverness, the bodies had been cleaned. Another theory Dirk played with was that the killer had intentionally returned the bodies to the families, as if he were bringing back a pair of hedge trimmers borrowed item from a neighbor.

There had to be something else the murders had in common. The theories nagged at him, like a clue hanging out in the fog of the case he could grab if only he were to reach out for it.

A noise from the back of the shop shook Dirk from his thoughts. Claire was still finishing up in the locker room, and he knew it would be a few minutes until she was ready to leave, so she didn't make the sound. Almost all the mechanics were gone from the day, and normally they were working on finishing up at this point anyway.

Dirk shook his head at the noise. It portended a series of events he was all too familiar with. *Here we go again.*

A mist poked out from under the door, filling the room rapidly. Dirk could tell from the smell it was not a fire or anything more alarming. He stared down at the papers, trying to refocus his thoughts on finishing an order form for gaskets and bearing grease.

Tendrils of white stretched out over the floor, circling his desk and his feet like a slow-moving serpent searching for its next meal. Starting out white, it turned green and made a retreat toward the corner of the room where it thickened, appearing solid and yet amorphous at the same time. Out of the vapor, two glowing orbs formed, swirling around each other until they settled where eyes should be if the thing were human. The mist issued a low growl, reminiscent of a wild dog about to attack.

Dirk, still trying to reengage on his paperwork, took notice of the fog and shrugged. "You really need some new material, you know?" Dirk signed a check and slipped it into the envelope with an order form.

"Fear me. Cower in terror at forces from beyond."

"Not interested. You did this last week, and it wasn't all that impressive then. Kind of Halloweenish if you ask me. Maybe I need to put you outside my house on Halloween? Five-year-olds might find it scary," Dirk said, faking an air of disinterest.

"Halloweenish!" The fog suddenly disappeared along with the eyes, and out of it an image of a man formed. "I'll have you know that routine scared the crap out of some kids a few years back! You should thank me. They were going to egg this crate you call a shop!"

The specter took on a more familiar shape to many of those who had spent a significant amount of time in the building. The spirit floated a few inches above the ground and was about the height of an average man. He struck Dirk to be in his thirties, but even the ghost was unsure of his real age. While he had appeared in a variety of clothes since Dirk had known him, this visit he was wearing an old pair of slacks and a loose cotton shirt. He spoke with the accent of an old Southern gentleman. He had a slight glow, as if he had accidently swallowed a flashlight.

He wasn't so much a nuisance as a source of bemusement. When Dirk bought the shop, no one mentioned the ghost haunting it. Dirk often said that realtors were supposed to reveal any reports of paranormal disturbances. Apparently "Victor" had slipped their minds.

After opening his motorcycle repair shop, Dirk noticed the windows were sometimes left open when he arrived in the morning, then the television began turning itself on. Tools went missing and were found in strange places. Dirk, always a fan of the paranormal, eventually made it a point to draw the thing out of hiding and talk to the entity. Sometimes he regretted it, but Victor also had proven his usefulness on more than one occasion.

The mechanics were warned about Victor and understood he was to be essentially ignored as a condition of employment. No one wanted to encourage his frequent tool-stealing and random appearances in the shop. The older mechanics would converse with him on occasion at the end of the day as they were finishing up. Victor, if he felt like it, engaged in the discussions.

"You know, Dirk, this whole murder business is pretty bad. A few of us over on the other side got to jawin' about it and—"

"Oh, not you too!" Dirk let out an exasperated sigh. "I can't get involved until someone hires me to investigate. The police won't tolerate me snooping around in cases unless I have a client. I could be arrested for police interference and lose my license."

Victor leaned forward and adopted an uncharacteristically serious tone. "Don't get your knickers in a bunch! Look, I'm being serious as the afterlife here when I tell you something ain't right. People are saying yungun's are gittn' to the other side and refusing to talk. They're scared out of their wits. Something spooked them in the land of the living. You have to get in the game. Ifn' you do, Dirk, be careful. This isn't your garden-variety murder. This is something else entirely."

Claire walked in the door and right through Victor, "Hey, Big V, how's the big sleep treatin' ya?" Claire had known Victor since she was a baby, and to her, he was about as scary as a cotton ball.

"Claire, I've told you before and I'll tell yeh ag'n, please don't go strolling through me. It's kind of creepy!" Victor said, shaking his fist at her.

"Wait, the ghost is lecturing me on creepy? Interesting," Claire replied, putting her hands on her hips and cocking her head to one side. "Uncle Dirk, I need to get home. Mom is going to be calling soon to ask where I am. And you don't want to be in trouble with your sister, do you?"

"Okay, we can go. Victor, keep your ears open. Let me know if you find out anything useful. The news says that a new victim has been found. If we do get called off the bench, I want to have all-hands-on-deck." Dirk picked up his keys and made his way toward the door.

As an afterthought, he reached into his desk and pulled out his Beretta 92C pistol along with a small bunch of business cards. Across the top were the words "Bentley Detective Agency". He had a hunch he'd need them soon enough.

"See ya, Vic." Dirk purposely walked right through him and out to the truck.

"Tarnation! The living are so annoying!" Victor shouted after Dirk, shaking his head.

CHAPTER 2
QUIET WORDS ON HOLY GROUND

Dirk thought about the murders while he navigated the roads toward his sister's house. A seemingly random pattern emerged with a few key facts the police kept under wraps. Keeping these facts a secret reduced the level of panic in the city, which was already reaching a fever pitch. Hiding clues from the public also allowed the Caral City Police Department a litmus test when the killer surfaced. *And the killer will most certainly surface.*

The victims went to the same school. This was not a helpful fact since almost everyone in the city went to the same schools. Detectives working the case still weren't able to uncover any specific activities tying the victims together. Although, as could be the case, they may not have been asking the right questions. The lack of physical similarities between the victims made it unlikely they were chosen based on those factors alone.

And yet, there were clues consistent with the work of a serial killer. In addition to being found in high-traffic areas, the more recent victims wore identical red dresses. Every victim had been completely drained of blood with no visible indication of significant trauma.

Neither the crime scene techs nor the medical examiner were able to come up with any meaningful evidence aside from small puncture holes in the bodies, which were significant as none of the victims had surgery recently. No weapons were found at the scene, and there were no signs of a struggle. This indicated the murders had taken place at another location and the bodies were then moved.

The deceased were pristine when found. The medical examiner concluded, curiously, that they'd been washed just before they were murdered as he'd found soap residue suggestive of a common bath soap. Exsanguination was listed as the cause of death.

The puncture wounds on the bodies were precise, not jagged like a stab wound. The medical examiner found a small piece of rubber inside of one of the puncture wounds, suggestive of medical-grade tubing. Dirk reasoned this pointed to the murderer having had some sort of medical training. Although, leaving a small piece of surgical tubing in the wound was sloppy for a surgeon.

The police had sent out feelers across the country for other people who had maybe been killed in a similar fashion. To date, they found two more victims in the Pacific Northwest, a boy and a girl, which loosely matched the method of what Dirk considered an execution. Although he couldn't shake the feeling there were more.

Dirk desperately wanted to do some digging. The police would never let him investigate a case without the victim's family retaining his services and them signing the appropriate releases. And yet, Dirk was not without other avenues he could pursue. The news media, feeling a strong undercurrent of proverbial blood in the water, kept reporting every detail over and over again to the point where he could not help but think about the case. Instinct told him it wouldn't be long before someone asked for his help.

After dropping off Claire, he stopped at the gas station for a soda and then made his way toward the church which held Wednesday evening services for people who had busy schedules. He crossed town, cutting through the city center and an old school central city park, which had gone through different periods of use and redevelopment. A few abandoned storefronts, but most were occupied by small businesses and restaurants offering everything from Chinese food to traditional homestyle meals. Store owners and employees were locking up for the night, and a few couples still strolled the walkways of the park. It all looked too serene in a city where people were disappearing and being stalked.

And then there was Victor. Dirk let slip a laugh at the idea of his ghostly partner. The specter could be a major pain in the ass. As a matter of fact, he was often a gigantic pain in the ass. However, he was their representative in the spirit world. He'd never steer the team wrong. If Vic thought something was creepy about the case, Dirk could count on it. He'd proceed cautiously.

The ghost said that the girls were refusing to talk on the other side. From his chats with Victor, likely something had scared them into being mute. Victor had gotten lucky in other cases by poking around, and he had always managed to produce some sort of information from the dearly departed. Granted, it wasn't always apparent what the clue meant, but it often proved important. An investigation was just a matter of putting the pieces together.

The crowd outside the little Methodist church was starting to build. Old ladies wearing overcoats were being helped up the stairs by strong young men while kids ran around in their best church clothes, chasing each other around the large oak tree in front of the church. A few kids hid in the adjacent park and played on the swing set while their parents yelled at them to come inside. He could see Keith standing at the front door, shaking hands with his flock.

"Well, fancy meeting you here. What's it been, like, an hour?" Dirk said.
"Oh, just shut your piehole and take your seat. I think you need some savin' tonight, boy!" Keith responded while putting his hands on Dirk's head. Keith disliked the formal rigors of the being a pastor, believing ceremony got in the way of the real work of the church.

Dirk sat down in the back of the church like he always did, leafing through the order of worship. Nothing new. Regular hymns, someone old that he'd never heard of died in the nursing home, someone else gave birth, and the service committee was looking for people to do a project. Dirk liked the normalcy of it all. It was a relaxing counterpoint to the unpredictability of life.

The service went off as expected, ending with a rousing singing of "O For a Thousand Tongues to Sing." It was Dirk's job to collect hymnals and make sure all the bulletins were pulled. He'd been doing it for as long as he could remember. It gave Keith time to finish and then they would go have a beer. It was their routine.

"Mr. Bentley?" A voice called from the center aisle.

"Yes?" He looked up from his duties to see a woman standing a few feet away. She was wearing a summer dress and clutching a handbag. While her dress could be considered appropriate attire for a church service, her body language suggested something else. Stooped shoulders and tear-worn puffy eyes implied an unspoken brokenness.

"May I have a word with you? Pastor Keith said I should talk with you."

Dirk glanced up in the direction of Keith, who was still shaking hands with the people leaving the church. Keith shot him a glance, pursing his lips tight as he nodded in the direction of the lady. It was subtle, but it gave Dirk all the information he needed. This mother knew loss in a way Dirk couldn't possibly understand. This had to be the mother of the most recent victim.

"Absolutely, you have my attention. Shall we sit?" Dirk said, motioning to the pew.

"Yes, thank you," she said dolefully.

Dirk could usually tell a lot about people from the way they held themselves. In addition to her eyes having a telltale weariness to them, her makeup, which looked like it had been freshly applied, showed streaks where tears had left little valleys on her face. She carried with her the appearance of a woman who was shouldering the weight of the world, and with every step, she lost more of her strength. He would have thought she was beautiful it if wasn't for her defeated appearance. In her hand, she carried a small photograph.

"Mrs. Smithfield, I presume?" Dirk asked.

"Yes, how did you know?"

"In my line of work, I learn to pick up on things," Dirk said.

He didn't want to admit it, but the photo was a giveaway. He'd seen it before with parents suffering the loss of a child; the need to cling to something belonging to them. As if holding onto it meant clutching onto their last connection to their progeny. Releasing the item implied the unfathomable.

"What can I do for you?" Although he had the feeling he already knew.

"You see, well … I'm not sure how to begin. I'm sorry, this is hard for me. My daughter was murdered." She started sobbing immediately.

To find the strength to come forward was Herculean enough. The reason she was talking to him was because the police had run out of leads. He could help, maybe not by solving the case but by finding out more than the police could. The police were by no means incompetent, just constrained in many ways. He had methods they couldn't leverage and a few he was not supposed to use and still did anyway.

"I'm sorry, I shouldn't have bothered you with this. I'm sorry–" Her voice was starting to crack, and she stood to leave.

"Wait, the police gave you my name, didn't they? They told you to find me here, right? Look, I'm not sure I can be of assistance to you, but I'd really like to try. This is painful, but it's more painful trying to go through this alone. Talk to me a bit more, and maybe we can figure something out." Dirk desperately wanted a shot at this case. He hated murder in general, but he hated murderers targeting kids more. He *needed* to stop this or at the very least attempt to bring about a break for the cops to pursue. Even if this never resulted in a dime in his pocket, he'd be satisfied knowing this person was on their way to death row.

Keith had come over to stand next to her in the pew. Dirk was glad. Keith was a great mechanic, but he was an even better pastor. He put his arm around her and held her hand. Keith was in full-on pastor mode now, and he could comfort anyone in times of grief, something Dirk was not terribly comfortable with. She retook her seat, and Keith sat next to her, opposite Dirk.

"All you have to do is talk to me for a bit. Just give me the facts. I don't care how crazy or small the detail is, the more you can tell me, the better. Between the three of us, maybe we can figure out what happened to your daughter." Dirk could sense she was looking for something, and he highly suspected that thing was a little reassurance. Then the dam broke, and she told them the story.

The woman's name was Carla Smithfield, and her daughter Heather had been an intelligent child who always had a flair for the dramatic. The photo Carla held was of a beautiful girl. She was wearing her soccer uniform, and she was holding a soccer ball on her hip. She had a broad smile, which melted Dirk's heart instantly. He had to swallow a sudden upwelling of panic as he realized he could be looking at a photo of Claire.

Dirk and Keith listened while she retold the story of the last time she saw her daughter. It was enough to rip Dirk to shreds.

Carla wiped a few tears from her eyes. "Mr. Bentley, when she left that morning, we had a little fight about her sweatshirt. It was lying on the floor. I told her not to be so careless. She got mad at me. It was such a silly thing to argue about. If I'd only known…"

"Mrs. Smithfield." Keith held her hand as he spoke. "If we only knew when any last moment with our loved ones was, we'd all be different people."

"I would trade a million dirty sweatshirts for even one more minute with my daughter."

Dirk listened, and Keith played the role of a sympathetic pastor. She'd asked for his help, and that act gave him the green light he needed to open his own investigation. Subconsciously, he started formulating a plan. Details, places, and strategies fell into place as the investigator in him took over.

"With your permission, I'd like to start right away. It isn't going to be easy. We'll need to look at Heather's room, maybe talk to some of her friends. It could get very personal, and we may uncover things about your daughter that you don't want to hear. But I promise you, we'll work through it together."

Dirk hated to see anyone like this. She was gutted from the top down, and he knew that no matter how much he found or even if he could bring the perpetrator to justice, there was nothing he could do to fix Clara Smithfield and her husband. All he offered was a little closure. In a world too easily distracted by a million other things, the murder of one teenage girl barely warranted front page news anymore.

In any missing persons case, there was always the chance the person would be found. However, this was murder. Even if he caught the killer, there was no bringing back Heather. He hated these circumstances, but he had a chance to make sure it never happened again. And he had his suspicions the killer was far from done.

Handing her one of his business cards and writing down her phone number and address in his notebook, he promised he'd be in touch. He wanted to get a look at her room soon to see if there were any clues the police missed. But first he needed some answers, and for those he was going to have to talk to one of his police contacts.

Not just any police officer would do.

Dirk pulled out his cell phone and dialed Police Sergeant Carrie Pettygrew as he climbed in behind the wheel of his car. After a few rings, it went to voicemail, suggesting she could not be bothered. "You have reached Sergeant Pettygrew. Sorry I missed your call. I will get back to you as soon as possible." Dirk left a message and hung up.

Carrie was more than just a source in the police department. They had known each other since she was in pigtails and braces. They'd walked to school together as kids. He'd carried her books, and a few times she'd carried his. They were closer than friends. She told him things about cases she shouldn't.

For weeks, he'd been saving details of the case. Over the years of his life as a professional investigator, he'd developed a sense from the desperation in the media and stories he heard from police officers, and he knew when he was likely to get a phone call. As he spread the photocopies, printouts, and clippings out on his kitchen table, he drank coffee and reread his own unofficial notes he'd already read a dozen times or more.

He squeezed every word from what he had available in search of anything the police could have missed. Where there were photos of bedrooms or homes, he used a magnifying glass to see if anything stood out. So far, the chase had come up empty except for a few far-flung theories. Not everything ended up in the papers, and Dirk knew he'd have to visit the homes of the other victims to dredge up more clues. He just simply didn't have enough information at his fingertips.

An old doorbell rang out to announce the presence of a visitor.

Looking through the peephole, he could see the distorted image of a woman in a business suit. She was carrying a couple of bags. He'd have been okay with just a phone call, but showing up at the house was even better, and it appeared she'd brought dinner. Carrie understood him well enough to order his usual without even asking. He could easily do the same for her.

Dirk opened the door to let her in.

Stepping through the threshold, she handed him one of the bags she was carrying. The printing on the bag indicated it was from Wong's Chinese Takeout. She was wearing her blue pinstriped suit, a lace-topped sheer blouse, and wore perfume that smelled like heaven to Dirk. It was sexier than if she'd come to Dirk's door in nothing at all. Carrie understood what made him tick better than he did.

She was short, with medium-length blonde hair and gray eyes. Carrie could have been a runway model or an actress if she had been a little taller. She came from a long line of police detectives, and she was up soon to get her own detective badge.

She was the only woman on planet Earth who could reliably get him to do just about anything if properly motivated. For some reason suits did it for Dirk. She hated wearing them, which made Dirk suspicious. She normally changed before coming over.

"Uhhh, hello?" he said. He contorted his face the way someone would if he'd just opened the door to a three-eyed purple monster.

"What?" she said. "Can't a gal bring Chinese food sometimes? I thought you guys liked that kind of thing. Besides, you said you wanted to talk to me, so here I am. Suspicious much?"

"No, it is just that you never come over in a suit. You are usually dressed like—"

"Pick your next words carefully, Mr. Bentley, or I will take my Chinese food with me and go back to my apartment." Aware he was staring at her suit and simultaneously undressing her with his eyes, she continued, "I had court today, and I didn't have time to change. Besides, you dig a chick in a suit." She gave him a light kiss as she pushed her way into Dirk's house. "If I had a key, I wouldn't have to ring the doorbell, you know."

Dirk sighed at the drop of the hint. It wasn't the first time he'd heard it.

She took off her suit-jacket and unpacked the Chinese food, Dirk resisted the urge to say anything about the case. It would be the topic of discussion soon enough. Carrie had hinted a few times that the investigation, of which she had been involved in, was hitting a rough patch. While the police had plenty of bodies, they were lacking in any real evidence. The perpetrator had been very careful.

Carrie had accused Dirk of having an occasional mean streak. He could have just as easily told her he was already working the case, but that was too simple. He wanted her to beg for his help, and he'd be damned if he let that opportunity pass him up.

He had no idea how long he could continue. She was killing him. And yet, he was determined to not break first. It was torture but also a little fun.

"So, how was court?" Dirk asked.

"Well, it was kind of boring; you know how court can be. Judge comes in … I say my thing. Bad guy gets put in jail." She bit down on her bottom lip a little and then gave him a wink and her best flirty smile. Solidifying her hold on Dirk, she purposely ran her finger through the sweet and sour sauce and then over her tongue. Not in the way people do it in the movies; this was subtler, almost restrained. At the same time, intentionally sexy. His breath quickened, and he felt his blood pumping harder than ever. He was on the edge, and she knew it.

It's officially a standoff.

They sat down at the table and selected something from the contents of the paper containers. Dirk and Carrie had never gone to Vegas because Dirk knew she would be the world's worst poker player. She could never keep anything from anyone. Dirk read it in her eyes at the door. He wasn't going to just ask her what she wanted.

Over the previous week, she had repeatedly asked him about the case and what he thought. Carrie tried to be obtuse but lacked the gift of subtlety. The only time she'd ever done this before was when the police were stumped and needed some help. The department had retained his services in the past to see if he could get the investigation moving. He took her questions as a sign they wanted him to help, but in her mind, it admitted the police had hit an official dead end, and she hated that idea. To her, the police process was superior.

Carrie had one fault, and Dirk exploited it to the fullest; she was stubborn as a mule.

They ate in silence for a few minutes. Occasionally Dirk glanced up to catch her staring at him. It became more and more piercing as time wore on. He was enjoying it. He could almost feel her eyes, like daggers.

Slamming her chopsticks down on the table, she said, "Okay, damn it, I give up! Are you going to tell me what you and Clara Smithfield talked about or not?"

"Oh, I'm sorry, client confidentiality." Dirk loved it when he won. A faint smile crossed his lips.

"The woman was in my office crying, Dirk! I sat there with her as she looked through the pictures of her dead daughter."

"Interesting. So, you're telling me the police investigation has … I'm searching for a word here." Dirk raised both his eyebrows and his shoulders. The seriousness of the case hadn't escaped him, but getting her to admit they were at a dead end was just too much fun for him to pass up.

"Are you really going to do this? It's a sad case, Dirk. A girl is dead. Pictures, Dirk, pictures." She scowled at him.

"Yep, sure is."

Carrie, now getting a bit red in the face, threw her hands up in the air in exasperation. "Okay, fine. The police investigation has stalled. We're not sure where to go from here, and it's just spooky and weird.

"What do you want me to do? Do you want me to say you're great, and we suck? You can solve a case, and we can't? I know, how about 'Dirk is great' on official police department letterhead?"

Dirk sat back in his chair and folded his arms over his chest. His smile went from ear to ear. He loved every second of it. "Oh, so you're the one who sent her over to see me? The picture is becoming complete now. Do you think I could really get that on official letterhead?"

"You know what? You are a big stupid head, Dirk!" Carrie threw a wonton at him.

"Oh, real mature, Sgt. Pettygrew." Dirk picked up the wonton from the table and took a bite of it. He loved the idea of making her go this far for a case he'd already started working. It felt good to have one up on her for once. He learned years ago to never make the mistake of thinking he knew more than her. "I already took the case."

"You ass!" She threw a fortune cookie at him. "I came over here in this getup when I could have been dressed in sweatpants and a T-shirt. Then I bought you Chinese food, and you let me go on like that? Dirk Bentley, you are a complete jerk! Worst boyfriend ever."

Dirk held his sides from the laughter. "Okay, I'm sorry, sweetie. But it was really funny. And you are so hot in that suit, and maybe we can see about taking it off later." He leaned in close and gave her a soft kiss on the cheek. She was irritated, but he knew how to talk her down from the ledge. "Thank you for the Chinese food. Now, let's get on with this case."

"You're welcome, and besides, I was hungry. You arrogant ass. It's not all about you. Stupid boy," she said.

While they finished up dinner, they compared notes on the overall timeline. Dirk wanted to walk through every detail they could remember from the first time anyone heard of the cases until now. She'd brought along the files of the murdered girls for him. She knew he would request them anyway, and the department couldn't withhold them if the parents sought their own investigator. While he looked through them, Sgt. Pettygrew stripped out of her suit, took a shower, and put on one of his T-shirts and robe, reentering as Carrie, Dirk's high school sweetheart.

By the time she rejoined him, he'd already begun to make photocopies of a couple of things from the files, arranging them on the floor. Carrie laid down on the couch and watched him work. He moved papers into piles and then smaller groups, sorting them based on his own system.

Most investigators lost themselves in the minutiae. They looked at one piece of evidence in great detail, truly believing it held the key to it all. But the same investigator couldn't tell you the color of the house the murder took place in. Dirk summed up his method by remarking that the devil wasn't often in the details. Dirk took more of a holistic approach.

Carrie observed him from the couch. She once told a colleague that he was one of the most brilliant investigative minds she'd ever seen, and he spent most of his day disassembling carburetors and putting new tires on motorcycles. His talent for solving riddles was one of the things she loved most about him, and crimes were more often than not a puzzle needing to be solved.

Each police report came with a short bio, which he copied along with the evidence list from each of the girl's rooms. He also scanned the photos. Dirk couldn't shake the feeling the photos were going to be mostly useless in cracking this case. Crime scene photographers largely just photographed what their training told them to and missed out on little details that suggested how the deceased spent their final hours and days. Dirk needed to get in their mindset to unravel the route they took to their final destinations.

He felt Carrie spying on him. She lay on the couch with her head on one of the throw pillows she'd made him buy. In many ways, he was the consummate bachelor, but she was working on changing that. She smiled at him. "I love watching you investigate. It's kind of hot."

"Says the woman on my couch in my robe," Dirk answered.

He finally sorted through the last of the interesting parts of the case files. He reassembled the files and double-checked to ensure he hadn't missed anything. He smiled at Carrie, still lying on the couch, and gave her a wink. Dirk thought the older they got, the more amazing she was. Their eyes met. The time for work had come to an end, and she took him by the hand, leading him to the bedroom.

As they lay entwined together, he thoughtlessly stroked her hair as his mind churned away at the piles of paper sitting a couple of rooms over on his kitchen table. "Victor warned me …"

"Victor!" She immediately gave him a dirty glare.

Ooops, bad form.

She was seemingly the only person on planet Earth Victor had yet to reveal himself to. She wasn't sure if her boyfriend was insane or if she should be offended by the rudeness of the specter.

"I know you think I'm crazy," Dirk said.

"Oh, you're crazy alright. There is not speculation involved."

Ignoring her, he continued, "He warned me to be extra cautious about this case. He said something didn't seem right about it," Dirk continued purely for his own benefit.

"So, the ghost talks to you at the shop, the non-physical entity guy, and you told him you took this case before me?" She hit him in the head with a pillow. "You're an ass!"

"I'm being serious. I'm not sure why, but it's enough to spook a dead guy." He didn't need to continue. "I may be an ass, but I'm your ass... wait, that didn't come out right."

"Oh, geez, honey." She moved closer to him and wrapped one slender arm around his waist, pressing her body against his. "Hey, just be very careful, okay? You know I love you, right? You don't want to tell me you do too because you're a big chicken. We can work on that. Please, try to not do anything stupid. Whoever's doing this is an evil bastard, and it's hard to predict what someone like that will do if cornered. It's hard, but don't be a hero."

Dirk saw a conversation hurtling toward him at impossible speeds. One of the few issues he hated dealing with was the idea of love. A topic of discussion he generally avoided. "Evil bastard, huh? Wow, there's a phrase you don't hear very often."

"Sort of like the people saying, I love you? Fine, you win. Tell you what, we can talk more in the morning. I am not on until afternoon tomorrow." Carrie let him off the hook for now and rolled over, drifting off to sleep.

She dreamed of a wedding.

He dreamed of four slain bodies, dressed in red, floating by him on lily pads.

Dirk stood on a small island in the center of a pool. One by one, they moved around him, just out of reach. Each corpse opened its mouth as if screaming. And still, no voice came.

They swirled faster and faster, creating ever larger wakes in a circular pattern. With every circle, they moved farther out of reach. Dirk's small island started to sink into the lake, the water quickly grabbing at his legs, threatening to pull him under.

The island vanished below him, replaced by unseen tendrils working against his ever more fevered swimming. Random flotsam moved past him, and as he made a grab, the bodies lurched just out of his grasp. Any source of salvation remained stubbornly a few inches out of reach.

The more he struggled, the heavier he felt. He tried to scream just as the water overtook his head and filled his lungs.

Dirk sat bolt upright in bed, letting out a gasp as he did.

"You okay in there?" Carrie's voice came from the bathroom. He glanced over at the opened door and saw the fogged mirror on the opposite wall. A consummate morning person, Carrie was showered and sliding her HK45 pistol back into its holster. "Bad dream, huh?"

Dirk's process of investigation occasionally prompted nightmares. The first few times it happened, it had frightened her so much she left his house and went back to her own apartment. She reasoned that this was his brain starting to unravel the details of the case on a subconscious level.

"Yeah." Dirk rubbed his eyes and threw back the remaining covers. "I should get to the shop. A little work will help me clear my head. I need to put my thoughts and an old carburetor together. Maybe I can start by talking to the parents and see if they remember anything else."

"You'll figure it out, honey. I have faith in you. And keep me apprised of your case. I need to let the chief know if you figure out any new leads." She slid her cell phone into her breast pocket.

"The chief? Are you telling me that you used me to get to my brain? I'm hurt that a member of the police department would undertake such a sneaky approach. Having sex with me for my crime-solving abilities! Granted, I'm not opposed to it. I think I kinda like it. Finally, someone wants me for my body. I'm kind of like a crime fighting man-whore."

"Yeah, that's what you are, a man-whore. Precinct called. I need to head in early. We got a drug bust apparently. I'll see you later." With a kiss, she left for the station.

Dirk poured some coffee from the carafe into a cup had Carrie pulled out for him. He watched her walk out the door, and as the door closed, he said to the empty house, "Love you."

He had no idea why he couldn't say it to her face. He knew he'd truly loved her since their first date in high school and yet the words wouldn't come when she was around to hear them. It frustrated him as much as it most certainly frustrated her.

He brushed the thought away as he downed the coffee, ignoring the searing heat of the still-hot liquid. There was no time to obsess over their relationship now. He had more than enough work to do and not enough time to do it. At the shop there were always projects needing to be completed, forms to be filled out and then there was the case. Another life could already be at stake in whatever game this lunatic was playing.

CHAPTER 3
FOLDED CLUES

Dirk did his best thinking on the road. The drive to the shop provided ample time to consider his meeting with Clara Smithfield. Based on her characterization of her daughter, he didn't think it was an addiction issue. He had a pretty good sense for when parents were living in denial of an unaddressed familial drug problem. Other things could plague a young life and disrupt their normal behavior.

Victor had told him once it was obvious if someone had died from an overdose. They just had a certain "dirty" feel to them. If he was wrong about the drug problem, Victor would hopefully say something. That is if he could find the Smithfield girl at all. Keith believed Heather was likely clean too. He knew the family a little, and they'd always been loving. That fact didn't necessarily rule out any one angle at this early stage of the game. Kids were fantastic at hiding things from the watchful gaze of their parents.

He'd need to see their home firsthand and have a look around. There were all kinds of clues the police department routinely missed. It wasn't incompetence so much as it was not seeing evidence the way Dirk did. Luckily for him, grieving families rarely touched victims' rooms for quite a while after they died. Some of the more interesting traces could still be there.

The morning was slow and predictable. He had a carburetor and clutch job needing some attention. He worked through the repairs before heading into his office. He met Carrie for lunch three times a week, but today she was busting some drug dealer's door down. As he ate a sandwich he'd brought from home, he made an appointment with the Smithfields at around half past one.

Dirk headed to the locker room and washed the grease and oil off his face and arms. After reapplying some deodorant and a quick spray of some off-brand cologne Carrie kept him in supply of for his birthdays and Christmas, he was ready to go.

Dirk cut a path through the urban city center into the more placid suburban landscape of the outer rims of the city to the Smithfield's two-story colonial single-family dwelling with a big yard. Each window was framed by a set of perfect wooden shutters as an ultimate testament to the suburban credentials of the home. It was all so devastatingly ordinary. This should be a place of happiness, where a loving family raised their children.

A sign in the yard summarized the overwhelming sadness of the situation. It read "Class of" with a photo of a smiling girl whose date with the graduation stage was cut painfully short. It was the face of optimism encapsulated in a beautiful young woman who'd never come bounding down the halls of their family home, fall in love with someone, or find that perfect first job. The realization that the weight of the Smithfields's world suddenly rested on his shoulders sent shivers down Dirk's spine.

Mrs. Smithfield met him at the door. Mr. Smithfield sat in a chair in the front room but didn't get up or acknowledge his presence. According to what Mrs. Smithfield told Dirk, he'd been sitting in that chair almost consistently since he learned of his daughter's death. It had hit the family hard, but it left Mr. Smithfield destroyed inside. Dirk didn't need to hear it from him. He felt it the moment he laid eyes on the man.

Before being led upstairs, Dirk had a few moments to scan the living room for any pertinent details. Pictures hung on the wall, most featuring Mr. and Mrs. Smithfield, Heather, and her brother. The obligatory family Christmas photo hung above the fireplace, each of them dressed in an ugly Christmas sweater. A few photos on the wall were from various family vacations to warm beaches throughout the Caribbean.

In one photo, Heather and her brother sat together on a bale of hay. The two had goofy expressions, and they were making rabbit ears over one another. It was certainly not what the photographer was going for, but the result was funny enough that the family had bought a copy. Ordinary trappings of an ordinary family screaming out memories of a happier time when they were together.

This was the picture of two perfectly normal kids. Police crime scene photos never did people justice.

On a shelf, boxes of family games were stacked, waiting to be used. All of them were taped back together with packing tape after what he imagined was a raucous night of family time. It occurred to Dirk how most families had a collection of board games shoved into a cupboard. No one even contemplating this may be the last roll of the dice for them as a complete family. The realization was chilling.

He pulled himself away from his impromptu inspection of the living room at the sound of Clara reentering the room. "Can we go upstairs, Mrs. Smithfield?" Dirk didn't want to take up more of the their afternoon than he had to. Aside from that, every moment spent in this house felt like a pile of stones being stacked on his chest. With every exhalation, it was harder to bring in more air.

She nodded at him but still had not said a word. At the end of the upstairs hallway, she shopped short of the door, her hands at her sides. The look she gave Dirk was one of fear and trepidation. No force on heaven or earth was powerful enough to make her touch the doorknob. It wasn't uncommon for parents of a deceased child to shut the door to that child's room. As if borrowing a page from Dr. Schrödinger, it made it possible to believe the deceased could walk out of the room at any time. Opening the door meant Mrs. Smithfield would have to admit Heather was gone, and they would have to face that cruel reality. This was deeply emotional water Dirk was treading. Tears cascaded silently from her eyes.

Dirk took grasped her hands. They felt cold as ice and trembled to an extent where he wondered if he could even hold onto them. "Listen to me. I promise I'll do whatever I can to find whoever did this to your daughter. I'll make sure they pay for this."

"Mister, you get this son of a bitch." The sputtering voice of Mr. Smithfield came from the bottom of the stairs behind them. Dirk turned to see a man whose eyes were filled with tears, rage, and determination. While Mrs. Smithfield looked sad and broken, Mr. Smithfield's countenance suggested unfettered anger. "I want you to get whoever did this, and I want to see him suffer. I want him to know how bad he's hurt us. Although, I doubt that's possible." It was all he could manage to say, and he leaned against the handrail, as if the exertion of coming up the stairs had been too much.

Dirk suddenly felt as if he were connected to this man on a spiritual level. Mr. Smithfield's pain became his, even if only for a fraction of a second. Dirk wondered how he could even live with such a torment as losing a child to murder. "I promise to try everything I can think of to make this guy pay for what he's done, Mr. Smithfield."

The father of the killer's most recent victim nodded, seemingly satisfied by Dirk's assurances. He pushed his way up the final few steps, past the two of them, and opened the door to Heather's room. Turning to his wife, Mr. Smithfield enveloped her in his long arms. It may have been the saddest thing Dirk had ever witnessed in his entire life.

Dirk peered into Heather's room the way a historian carefully peeled back the lid of a time capsule. Upon the conclusion of the forensic evidence team making their sweep, the door had been shut, and the word had stopped until today. A light layer of dust coated the desk and chair. A police department pen had been left on the desk, and a measuring tape, which likely belonged in a crime scene technician's box, sat unceremoniously on the dresser. At the bottom of a wastebasket, used rubber gloves from the investigators waited for someone to determine their final disposition. A detective's business card had been left on the bed. They were thorough enough for normal police investigations, but they were terrible housekeepers.

What made Heather Smithfield tick? Likes and dislikes all helped to push his mind in one direction or another. Trends, things out of place that shouldn't have been, or other slight misalignments in the room, often ignored as being only trivial by the police, were his bread and butter.

He began by looking at the bed. Beds, particularly mattresses, could be a treasure trove of clues. People, especially kids, tended to hide their most intimate of secrets in between mattresses. A favorite hiding place was on the underside of the box spring, inside the felt tacked onto the bottom. He gave the mattresses a thorough check but found nothing of interest.

He laid down on the plush carpet so he could see directly under the furniture. He searched for anything suspicious, like loose sections of carpeting or things dropped behind the bed. Something on the floor behind the bookshelf caught his eye. He reached under and pulled out a photo of the family together on vacation. The frame had a wire hanger on the back, as if it had been hanging from something like a hook or a nail.

He continued searching the floor and came up with only the usual trappings of a teenager. In addition to a few clothes, there were pencils and pens on the desk and a collection of stuffed animals. A few pictures from friends were piled neatly on the desk, suggesting they'd been special to her.

The bookshelf was full of books from school, as well as books she'd probably had as a small child and didn't have the heart to throw out. Every shelf was in order, and every book seemed to have its place, except for the middle shelf. The frayed edges of the books suggested repeated use. The overwhelming theme of the shelf was theater arts. Some of them were books a school would have and some were scripts of common plays everyone knew.

He sat down on the bed and pulled one from the shelf. The corners had seen better days. *Perhaps this was a book the school was getting rid of?*

Absently flipping through the pages, a folded piece of paper slipped out and fell to the floor. He picked it up and unfolded the note. The paper was a thicker stock and was clearly printed for a desk note set, like a larger organization might have to give out to people. Across the top of the paper was the name "The First Transformational Church". The address was scrawled on the bottom in a cutesy font meant to give the impression the congregation was fun and didn't take itself too seriously. Churches were more Keith's area of expertise, but it struck Dirk as odd that the girl would have notes written on paper from a church in her theater papers. The name of the church did not ring a bell, but it could be worth checking out.

Dirk took the piece of paper and shoved it into his pocket. The Smithfields were downstairs in the kitchen when Dirk left the girl's room. They were both sitting at the table, coffee cups in their hands. Dirk sensed they had been talking as both of their eyes were puffy and red. A pile of wadded-up tissues lay between them. Maybe it was the start of the healing process for them. Perhaps opening the door to the girl's room was the first thing they needed to do. Dirk cleared his throat to announce his presence.

"Excuse me, I'm done in the bedroom. I just have a couple more questions. I was wondering, does your family belong to the First Transformational Church?"

They looked at each other in puzzlement. Their glances suggested neither one of them had given the place as much as a thought in a while.

Mr and Mrs. Smithfield exchanged glances. "No, but we did attend once. Does it matter? We were only there the one time, church shopping, you know. We didn't like it though."

"Church shopping?" asked Dirk.

"Yes, we were considering different churches to attend a while ago, so we were trying a few out," Mr. Smithfield answered.

"Also, did Heather have an interest in the theater?" Dirk asked.

Mrs. Smithfield smiled. "Not so much an interest as much an obsession. She wanted to be a Broadway star. A few months ago, she started taking private lessons from her theater teacher. He said she had huge potential."

"Interesting. Where did these lessons take place?" Dirk pulled out his notebook and made a few notes.

"At school, with a bunch of other kids in the theater program. He called them his 'muses'. He was a creepy sort of fellow," Mrs. Smithfield said.

"I'm sorry, what?" Dirk lowered his notebook and gave Mrs. Smithfield a quizzical look.

"Muses, you know the entity that serves as someone's inspiration. You don't think the theater teacher had anything to do with this, do you?" Mrs. Smithfield suddenly became awash in panic, as though paying for private lessons had somehow sealed her daughter's fate.

Dirk was about to say something when Mr. Smithfield interjected, talking to his wife, but his eyes were firmly affixed on Dirk, "Now, honey, no one suspects Mr. Tenebris. At least, the police didn't seem to think it was worth looking into."

"Is Mr. Tenebris the theater arts teacher?" Dirk asked.

"Yes, that's his name," Mrs. Smithfield said.

"I'm guessing you weren't as convinced as the police were that he wasn't involved?" Dirk said, raising one eyebrow toward Mr. Smithfield.

"Let's just say I had my reservations about him. Something about him was just kind of off. Have you ever met someone who struck you as phony?"

"Phony how?"

"Like he is hiding something he desperately doesn't want you to know, but the weight of it is crushing him?" Mr. Smithfield stood from his chair.

Dirk took this as his cue as leave. "Yes, I have. Thanks for that. I'll be in touch when I have more. By the way, what didn't you like about that church?" Dirk wondered if one visit to a church was truly enough to form an opinion about a church.

"Hard to put my finger on it." Mr. Smithfield was thinking out loud at this point. "The whole thing seemed odd. The preacher, just like Tenebris, felt like he was being phony. Like he was putting on a front to hide who he really was. Something was just wrong with that guy. It is hard to explain."

On his way to the car, Dirk thought about the visit. While hadn't really produced any solid leads, Dirk had a few strings he could pull. That was more than he started with.

Time to head back to the shop to fill in Keith and Victor on what he'd found. Maybe Victor had more information for him.

Pulling up in front of the shop, he could see the regular staff finishing up and getting ready to close. Keith was in the office, laser-locked on a catalogue, writing in some information on order forms for parts. He was cradling his head in his hands.

"Hey, Keith, are the catalogues really that hard to understand? I requested the picture book editions, just like you asked. Do I have to start reading them to you again?"

"You should consider doing these forms yourself one of these days instead of leaving them to me to do. Then you can deal with the tremendous headache. Sort of like the one you give me."

"I think you mean that I add excitement to your life. Anyway, I just met with the mother and father. I also got a good look at the girl's room. Not a ton of stuff but a few things that could be interesting."

Keith set the pen down. "Ah, do tell."

"There was something I found while going through her books. Check this out." Dirk handed the folded-up piece of paper with the name of the church on it. Keith read the words aloud and shrugged. He had a similar reaction to the paper that Dirk did.

"I've never heard of this place. It really doesn't take much to set up your own church these days. Did the family know anything about it?" Keith asked.

"They claimed to only have gone there once. They said it was weird."

"Weird, huh? I'll see if it means anything. Could be a lead of some sort." Keith kept abreast of the church scene, and if he hadn't heard of it, then it was probably new. He was a member of the local church council, which he described as clergy getting together for coffee and breakfast once a month.

"And there was something else, Keith. The kid was obsessed with the theater. The parents were even paying for private acting lessons on the side."

"Hmm … interesting. People's obsessions have been known to get them killed from time to time," Keith replied.

"But school is supposed to be safe."

"Sadly, my friend, very few places are safe anymore. It is the world we live in."

On the other side of the room, a broom handle fell as the corner took on a golden hue. Victor floated out of the wall dressed in his Confederate captain's uniform, complete with a slouch hat, sporting a "CSA" pin on the front and a musket.

"I'm sorry, little boy, we're out of candy. Didn't you see we turned off the porch light?" Keith tried to keep from laughing, but when he said this, he smiled and let out a little chuckle. He loved to poke fun at Victor's more interesting appearances.

"Stuff it, knothead!" Victor shot back.

"Hey, Victor, any luck with the girl?" Dirk asked before the two could bring the insults to a frothy boil. He was powerless to stop it from happening anyway, but he wanted to get an update before the real shouting started.

"I haven't talked to her yet, but I know where she is," Victor said, leaning on his rifle. "A few have tried but have gotten nowhere. I need information to go on, a little information to break the ice. A name or something could get her started. A few details to make a connection will help to open her up."

"Heather Smithfield, her name is Heather. She loves the theater." Dirk filled Victor in on the rest of the story.

"Just be careful, teens are somewhat sensitive creatures," Keith said. "One wrong word and they can fly off the handle. I mean, you guys lost a war. Do you think you can manage a teenager?" The war was one of Keith's favorite taunts since it got under Victor's ectoplasmic skin.

"You take that back!" Victor roared.

"I don't think so. Besides, what are you going to do about it?" Keith picked up a stress ball shaped like a motorcycle that Dirk had brought back from a convention and threw it through Victor.

The obvious slight at Victor wasn't to be ignored by any Southern gentleman. He glared at Keith, menacingly shaking his fist. Then picked up the musket he was leaning on and fired it right at Keith.

The room exploded into a surprisingly realistic blast and elicited some yells and the sounds of dropping tools from the mechanics working in the garage area. The office filled with a smoke from spectrally-fired gunfire which looked more like the fake fog they used at haunted houses.

"Victor! That's really too much, this is a place of business," Dirk said, wiping away the ectoplasmic smoke left lingering in the air. He opened the door to the shop and shouted, "Sorry, guys, it was just … well, you know." Three of his mechanics had been working, and the spectral rifle blast had sent them all hiding under the grease racks.

"Johnny Reb over there started it! Ain't no way to talk to a veteran," Victor shouted.

"For the Confederacy. News flash, you guys lost!" Keith shot back.

"Yeah, well at least I have the common decency to serve in my armed forces!" Victor said, standing slightly more at attention.

"Exactly how many battles have you won, oh mighty warrior?"

"I've done about had it with you!" Victor's Southern drawl became more pronounced as he became increasingly frustrated with Keith. "I'll show yah!" He picked up his rifle and started reloading it.

Keith laughed. "Oh yeah, shoot me with the ghost rifle."

The exchange was almost rehearsed at this point. The two had this argument before, but the rifle was a new twist. Dirk suspected it would someday go on in the afterlife as well. It was Keith's favorite way to get Victor to leave him alone, but Dirk suspected they both actually enjoyed it on some level. If it was allowed to move to its crescendo, Keith would stop talking to Victor, and the spirit would vanish in a huff.

Normally the two battling it out amused Dirk, but not this time. He was preoccupied by the girl and the case. He needed to dig deeper. The information he sought could only be found with access to the other girls' rooms. He wondered if there were any further ties to the church. For some reason, the paper he had found bothered him.

Something about that paper suggested a deeper meaning he could not put his finger on.

He started making lists of addresses and phone numbers, understanding that not every parent was going to let him nose around. If only a few did, it might just be enough.

In the background, he could hear Keith and Victor needling each other. The ghost was in a sparring mood, and Keith was not one to back down. Dirk yelled paternally, "Would the two of you stop it? I have a lot of work to do and so do the both of you. Keith, get with any local churches which could have a dubious following and find out about this First Transformational whatever. Victor, get your phantom butt back to the other side and talk to Heather. Maybe she will open up to you. She could break this case wide if she starts to remember things. I'm going to see if I can talk with the parents of the other girls."

Victor nodded and vanished into air, pointing his finger at Keith as he did, suggesting this fight was far from over. Keith left for home to reach out into his web of pastoral connections to see if he could add to the evidence pile. It was time to pry for some answers from this case, which was reluctant to give up its secrets.

CHAPTER 4
A SOUL IS FOUND

Victor whirled through the tunnel that served as the portal between the world of the living and the dead. A swirling vortex of blues and grays offered occasional glimpses of things from his own life. He suspected people only saw parts of their existence as they passed through the tunnel, but he never gave it much thought. The other side was a black hole surrounded by a white mist, which contrasted the blues and grays.

The way he saw it, there wasn't really a heaven or a hell. Some people were simply in a better place. And some people, people not playing by the rules, were where none would go willingly. He had no doubts where this murderer would end up when he was ultimately judged. Everyone faced their judgement eventually.

Exiting the tunnel, he found himself standing on a field of green in a familiar light and warmth he knew as the afterlife. The living who narrowly escaped death went on about a calm luminescence, but Victor always thought it would burn his eyes out until he had a moment to adjust. Off in the distance, trees and hills dotted an impossibly blue skyline. Low shrubs formed lined paths filled with people. Animals of an infinite number of different species played in the distance.

Heaven, the Afterlife, Valhalla, the Great Beyond, whatever you wanted to call it, was all essentially the same place. What mattered was what you made of life before you got there and what you made of your afterlife once they laid you into the cold ground.

Unless, of course, you were in the bad place, and most spirits chose not to talk about what happened if the eternal judgement did not work out in your favor. It did not matter what you did—it was not where you wanted to be. It was cold and impossibly dark, and he really didn't need or want to possess any further understanding of the matter.

When he'd died, it had seemed to take forever for him to get used to roaming around this expansive landscape. Impossible for the living to comprehend, Heaven was eternally big, always warm and inviting, and filled only with love. You'd be skiing in one minute and then take a month-long stroll in the woods the next. Victor once tried to describe it to Dirk, and all he could come up with was to tell Dirk to imagine being at your grandma's house on the couch, watching your favorite TV show with quick access to fresh chocolate chip cookies and milk, and your dog was sitting right next to you. That feeling stretched on for eternity.

The afterlife should've been more crowded than it was. Without the strict cinctures of time and space, spirits of the formerly living found their own places. It also seemed to offer countless destinations or no destinations at all. They congregated with the people they knew in life, friends they made in death, and places they liked to be.

An old sea captain could sail a mighty ship, commanding it with ease, farmers had farmhouses with fields as far as the eye could see, the homeless took up residence in a house with many rooms, and people who had suffered mental illness enjoyed a life free of malady. The afterlife, as it turned out, was a highly individual existence.

Victor recalled his entrance into the afterlife. The Civil War, or the "War of Norther Aggression" as the Confederacy called it, had reached a point where most accepted a Union victory over the South. He had served as a Captain, commanding an infantry company made largely of children. Victor did the best he could. It wasn't an ideal situation, but everyone was fed, clothed, and as warm as he could make them. In a hell on Earth, he'd maintained a kind heart.

His force was grossly outnumbered, they had no extra ammunition, and only every third gun was even loaded. Most of his green soldiers were committed and could be counted on to fight to the death. However, Victor also knew, through talking with other commanders, that no amount of blood spilled would never change the outcome of a war teetering on its final battles. The decision weighed heavily on him, whether it was better to just give up his strategically insignificant piece of real estate and wait out the rest of the war in a Union prison or fight with a bayonet and likely join the war dead.

Most of his troops were barely old enough to shave.

As the battle looked like it was upon him, a Union courier showed up requesting his conditions of surrender. The opposing commander, a man by the name of Major Anderson, was known to be an honorable warrior. He saw little sport in slaughtering soldiers who were no more than kids.

It was then Victor's own life had ended abruptly. His rifle, placed against a tree, fell over, and a sudden explosion from the barrel rang out over the valley. Victor, battle hardened and tested, looked own at his own shirt and understood instantly what happened. Seeing this, his lieutenant grabbed the paper from his dead captain's hand and gave it to the courier without a word. He took it as an omen of the impending battle. It was locally known as the "Battle of One Shot."

Many years later, a small motorcycle repair shop would be operated on the location where Captain Victor fell to his own musket shot.

Oftentimes, a recently deceased relative would be on hand to greet you after you crossed over. People preceding their parents in death didn't always have someone recognizable to help them through the transition.

Normally the deceased were met by cherubs, but Victor always thought of them as hopelessly lazy. These were the same characters the Greeks depicted as fat little babies who spent most of their time eating and playing harps. Victor considered it a pretty dead-on description. When the cherubs finally realized they had a job to do, they typically surrounded the poor person and tried to convince them how wonderful it was to be dead. Not something you really wanted to hear if the last thing you could remember was your car hitting a guardrail or gasping for breath in a hospital room.

It was much easier when the person had a deceased relative to meet them to make things go a lot smoother. Victor had his uncle Hal. Hal had died before the Civil War. He was a celebrated barkeep. He was a good friend of the Holliday family, who would produce one of the most infamous gunfighters in U.S. history. Hal greeted Victor by saying, "Yer dead, boy. Git up off yer arse."

Most newcomers to the afterlife arrived in the same area, a rolling meadow near a park. People just remembered waking up there without little fanfare at all. That was the place to look for the latest victim. If no one had been there to greet Heather and no one else seemed to know anything about her, then this would be the most logical starting point.

True to form, the cherubs were nowhere to be seen. *Lazy little fat bastards.*

Newcomers were often scared or angry and always very confused. Being left alone in a meadow and bum-rushed by fat flying babies really didn't help matters. Victor knew Dirk was probably right about using her real name. People often underestimated the power of someone just caring enough to learn someone's name.

Surrounding the girl were a couple of angels. They were trying to help the girl the best way they could. Angels hated to see people sad. It was in their programming. God created them to assist humans, and they still regarded her as essentially that human.

"Hey, scram, guys, let me talk to the girl, huh?" Victor said. The angels left, looking a little put-out. He had a twinge of guilt. It wasn't their fault she would not respond to them. But time was not on anyone's side, and he needed to get into the game.

The young woman sat with her head in between her legs. Light brown hair fell around her face and danced around her knees like strange window dressings. The rest of the young woman, whom Victor mused was now a perpetual teenager, didn't move a muscle. He suspected she had been that way for quite a while now.

He sat down in the grass, next to Heather. Victor gave her a few moments to get used to the idea of someone being so near her. "You know you're safe, right?" Heather drew her knees up closer to her body and tucked her head in as far as she could in response. "It's been a while for me, but I remember what it's like when you're new and no one comes to meet you. Believe it or not, I'm here to guide you through this."

She remained like a statue as he continued, "I have some friends on the other side who really want to be there for you too. However, we need your help or whatever happened to you will probably happen again to someone else. So, can you work with me a little?"

Heather continued to sit with her head between her knees, her gaze likely firmly fixed on the ground or perhaps shuttered behind eyelids. Victor understood her point of view at least. He had seen it before. She was past the point of being frightened and was just avoiding dealing with the world around her. In some ways, it made sense. If she didn't look around, she'd needn't acknowledge her new reality.

"My name is Victor. I have a secret to share with you. See, I am special around here. That group of friends I mentioned, they told me your name. It's Heather."

The girl raised her head from in between her knees. She squinted at Victor, and with a small, squeaky voice hoarse from her own crying, she said, "You ... you know my name?"

Victor was unusually taken with the girl. She reminded him a bit of his sister at her age. "Yes, child, I do. I really do want to help. But we need to discuss a few things first."

A mix of panic, anger, and sadness washed over her face. "I can't remember anything. All I know is I woke up here. And now I'm…" Heather stopped herself. She didn't really need to finish the sentence.

Victor understood the rest without her needing to say it. Everyone said the same thing when they get here, *they just understand they're dead.*

Victor drew a breath of relief that the girl was finally communicating. "Well, yes, I reckon it takes some gettin' used to. The memory loss isn't permanent. All the memories you had will return. It's just a matter of time. Now that you are talking to someone, it'll come back faster."

"And those other terrifying flying things?" Heather pointed into the distance.

"Oh, angels and cherubs, yeah, I get how they can be scary. The best I can tell you is to not pay them any mind. Annoying? Yes. They mean well though. The angels will do anything for you. And I mean it. You want a coke with a slice of chocolate cake? They will bring you one, just ask. Really, it is partially why they're here. Their problem is they don't understand how this can be scary to someone. Right now, let's just sit and relax. Maybe I can show you around? There's a lot to see. You'll be shocked how big it is."

Victor could see the faintest glimmer of trust in her eyes, but he wasn't expecting miracles. This was all new for her, and she seemed to relax slightly, which was a small victory. He just hoped her memory would return soon. The life of another might depend on it.

CHAPTER 5
PASSIONS FOR OTHER THINGS

Dirk watched Carrie cleaning up from dinner in the kitchen of his house while he made the phone calls he dreaded most. How does a person call a grieving family and tell them he wants them to walk, step-by-step, through the life of their child who had been murdered? It was never simple, and despite what television wanted you to believe, it never got easier for the investigator either. There was no such thing as a "hard-nosed" detective in real world.

He made his way through his list of families who had their kids go missing. Out of his calls, he was able to get three of the parents to agree to help him. The rest simply hung up the phone. Dirk theorized that immediately after the call ended they'd likely descended into a fit of tears.

This part of the job just sucks.

"Well, I suppose I should be happy that I got three of the families to speak to me," Dirk said, leaning back on his desk chair.

"Yeah, but now you have to actually talk to them. Want me to join you?" Carrie asked.

"You can't and you know it." A police officer coming along with him to a murder victim's home was the kiss of death for his investigation. Police officers looked for suspects while private investigators just searched for the answer to a mystery they were hired to unravel. It was a subtle but critical difference. People tended to open up to private investigators about details and theories they would never share with the police. "Besides, you have the whole cop thing you do. Someone has to make a living around here."

52

"Well, I've been thinking about giving it up and just being a stay-at-home wife." Carrie flopped down onto the couch next to him.

It was a joke, and he recognized her attempt to add a little levity to the situation. Still, her joke fell flat given the seriousness of his task at hand. The stress of what lay before him was written all over his face. "Hah, you should consider a stage act in Vegas. Talk of marriage later—right now I want to catch a killer."

She gave him a kiss and stood from the couch. "Always the way, isn't it? Girl meets boy, boy meets girl. Girl loses boy to homicide cases. Oh well, all for the best I suppose. I have a few errands to run before work. Besides, you need some sleep, and I have the whole 'job thing' tomorrow, as you put it." She bent down and looked into his eyes. "Just be careful, okay? And remember, if you need me, I'll be there. I love you, Dirk Bentley, even if you are a big chicken who hates talking about his feelings." With another kiss, Carrie left.

"I love you, Carrie," Dirk said. He repeated it a few more times. He'd say it while she was out of the room and yet he couldn't bring himself to say it to her. Why not? He thought she was the most spectacular creature on the face of the planet, and he'd die for her. But he couldn't muster up the courage to tell her. "Damn it!"

He finished his beer, brushed his teeth, and went to bed. Maybe the morning would bring a little more clarity. As he lay in the dark, he thought about the next day. The first interview was scheduled for the early afternoon.

Outside the house, the late evening was threatening to capitulate to the night. Cars drove by on the highway a few streets over. Automobiles filled with commuters driving home from a late day at the office or going to their night jobs. People off for late dinners, coffee shops, and a myriad of other places. Any one of those cars could contain Heather Smithfield's killer. If he were a magician, he might just be able to reach out and identify them, but he knew the only solution to this case was good old-fashioned detective work. The answers were there—he just had to drag them out from the rocks they were hiding under.

* * * *

Victor was pleased with the amount of progress he'd made with Heather. She was starting to recall a few things. The memories were slow in returning, but at least they were coming. He explained to her why it was so important for her to remember as much as she could as quickly as she could. He felt there was no need to overwhelm her with the details. The part about the murder could wait for now. He simply commented on her death by explaining "It was something bad."

He knew from experience it could take weeks for new arrivals to get back their full recollections. Thankfully, usually not that long, but it could be a while before she remembered any specifics about the murder. There was no guarantee she'd call to mind anything important. She might not have even seen who attacked her.

The angels came back to see if she needed anything. She was able to answer them, giving them a polite "No." They left in a bit of a huff because they knew Victor had gotten her talking and not them. Angels just didn't get how a newly dead person might be a little freaked out by them. Cherubs could be comical, but angels were terrifying.

Victor and Heather walked a little past a few shrub-lined pathways and through a park area. There were no streets as much as wide paths for people to use when strolling. "You know, kiddo, there is tons and tons more to check out. You could literally spend the rest of eternity exploring and never get to the end."

"But we don't have to see it all today," Heather added, scrunching her eyebrows together.

Victor laughed. "No, we definitely don't need to. You could pick a spot on the horizon and go all day and all night and never get there." Secretly, Victor was hoping she'd see something or meet someone to jog her memory. They had been together for hours, and still nothing dislodged even a hint of a recollection.

"How much of it have you seen?" Heather asked.

"Not sure. I've been here for a while, and I haven't found an end to it. So, I guess there's no real way to tell," Victor said. "So, anything feel familiar?"

"Not really, I just can see pictures and glimpses of things but nothing specific. Why are you so worried about me remembering things?"

"Well, it's my job."

"You know, Victor, in my day and at my age, we already have more education than most adults during your time. I'm not stupid, okay? There's something you're not telling me." Heather turned toward Victor with a hurt look across her face.

Victor sat down on a bench near a green soccer field. "You're right. You've got to trust me on this. I'm keeping a couple of things from you because I don't want to overwhelm you right now. You'll have all the time in the world to deal with what happened to you, and then we can talk about it. It's best to let you get your memories back on their own and not pressure you too much."

"Fair enough, I suppose I can wait a little longer," Heather said with a bit of a pout. "I mean, I suddenly find myself with all kinds of time on my hands."

"Alright, deal. You let your memories sink into your noggin, and I'll try to coax them out when I can. Look, I've got to go for a little bit. I'll be back soon enough." The instant he spoke those words, he saw a flash of panic return to the girl's eyes.

"Can't I come with you?"

"No, not yet. We don't let spirits just march through to the world of the living whenever they get a hankerin' to. It's kind of a rule around here. You can do it eventually, but you likely won't want to. You're one of the first people in your immediate family to end up here, and it's only natural you would want to go back. Mark my words, there'll be other members of your family coming through, and you'll be responsible for helping them. You'll show them around, like I'm showing you. Thankfully, you've got me. You're very brave to go through this." Victor got up off the bench.

"How'll I find you? I don't want to be alone." Her eyes welled up with tears.

Victor was suddenly reminded that the girl standing in front of him was only about fifteen years old and not anywhere near a full adult yet in terms of life experience. "Oh sweetie, you ain't alone. Look at this place. Can't swing a polecat without hittin' someone around here. There are literally gazillions of others for you to talk to. I'll find you. Don't you worry 'bout a thing. I'll be back sooner than you think. Then we can resume our tour."

"Don't be long, alright?" Heather asked meekly.

"I promise, I just need to talk to some people," he said. With a snap of his fingers, Victor vanished in a wisp of vapor.

Heather sat on the park bench for a while longer, looking at the grass and the sky. In front of her were a group of kids who seemed to be her age, playing soccer on the greenest field she had ever seen. A tear rolled down her nose and dropped off toward the grass. In a flash of memory, she suddenly recalled being passionate about playing the game and how much she loved performing in the theater.

CHAPTER 6
WADING THROUGH A MINEFIELD OF EMOTION

Dirk rolled around in his bed in a fitful sleep, alternating between a fever and then freezing. Cases always had a way of invading his slumber, as if his brain would not allow him even a moment's rest until the case was solved. Eventually he capitulated his battle for rest and got dressed for the morning at the garage. He'd put in a few hours at the shop before his first meeting with parents. Dirk's strict work ethic would not allow him to take the day off, even if he truly deserved it.

Dirk wondered where he got his own strict work ethic, given that his own parents valued more of a work-life balance. These thoughts occupied his brain and kept his mind off the murders as he cascaded through the streets and finally up the long driveway to the shop. He pulled in next to Keith's motorcycle in its usual spot.

"Rough night of sleep, buddy?" Keith said. Dirk's slumped posture and unkempt hair told the story to anyone daring a look.

"Yeah, I suppose so," Dirk said. He opened his tool chest and started disassembling a transmission, which had been patiently waiting his skilled hands. "Normally cases don't bother me, but this one is tougher than usual. These are just kids. This time it feels personal."

"I know what you mean. Anything involving kids has a finer edge to it. That is why so many cops leave after the first investigation where they face that reality. Kids are supposed to be innocent. Then, we find out the world isn't anything like we think it should be. The murder of a teen, even an older one, upsets our lives in ways that nothing else can."

"Well, I have to talk with three sets of parents today. See if I can maybe get them a little closer to bringing them some sort of closure."

"I get to interview with three fundamentalist rejects today. Wanna trade?" The night before, while Dirk was trying to sleep, Keith had texted him the details of ministers in the area who might have some additional insights on the church Dirk had given him information about. Each of them sat teetering on the fringe of the town's religious scene.

They both descended into their own thoughts as the sounds of air ratchets and newly arriving workers moving heavy metal pieces around the shop and putting motorcycles filled in a more comfortable soundtrack to their routine. All around them, bolts were removed, gaskets were replaced, and batteries recharged.

If only fixing people were that easy.

Victor materialized out of a rack of tires in the back of the shop without any of his usual fanfare. "It's about time you two quit screwing around and get to work." He hovered in the center of the room, holding up his hand, commanding their attention. Victor recounted the time he'd spent with Heather and voiced concerns over the girl's lack of memory.

"Good work, Vic." Dirk knew he needed to reassure the shop's resident specter he was headed in the right direction. "Keep doing what you're doing until we have something a little more concrete." They agreed to meet again later to see if anything more had come from their separate investigations.

Victor vanished, although they were unsure if he had returned to the other side or hung around to annoy the mechanics a while. Keith left to tend on a Honda V-Star with starter problems, and Dirk continued trying to fix a stubborn transmission. By noon, both projects were complete, and the friends cleaned up to attend to their appointed tasks. It was time to catch a murderer.

Dirk drove across town to the home of Lindsey Wales, one of the many victims. The Wales's home was not too dissimilar to the Smithfield home. A large colonial in an upscale neighborhood. Most certainly not the high end of the economic spectrum but not the low end either. Manicured lawn and fenced-in backyard made it look like postcard neighborhood for raising children.

He knocked on the door, and through a small panel of glass, he could see movement inside of the house.

"Yes, can I help you?" A man answered. He was of average build, wearing a blue button-down dress shirt. He had short black hair and a worried look on his face. Under normal circumstances, he would have struck a forgettable figure. Anyone could see from his appearance that life was wearing him down in ways that most people could not possibly imagine.

"Hello, my name is Dirk Bentley, and I'm working with the Smithfield family on the murder case of their daughter. I know it's…"

The man who answered the door put his hand up as if doing so would instantly force Dirk to vanish. "We don't know the Smithfields, and my wife was a little premature when she said she'd talk to you. I don't think we will. Painful enough for us and you can certainly understand why we wouldn't want to go through this again. Thank you for stopping by." He stepped back and moved to close the door.

Anticipating his response, Dirk put his foot between the door and the frame. "I don't even need to really ask you many questions. I just want a quick look around her room, and you can stay with me the whole time. I think it's possible these murders were linked, and if they are, we can catch whoever did this." Dirk suddenly remembered the

Wales murder had only been weeks before the Smithfield murder. With these two, the wound of loss was still very fresh.

"You're not getting it." The man's face reddened, and Dirk could feel the door of opportunity figuratively and literally closing. "We are tired of the police questioning, the constant reminders, the media coverage, all of it. Please, just leave us alone."

He could see Mr. Wales's point of view. In that respect, Mr. Wales was wrong. Without a killer, the media would never let this story rest. The news was relentless in hounding the families.

"Mr. Wales, I understand what you've told me. Please understand what I am telling you. This is going to happen again if someone doesn't do something. Just give me five minutes, then I'll be gone." Dirk knew he was overstepping his legal bounds by putting his foot in the door. And yet, if there was any chance this guy would relent, it was worth the gamble. This investigation could stall out before it even really started.

"No, I'm sorry, we just don't—"

A woman appeared and cut the man off mid-sentence. "Another girl, another baby? Like my Lindsey?" The woman pushed the man out of the way with a force that seemed unnatural to her stature.

She was a mess. Her eyes were red and puffy. In one hand she carried a wad of tissues. The similarity to the victim was striking. This had to be Lindsey's mother or a very close relative at the least.

The husband tried to step in front of his wife again to reassert his dominance. "Honey, I really don't think—"

"Shut up, Harold," she shouted. "Oh, God, not another. I can't bear the thought of anyone else going through this. Please, Mr.

Bentley, come in. When I read about the Smithfields, it was like it was happening to us all over again."

Harold complied with a comical sweep of his hand into the house.

Mrs. Wales stared at her husband, driving her point home. "If we can do anything to stop this son of a bitch from putting someone else through this, then I… we will certainly help."

"Thank you both, really." Dirk looked up into Harold's eyes, hoping to broker some sort of peace settlement. He'd need both of their cooperations.

"I'm sorry, Mr. Bentley. My husband is worried about me."

"I understand completely, Mr. and Mrs. Wales. I promise I'll be discreet and fast. We won't drag this out any longer than necessary." Dirk followed Mrs. Wales upstairs to the girl's bedroom.

"Mrs. Wales, did your daughter act any differently before it happened?" Dirk wanted to get to the heart of the matter. He wasn't sure how long the woman could keep it together or Harold would tolerate being sidelined.

"Well, she seemed fine to us. Maybe she was spending a little too much time at school."

"I'm sorry to have to ask you this, because I'm sure the police did too, but did you suspect drugs or alcohol or anything?" Dirk hated asking the "the drug question" in a murder case, but any small detail could help direct him to an important clue.

She sighed deeply. "No." The look on her face told Dirk he was right about the police going over the question before, and she was tired of people suspecting it.

"This is going to seem like an odd question, but did you notice your daughter hanging out with a different crowd? Maybe she had changed something significant about her friend group or something?" Dirk could see both parents were shocked by this line of inquiry. It was likely the police hadn't asked them anything like this.

"Most certainly not. My daughter was a good girl." Mrs. Wales was incredulous.

"I absolutely believe that is true, Mrs. Wales. I try to leave no stone unturned in any case I work. I want to make sure we know everything," Dirk said.

"Here is her room. Please don't make a mess. She never liked disorder; she wouldn't stand for her room torn up." She sobbed, and Dirk understood the time for questions was ending. Mr. Wales came to the bedroom door and put his arm around her. Dirk sensed Mr. Wales still harbored deep suspicions. If he was in Harold's shoes, he would feel the same way.

The room looked exactly as Dirk imagined a typical teenage girl's room should. Stuffed animals, pictures of boys cut out of magazines. A yearbook was open on the desk to the theater department's page.

"Mrs. Wales, not to sound indelicate, but were you, or anyone else, reading this book on the desk?"

"No, it was like that the day she left for school. You know the day she… you know, she…"

Dirk sat in the desk chair and stared at the page. On the face of her theater teacher, she'd scribbled out two pointy horns and a beard, obviously intending to make him look like a devil. Under the picture was the name Mr. Arthur Tenebris. Dirk could remember doing the same to a few of his teachers.

Some things never change.

Still, Dirk noted, Victor should ask the girl for information on Mr. Tenebris. Maybe there was more to it than just a student irritated at an overly demanding teacher.

A long shot, but stranger connections had been made during investigations, and if both Lindsey and Heather's parents didn't particularly like Tenebris, it would be worth checking into him. Dirk wrote a reminder in his notebook to have Carrie take a quick glance at his police record. Maybe there was something more to him than met the eye.

Dirk searched through the desk drawers, being careful not to mess anything up as the parents had asked. Unlike the parents, he might have to account for his actions with the spirit world. The last thing he wanted was another spirit haunting the shop because he forgot to put a stuffed bear back where it belonged or left a favorite pen in the wrong place.

He gave her bed his usual examination, not seeing anything of value. On the bookshelf was a collection of teen magazines, where she had dog-eared some of the pages. Most were the usual topics of interest to teenage girls.

The rest of the bookshelf contained the normal resources of a high school student's life. Math, science, and theater arts textbooks all lined up in a row. Searching through his notes and the photos on his phone, Dirk realized a couple of them were the same ones Heather had on her shelf in her room. Although, leafing through them, little caught his attention as being out of the ordinary.

When he went to place one of the books back on the shelf, he spied a piece of folded paper tucked away behind the books. He pulled it out, and what he saw stopped him dead in his tracks.

The stationary carried the embossed name, address, and phone number for the "The First Transformational Church."

The note suggested it was a reminder of an appointment to take place on September 10th, the day Lindsey was first reported missing. What struck Dirk as the most interesting was the last item. The words "4:30, Mr. Tenebris."

Dirk pulled out a notebook and wrote down the information. He also took a photo of the note to print off for his own evidence folder. Could it be that she had a meeting with Tenebris that day? The odds of anyone else in her life having the same last name had to be remote. The coincidence was too much to ignore.

Continuing his search, he lay down on the floor and did a quick scan. Some dirty clothes forgotten under the bed but nothing else of use. Looking over the rest of the desk, he saw the normal trappings of a teenager's life.

He then picked up the yearbook from the desk and carried it to the door where Harold stood sentinel over the activities in his daughter's room.

"Mr. Wales, just out of curiosity, did your daughter ever mention anything specific about this teacher?"

"Not that I can think of. I believe he is the theater teacher, but I'm not sure. I do know she took some special acting lessons with him."

"Okay, thanks. One other thing, and this is an odd question, but Mr. Wales, do you attend church?" Dirk asked.

"No, we're not a very religious family. I suppose you could say we're agnostic," Mrs. Wales answered the question from the bottom of the stairs.

"Have you ever been to a place called The First Transformational Church?" Dirk wondered where the girl would have gotten a piece of paper from if they never attended church.

"No, as my wife said, we are not churchgoers. I think Lindsey may have gone with a friend once or twice," Mr. Wales said.

"Interesting. Do you mind if I take these with me?" He indicated the yearbook. "I want to make copies. I will bring them back when I am done."

"Yes we do, but I can just make you a copy on our copier if that is all you need. Why? Do you think it's important?" Mr. Wales asked.

"A copy of this page would be great, thank you. Possibly important, but right now I'm trying to find a few puzzle pieces to put the whole picture together. It could be one of them." Dirk handed over the yearbook. "You mentioned that you didn't know the Smithfield family, but is it possible Lindsey and Heather were friends?"

"I suppose. Now that you mention it, I am sure they were both involved in that theater program.," Mr. Wales said.

Interesting.

Dirk turned toward Mr. Wales and handed him one of his business cards. "Sir, I have taken enough of your time. Again, thank you so much. I'll do everything I can to find out what happened. I promise to keep digging until I have some answers."

Before getting into his car, he flipped open his cell phone and called Claire. "Hey sweetie, I need a favor."

"Of course you do, Uncle Dirk. What is thy bidding, my master?" She laughed at her own poor impression of Darth Vader.

"You're a funny kid, you know that?"

"Yeah, I think it runs in the family. Seems like I have a weird uncle or something. So, what's all the hubbub, bub?"

"I need you to hightail it over to the shop. See if you can get Victor to talk with Heather about a guy by the name of Tenebris." Aware the Wales were watching from the window, he turned his back to them.

"Tenebris?" Claire repeated the name. "Tenebris. You don't mean the theater arts teacher? I've never had him, but theater arts is filled with all kinds of freaks. I bet one of them could be your bad guy. He is an odd little fellow. You want me to go over there and break into his office, maybe rough someone up?"

"Easy there, Lara Croft. Just go tell Victor I need to him to check out the general feeling on the other side about Tenebris. Maybe it'll help jog Heather's memory a bit. Also ask Victor if he can track down the Wales kid for me." He loved his niece, but sometimes the fact she was a teenager could be exhausting.

"Alright, I'm on my way. I'll see you later. Love you." With that, she hung up on him.

Dirk knew she would likely see Victor before he did as Claire been spending more time lately at the shop, doing low-level repair work. He also wanted Victor to see if he could track down the Wales girl to ask about Mr. Tenebris. He left the Wales home and made his way to his next appointment with Mr. and Mrs. Ramsey.

Dirk pulled up in front of the Ramsey residence on Pine Tree Lane. The short drive gave him a chance to consider the interesting theater and church connections. Potentially, these were only coincidences, but in Dirk's mind, it was highly unlikely. The odds of finding two identical pieces of evidence in both girls' rooms was too astronomical to be coincidental. And yet, stranger things had happened.

He was starting to develop a few ideas to test out. Not fully formed theories but enough to bounce around inside of his head and take up precious room. He still wasn't sure he had it all falling into place quite yet. Intuition screamed he had a potential connection, albeit maybe not a vital one. The solution wouldn't just simply stumble out of the woods and announce its presence.

A man made his way around the side of the house as Dirk approached. In his arms, he was carrying a box of random items. A teddy bear, a photo in a frame, a small wicker basket looking like it used to have a top. Items a teenage girl might have in her room. Dirk's heart sank.

The man stopped when he saw Dirk and smiled at him. "I'm sorry, did we have a meeting?"

"Yes, this is the Ramsey residence, correct?" Dirk responded, still eyeing the box.

"Well, I don't recall making an appointment for today, but the store is always open, as they say. Do you remember what you were interested in?" he said as he dropped the box to the ground. "You look like a Bayliner kind of guy or maybe a Boston Whaler? Oh, I'm sorry, the name is John Ramsey, Nautical Adventures. You are here about a boat, right?"

Dirk looked at the box. If these were indeed the belongings of the deceased girl, this meant someone was in the process of cleaning out her room and possibly carrying away precious evidence. "Interested in a Boston Whaler? I think you misunderstand me. My name is Dirk Bentley, and I'm investigating the murders of the girls. I made an appointment with Mrs. Ramsey." Dirk handed him his business card.

"Oh, yeah. She's inside." He absently pocketed the business card and picked up the box in disgust. Not exactly the response Dirk thought he'd see out of a grieving father. Although everyone grieved in their own way. Mr. Ramsey quickly walked toward the front of the house and opened the door, letting it fall closed behind him before Dirk had the chance to walk in. He got the impression that Mr. Ramsey was less than happy with his presence there. Or perhaps he could simply not be troubled with him.

Mrs. Ramsey sat on the couch, staring out the window at nothing. Dirk imagined she had been an attractive woman at some point, but stress, grief, and loss could destroy even the heartiest of people. She had long blond hair and gray eyes and was wearing a simple blue dress. She had a drink in her hand that looked more at home in a bar than in the fingers of a grieving mother. And yet, it was hard to sit in judgement of someone in her situation.

It was likely she'd seen the whole exchange between her husband and Dirk and yet she didn't even seem to acknowledge what had happened. Her eyes were red from crying with the thousand-mile stare of someone who was simply in another time and place.

"Mrs. Ramsey, my name is Dirk Bentley. We spoke on the phone." Dirk bent over slightly to try to get her attention, but she continued to stare off into the distance.

Slowly, as if speaking through a dream, Mrs. Ramsey opened her mouth and began to form words. Each syllable felt airy, like every sound was the product of a deflating lung and nothing more. "I'm sorry, Mr. Bentley. I should have called to cancel." Her gaze out the window remained fixed on a point in space only she could see. "I'm not sure we have any additional information for you, really. I'll pay you something for your time." She paused to draw in a ragged breath. "My husband and I feel it's best to just move on and look toward the future."

"Mrs. Ramsey, I know this is hard, but I also have a suspicion multiple girls were murdered by the same person. I'm trying to figure out who did this so we can keep it from happening again. All I want to do is ask a few questions and look in her room. I promise I'll be done as quickly as possible." Based on the anguish on her face, he guessed his phraseology had been chosen poorly. And yet, the statement penetrated to a place somewhere behind the stare.

"You know this is hard? Mr. Bentley, I'm not even sure you have any idea of what 'hard' really is. My daughter is dead. Some bastard murdered her, and all the police have provided are excuses."

Dirk felt like he had been punched in the gut. On one hand, he completely expected it at one point in this case. On another level he felt reassured that at least on an emotional level she had found her way through the grief and potentially alcohol-infused haze.

She was giving him more regard than she had during his entire visit, so Dirk seized the initiative. It was not a great opening, but it was still the chink in the armor he needed. "I'm sorry, Mrs. Ramsey, but I think I can help. I'm not looking for your money or any kind of support. I just want a little assistance searching for some answers."

Mrs. Ramsey's bloodshot eyes drilled into Dirk, accusing him, berating him. She continued, "Do you have any idea what it's like to have someone punch their fist into your chest cavity, grab your heart, and pull it out? No, I sure as hell don't think you do." She took another drink. "Here's the funny thing. I mean, it's really fucking funny. C'mon, you're gonna laugh your ass off here. You'd think that after someone has ripped out your reason for living, you'd die. But you don't. Every morning you wake with the catastrophic realization that your life has been destroyed, completely and irrevocably destroyed.

"I keep expecting her to walk out of that damn room, and I'll remind her to do her laundry, homework, or some other meaningless shit. I can't. She's dead. Rotting under a piece of well-watered sod in Saint Martin's cemetery. Do you even have the capacity to understand how I am feeling?"

This was exactly why he hated this part of the job. It wasn't that he had to deal with emotional people. It was that he had been lucky in life, and he was terrified of one day having to face a loss like this. Briefly, images of Claire and Carrie flashed through his mind since they were *his* reason for living.

"I'm sorry, Mrs. Ramsey. It was wrong and insensitive of me to put it that way. I have someone in my life who is about your daughter's age. Her name is Claire, and I'm worried sick that something could happen to her if I can't find a way to stop this. I can't do this alone. And you have the best chance of helping by letting me into your daughter's world. I truly meant it—I'm not looking for anything outside of answers."

Mr. Ramsey came downstairs, carrying another large box in his arms, seemingly oblivious to his wife's outburst. Again, they looked like girls' things. Dirk hoped Mr. Ramsey wasn't tearing apart the girl's room, but he knew he likely was. Maybe, since he was a stepparent, he was unsure how to deal with her death. His response might be to try to delete his stepdaughter's life.

"Mr. Bentley, I think you have wasted enough of our time. I have clients coming any minute. Phyllis, I need you to make them some coffee." Dirk remembered him saying he didn't have any appointments today. He'd only known this man for about ten minutes and already wanted to throat-punch him into tomorrow.

It didn't take a genius to see what was going on. Mr. Ramsey was a controlling husband, used to having everything his way. Dirk had seen it a hundred times before in spousal abuse cases, and it made him instantly see red. He found out she had agreed to talk with Dirk, and he probably had flown off the handle. Dirk didn't see any marks on her, but that didn't mean Mr. Ramsey wasn't abusing her either.

Mr. Ramsey was her second husband, Dirk had found out. He must have talked her into just trying to forget the whole matter. Based on his one interaction with the man in the front yard, Dirk decided the murder was nothing more than an inconvenience for Mr. Ramsey. One of those pesky life events that didn't fit his narrative of the world. A fifteen-year-old girl was dead, someone he was supposed to care about.

Dirk pulled his attention away from Mr. Ramsey's interruption. "Look, Mrs. Ramsey. I have a suspicion this is going to happen again. It would be hard to live with yourself if you could have done something to stop it." Dirk thought of the reaction he got at the Wales household. Maybe he could guilt them into helping.

Phyllis looked up at Dirk, as if something he had said had penetrated the alcohol-induced haze. "I'll tell you what I can remember." There was an audible grunt of disgust from her husband as he stomped his way back upstairs.

"Did your daughter act any differently before her murder?"

She drew a ragged breath. "Not really. She did all the same stuff, school, theater after school, and she had her violin lessons. She was good, you know." For the first time, Dirk detected the merest hint of a smile. A recollection climbing to the surface, which she could draw some happiness on.

"Theater? She was in the theater program at school? Was she friends with Heather Smithfield?" There was the theater again. Dirk began to see a coincidence which seemed a little too strong.

"I think so. They weren't really in school together necessarily, but they were in the after-school theater program together."

"Can you tell me if she had any issues with her teachers or anyone there at the school?" Dirk asked, wondering if there were any conflicts between the family and Mr. Tenebris.

"Funny you should mention that. She was telling me about someone just before she—well, before it happened. She didn't like him, but when I asked her to elaborate, she just claimed he had a weird vibe. She also said he was hanging out with some strange man all the time. A bald guy. I figured it was just like the way many other students don't like their teachers. I didn't really give it much regard. The teacher's name was Mr. Tallumbear … Teninbaum … or …"

"Mr. Tenebris?" Dirk offered.

"Yes, Tenebris was his name." Recognition momentarily flashed across her face. "You don't think he's hurting anyone, do you? He seemed like a nice enough man when we met him at the school."

"I'm not sure of anything right now, but it's a lead I am going to follow up," Dirk said. "Did you catch the name of the other guy?"

Mr. Ramsey walked by, dragging his feet across the floor as he did. "You've taken up enough of her time, Mr. Bentley. Phyllis, you need to make the coffee. This is business, which is more important than this joker."

Phyllis stood from the couch faster than Dirk would have given her credit for. Her eyes, no longer affixed on Dirk, bored into her husband. The uncomfortable stare down had its intended effect, and he left the room quickly with his tail between his legs.

"No, she never really knew who that other guy was," Phyllis answered the question lingering between her and Dirk. "And as far as looking at her room, I'm sorry, Mr. Bentley, but most of my daughter's things are in the garage now. My *husband* thought it'd be better if we got them out of the house. He's going to go through them and send her stuff to charity or throw it away." She cast her eyes down toward the floor. The way she said the word *husband* made him suspect she wasn't on board with what he was doing, but she was more or less just following his lead.

"I work a lot of murder cases, and in all of them it takes time to heal. I'm going to give you my card, and on the back of is the phone number of a friend of mine. Just call the number and ask to make an appointment. He will meet you whenever or wherever you want. He's good, and he really knows how to navigate stuff like this. Just tell them you want to meet with Keith on a personal matter." Dirk had a few cards in his wallet with Keith's number written on the back for just such an occasion. Grief counseling was his field of expertise.

"I don't really need any help. I'm strong, and I can handle this. I'll make it through." Phyllis parroted the mantra as if she was trying to convince herself more than Dirk. Perhaps she was chanting a mantra provided by her husband who had made her repeat the words a hundred times a day and she was desperately trying to believe them. She glanced at the number and then put it in her pocket.

"You know, if you need help, you only need to ask for it." Dirk searched for some understanding in her eyes.

She suddenly caught his meaning, and a momentary flash of anger softened to a more conciliatory look. "Mr. Bentley, it really isn't like that."

"Mrs. Ramsey, it never is. Can we go see the room?"

"Okay, but a lot of her stuff is in the garage. My husband is going to use it as an office."

The room still had marks on the wall where posters, pictures, and other things had previously hung. A few items remained, but for the most part, the room was bare. Dirk could tell there wasn't much left for him to examine.

Time to head to the garage.

Through the living room, Dirk saw photos of the family on the wall. They were everywhere. Mostly on boats but a some pictures were taken at Disneyland, one in Berlin, and a few in the Rockies. A disproportionate amount of the photos featured the girl and John Ramsey. The scene felt out of place after seeing his temper tantrum earlier.

"My husband and I got married when she was just five years old," Mrs. Ramsey said, smiling at one of the photos. "They loved each other. They really did. They were never like stepfamily. The two were like flesh and blood. Inseparable actually and he'd have done anything for her.

"They shared secrets, you know. Secrets from me. He would tell me about them at night when we were in bed. She asked him for advice about this or that. I didn't mind. I loved that they were close."

Dirk wondered how he could act so cold when someone he professed to truly love was murdered. He was really angry at Mr. Ramsey now, and his face must have shown his emotions. Dirk fell into a smoldering silence.

Mrs. Ramsey spoke up. "I know how he must strike you, Mr. Bentley, but he's hurting. He's just having a hard time showing it."

She seemed to be pleading with Dirk for understanding and perhaps some help, maybe not for her but for her husband.

Maybe Dirk had misjudged the situation. Maybe they both needed to talk with someone. In one way, it made sense. The moving of the girl's belongings, the seemingly overdriven work ethic, and his overall demeanor were suggestive of someone hiding their true emotions. He discreetly scanned Mrs. Ramsey again and found nothing to suggest physical violence.

In the garage, Dirk opened a few of the boxes, looking through the things you would normally find in a teenage girls' room. A collection of clothes, hairbrushes and hair bands, stuffed animals. Mrs. Ramsey sat stroking one of her daughter's stuffed animals.

Out of the pile, he'd found notes she'd made on pieces of paper. He'd also located a day planner with several entries on theater. One simply said, "T-Meeting Sept 15th". It was similar to the other reminder he had found. Dirk took a second to think through the information. September 15th was the day she was reported missing.

Just then, Mr. Ramsey entered the garage, and he was red in the face. "Bentley, I told you to get the hell out of here. Now look at the mess you're making! I need to sort this, and you're destroying it all."

"John, he's just trying to get some answers," Phyllis said, turning to her husband.

"Phyllis, go back in the house! No one is going to help. I'll get us through this. Me."

"John, calm down. He only wants some information."

"Don't tell me to calm down!" He backhanded her across the face.

Dirk could tolerate a lot. He'd seen people have full-blown fistfights in front of him, and he'd chosen not to intervene in those, but he couldn't tolerate a man raising a hand to his wife. Dirk slugged Mr. Ramsey so hard he knocked the man down, tumbling into the orderly stack of boxes of the dead girl's belongings. Dirk took a step back, bracing for the retaliation he was sure was coming.

One of the boxes tipped over, spilling its contents out, and a small picture frame slid across the floor to where Mr. Ramsey had landed. The photo was of a seven-year-old version of the girl and a slightly younger version of Mr. Ramsey. They were both standing beside a stream, wearing fishing hats. Instead of getting up to continue the fight, Mr. Ramsey just sat there, his eyes laser-locked on the framed picture. Tears pooled in the corner of his eyes and quickly streamed down the sides of his face.

He looked up at Dirk and then turned to his wife. "I loved her so much, you know? So much I can hardly stand it." Mr. Ramsey raised his hands to his face and held them there. "Oh my God, Phyllis, I'm so sorry. Every morning I've woken up and wanted to run into her room and tell her to get ready for school. Every night I have to look at her stuff and not see her. I loved her, Phyllis. I loved her more than any father has ever loved a child. I would easily die for her, take her place, do whatever I could. I just want this pain to stop. I want it all to go away. I want our baby back."

Phyllis fell into her husband, crying just as hard.

The situation hit Dirk like a ton of bricks. It wasn't Mr. Ramsey keeping his wife from grieving, it was Mr. Ramsey keeping *himself* from grieving. He could never accept that his daughter was gone.

Coming to terms with her murder it would mean letting in the pain. While Mr. Ramsey tried to shield himself, his wife had gotten caught in the emotional crossfire. No one could battle back the weight of such tragedy indefinitely.

Dirk suddenly felt for them. "The number on the back of the card is for someone who can help you. You both need to consider talking to a professional. Please call him."

Mr. Ramsey said in a voice, barely above a whisper, "Okay." He seemed defeated and vulnerable, not like the cocksure man he'd seen earlier. Dirk remembered someone saying something about how the first step to rebuilding was admitting that something had to be rebuilt in the first place. He prayed it was true. That meant there was a chance for what was left of this shattered family. Maybe all Mr. Ramsey needed was someone to punch him hard enough to bring him to his senses.

As Dirk finished rummaging through the boxes, he got a look at the girl's yearbook. Nothing of specific interest outside the note. Mr. Ramsey stood with him and helped search for specific things. He had tears in his eyes while doing it, but at least he at least was finally being cooperative.

Finishing up, Dirk turned to face him. "Thank you, Mr. Ramsey. Sorry I hit you."

"I'm sorry you had to. I deserved it. Thank you for understanding and maybe giving me a little of what I needed. If you catch this son of a bitch, I wouldn't be the least bit sad if you left him tied up in my garage. I'll take good care of him." The way he said it convinced Dirk he meant every word of it.

Dirk fished his keys out of his pocket. "Oh wait, one more question before I leave. Have either of you ever attended The First Transformational Church?"

"Yes, we're regular members there," Mrs. Ramsey said. "Why, is there something we should be concerned about?"

"No, not really, I was just curious. Just a loose end I'm trying to tie up." Dirk didn't want to raise any warning flags. This would mean the third victim who had at least some connection to the church.

Dirk thought about Mr. Ramsey's offer. He had to admit it had a certain appeal. Then again, whomever was killing these kids deserved to sit on death row. No easy way out for this guy.

He left the Ramseys with a wave, and it was a short drive to the next appointment.

Dirk pulled into the driveway of the last house on his list. The first two interviews had been time well spent, and he had no reason to believe this one would be any less so. As if on cue, at the appointed moment, the parents of Rachel Delgado, appeared at the door. The mother was wearing a dark, long conservative dress, and the father was clad in a dress shirt and bowtie. They both looked like they were going out to attend a formal occasion.

The residence was a one-story ranch-style house. The front yard was the size of a postage stamp. You could tell the neighborhood had been planned in every boring detail by some faceless developer who retired with his fortune shortly thereafter. The houses were practically on top of each other.

"Good afternoon. Mr. Delgado?" Dirk addressed the man standing on the front porch.

"Good afternoon. Mr. Bentley, I presume." He scanned Dirk up and down as if he was judging the appropriateness of his clothing.

"And Mrs. Delgado, correct?" He motioned to the woman standing beside the man.

"Yes, you are," she said politely but in a way of sounding a bit short. It was going to be an odd conversation. These two made Dirk instantly uncomfortable. He was reminded a little of Morticia and Gomez Addams from *The Addams Family*.

"I'm sorry if I'm interrupting anything. I can come back tomorrow if you'd like." Dirk found himself actually hoping they'd take him up on the offer.

"No, Mr. Bentley, a return visit will not be necessary. We agreed to an appointment," Mr. Delgado said. Given the directness of the answers, Dirk wondered if he would be doing most of the talking. They didn't strike him as being big on chit-chat.

"You see, it just looked like you were both going out or something, and I didn't want to interrupt." He wasn't sure why, but he felt compelled to explain himself.

Mr. Delgado continued. "Mr. Bentley, if you are referring to our attire, this is the way we always dress. We don't take to a slovenly style. Sloppy dress leads to a sloppy mind."

"Well, okay, you don't mind if I come in and ask you a few questions?" Dirk asked.

"Mr. Bentley, as we told you on the phone, we wish to talk with anyone who might be able to bring the person who murdered Rachel to justice," Mrs. Delgado said.

Dirk got the impression that their condescending tone was just the way they spoke and not necessarily directed at him.

They motioned for him to follow them into the house. The living room held all the traditional charm of a funeral parlor. Dignified and intentionally designed to be reserved and dour. It also struck him as odd how prepared they were for his visit. Unlike the others, this interaction reminded Dirk of something businesslike and transactional.

"So, I'd like to start by asking you a couple of standard questions. Did Rachel act any differently in the weeks before her death?"

Mrs. Delgado thought for a moment and then nodded. "Yes, she did. She started behaving more distantly. It's as if she went from being our daughter, who would tell us anything, to being closed in, silent. She seemed afraid of what we might say if she talked to us."

"I see. Can you think of anything changing in her life to make her react differently toward you?" Dirk wondered if she had parents like this that maybe she was rebelling.

"Yes, it was the damn theater group," Mrs. Delgado said.

"Marylyn!" Mr. Delgado snapped at her.

"I'm sorry, Harold," she said. "Mr. Bentley, we don't tolerate such talk in this house, and I should have known better. I apologize for my use of such language."

"Well, you did lose your daughter. I am sure you can be forgiven for a little profanity," Dirk said. At the mention of the theater group, Dirk's attention was immediately on high alert. A strange tingling sensation at the back of his neck made him instantly curious.

She smiled at Dirk in the way you do to people who had just pointed out the obvious. "Well, the good Lord is forgiving, thankfully for us. You see, it is that theater group she started working with which seemed to change her. She was spending more and more time with them. Obsessed with the theater, if you will. There was something about that club of theirs. It had her heart and soul. If you ask me, that's where you and those police should be looking."

"Did you tell the police this?" Dirk asked.

Mr. Delgado let you a deep sigh. "Yes, and they thanked us for the information, but I knew it wasn't going to go anywhere. They told us they'd spoken with the teacher, and he really didn't provide any additional insight. I don't trust they followed up on our suspicions. It was like I just was talking to a brick wall."

"I understand how it can feel that way. I have to ask you something, and it's personal. But it's a standard question—"

Mrs. Delgado held up her hand to indicate she now had the floor. "No, our daughter wasn't doing drugs, Mr. Bentley. I know my Rachel very well, and I inspected her room every day. There's no way she could've been into drugs without us finding them. The only time we really didn't have some control of our daughter was when she was at the theater group."

"I know this question is going to seem odd, but do you remember her maybe taking a religious stand you didn't necessarily agree with?"

Mr. Delgado answered. "Absolutely not. She was always such an exemplary girl. Maybe a little too enthusiastic about school sometimes, but besides that, she was perfect, a good God-fearing child."

"If you don't mind me asking, why didn't you go to the theater and see what was going on for yourselves? I mean, it sounded like you had your suspicions," Dirk asked.

"We tried, Mr. Bentley. Rachel begged us to stay away. She didn't want us coming down until the performance was ready. She was reaching the age where we felt she needed a little more autonomy, so we decided to give it to her," Mrs. Delgado answered.

Something happening once was not evidence, twice could be a coincidence, but three times was a trend. The theater was suspect number one at this point. Maybe find out a little more about this Mr. Tenebris.

These weren't absentee parents, Dirk could tell. Perhaps overly religious types, but they seemed to genuinely love Rachel. They might have been a little controlling, but he could imagine being the same way. "Let's take a look at her room, and I'll be out of your hair. Thank you for taking the time to talk with me."

Mrs. Delgado was trying hard not to let Dirk see her tears. Mr. Delgado quickly led Dirk up the stairs to Rachel's room. The door had been shut after the police had finished searching. A wreath of flowers graced the door, signifying the ending of a life. A photo of the girl lay in the center. Pretty girl with bright eyes. Her olive skin and hair framed the face of a beautiful young woman full of possibility. Mr. Delgado unlocked the door.

"I'm supposed to forgive him, you know," Mr. Delgado said. The words fell out of his mouth just above a whisper. Perhaps they were not meant for anyone, but Dirk felt more like it was a plea for understanding.

"I'm sorry, sir, what?" Dirk wasn't sure he had even heard him right.

Mr. Delgado repeated himself. "I am supposed to forgive whoever did this. The Lord says so. I am supposed to forgive others of their sins. Here I am, a strong man of faith, and I'm not sure I really can. What kind of monster does something like this, Mr. Bentley? Rachel was just a little girl. My little girl." Mr. Delgado stood there with a stoic and obviously hurt look on his face. Like Mrs. Delgado, he was not going to let his full emotions show in front of a stranger.

Investigations tended to make people face the impossibility of their situation all over again, even if they were trying to forget it. "Mr. Delgado, I don't have the answers. And I can't even begin to explain the reasons why someone does something like this. I don't know if I could forgive someone in this situation either. That doesn't make you less of a Christian. But it certainly does make you human.

"I'm not very religious, but I go to church every week. My best friend is the pastor. And he is smart. One thing he has always told me is that God doesn't prevent tragedies from happening, but he goes a long way to see us through the bad things when they do happen."

Mr. Delgado nodded and risked a smile. "You'll catch this person, Mr. Bentley. I know you will. We'll be praying for you."

Entering the room, Dirk said, "I can use all the prayers I can get, Mr. Delgado."

Dirk scanned Rachel's room. Again, it was the typical trappings of a teenage girl. He thought about the case files Carrie brought him. She'd been the first girl murdered of the ones he was able to speak to. It had been over two months since it happened. Thankfully, nothing in the room had been touched, so the little pieces of physical evidence the police tended to overlook would largely be undisturbed. A thick veneer of dust covered the surfaces.

The room had pink shag carpet. For a teenager, the room was surprisingly well-organized. Books were on the bookshelf, and papers were stacked and neat. The bed sheets were pulled tight to the bed.

Dirk began by scanning under the bed. On the floor, under the box spring, lay a small pile of papers. They looked like they were assignments from various classes. Dirk pulled out the stack. A spiral-leaf notebook at the bottom of the pile.

"Mr. Delgado, do you know if the police went through these?"

Mr. Delgado thought about it for a moment. "I think so. They didn't see anything important."

Dirk placed the stack on top of the bed and started flipping through the pile. On the top were papers, which looked like they were part of a math assignment. Under that were some worksheets, which had "Classical Literature 101" on the upper left-hand corner. He was about to set them aside when a smaller piece of paper fell out from in between the last loose page and the spiral notebook.

He picked the paper up off the floor. The writing on it was smudged so thoroughly that it was indistinguishable. The note was crushed, like someone had tried to stuff it in a locker without actually opening the door. Even with the note in such a poor state, Dirk recognized it right away. It was scratch paper from The First Transformational Church. Dirk's veins ran ice-cold. In addition to links to the theater, all three murders had come in contact with this church or maybe someone with access to scratch paper from the church.

The only book on the desk was her yearbook. Dirk flipped through it just as he had in the other girls' rooms. He found nothing consequential until he came to the theater arts page. The photo was of the theater troupe associated with the school. All the theater students were there, just like in the other yearbooks. In Rachel's yearbook, the face of Mr. Tenebris had been scratched out with a pen, and the word "Diablo" had been written next to him. It seemed universal that the students hated Mr. Tenebris.

"One last question, Mr. Delgado. Did your family ever attend a church called The First Transformational Church?"

"No, we have our own church, Mr. Bentley."

"Okay, well, thank you for your time, Mr. Delgado." Dirk walked out of the room and then toward the stairs.

Mr. Delgado said, "Wait, Mr. Bentley, just a moment if you please." He turned down the hallway and yelled to his wife. "Marylyn!"

"Yes, dear" came the response from some other portion of the house.

"Where was Richard and Deb's wedding? Do you remember the name of the church?" Mr. Delgado yelled back to her.

"Weird coffee shop. It was a place called The First Transformational Church or something like that." Mrs. Delgado's voice rang out. "Had that really odd man of the cloth who ran things."

"Mr. Delgado, it may not be important, but did you like the guy? I mean, did you notice anything off about him?"

He frowned. "Well, I don't speak ill about other people, but since you asked, he was a bit of an odd duck. Talked a lot about life forces and the soul. How we could transfer souls from one to another. It was just odd, is all. Not what the good Lord taught us. But Richard and Deb are good friends, so we went with it. The pastor seemed to be very fond of Rachel. He even said he knew the theater teacher, that Mr. Tenebris fellow."

Dirk had to shake himself out of momentary shock. The pastor had a connection to Tenebris. Tenebris could have belonged to the church. Maybe the church was where Tenebris was spotting his next victims. Only a hypothesis at this point but one worth testing.

As Dirk left, he handed Mr. Delgado one of his business cards in case there was anything else they could think of to help the investigation. Mr. and Mrs. Delgado stood hand in hand at the doorway, looking reposed, almost dignified. Dirk had the feeling as soon as his car rounded the bend that they would be crying their eyes out, in each other's arms, alone in their grief.

Three separate families, one numb, one trying to hide their pain, and another in full-blown mourning. Different stages of grief, different types of families. They all shared three things in common: the theater, the First Transformational Church, and a very tragic event.

Chapter 7
In The Fringes

Keith loved his data, and the database of churches he kept was a wealth of knowledge.

He glanced down at the paper from the First Transformational Church that Dirk had found. The writing on the paper was clean and precise. Obviously someone with good penmanship. The information placed on the top and bottom by the printing company was professional. A quick search of his own computer yielded no mention of the church with that name or anything matching that address or phone number.

If they were a small congregation, it was possible they'd slipped under his radar. A website for the church revealed it was a dead-end site which was last maintained a year ago. He would drive out to the address listed on the paper as soon as possible, but for now, he had to return to the task at hand.

Most of the people in his files he knew quite well and had for years. Small churches tended to rely on each other for support unless they were affiliated with a larger denomination. Bigger religious organizations always printed a logo on the scratch paper, so he reasoned the First Transformational Church was an unaffiliated congregation and likely a small one. So, asking the lesser-known churches in town about this place might be a good place to start.

He was able to winnow down the list quickly. Church figures of other religions, cults, even the local Satanic leader, Ed Pickins, could be annoying but not necessarily violent, let alone capable of murder.

There were three people he thought might give him something. All of them were local leaders of fringe congregations. groups who had the kinds of connections into communities that might share similar beliefs. Keith considered it unlikely that any of them were involved in murder, but he might get lucky. Maybe he was barking up the wrong tree, but being short on leads, Dirk and Keith needed a break.

Keith pulled into the parking lot of the "New Reformed Evangelical Church of the Holy Ones". He always wondered why a church needed such a long name. The head of the church was a fundamentalist preacher named Ryan Daily, who had taken to calling himself "The Light". The parking lot was empty, but it looked like an old pull-barn next to the farmhouse served as their sanctuary. It scared Keith a little bit, resembling a scene out of a Stephen King novel. He half expected a large dog to attack him as he stepped out into the parking lot.

And yet, it was time to get to work.

Shotguns were popular for home protection for three reasons. The first was that they were easy to operate. Secondly, you didn't have to be accurate to make it count. The third reason was that it made a distinctive sound when the slide was being moved. Those three things flashed through Keith's mind as he heard that noise. He froze in his tracks.

"That's far enough, get those hands up! You're on my property, and we ain't havin' services, so you just better git on your way." A voice boomed at him from the opening of the barn.

Keith had had a gun pulled on him several times during his frequent forays into the wilds of Virginia. By now he understood the drill, but it still didn't cease to scare him half to death. "Look, I just want to talk. I'm not from the government or anything, I promise. My name is Pastor Keith Marvin. You can call me Keith. I just have a few questions for you."

"You sure you ain't one of them court-appointed folks? You know, serving papers and all?" the gun-toting Daily asked as he approached Keith.

"No, I promise, a fellow pastor." Keith thought it best to leave out the private detective bit until Daily was unarmed. Even then, he needed to tread lightly. He felt a bead of sweat roll down his back.

"A fellow man of the cloth, huh? Okay, you can put yer hands down and come on over, boy."

A few minutes later, they were sitting on the porch, and Daily offered him lemonade as if nothing had happened. "Sorry 'bout the shotgun. Me and the law ain't on speakin' terms right now. Satan puts the gov'mnt in our way as a stumbling block."

Even without the shotgun, Daily painted an imposing figure. He easily stood six feet tall and was about four feet wide at the shoulders. Keith recalled Daily had been raised on a farm in Oklahoma, growing up baling hay and feeding cattle. All those bales of hay and hauling buckets of feed had made him a strong as an ox. He almost always dressed in overalls, and today he wore a straw hat, giving the impression he had fallen out of the backwoods.

"I see," Keith said. "Well, I'm here because I have a couple of questions. I'm helping investigate a murder, and I was wondering if you may recall anything helpful."

"Welp, whatta ya wanna know?" Daily asked, eyeing him suspiciously.

"I'm not with the cops. I'm working with a private investigator hired by the family of the girl who was killed most recently." Keith tried to reassure the mountain of a man. The last thing he needed was to have to flee the porch with a shotgun-toting lunatic running after him.

"The Smithfield girl," Daily said. "Been all over the news. Sad thing. Too bad about it. I'll admit to being a sinner, Keith. I can promise you I ain't no murderer, and it's the good Lord's truth."

"I'm sure of it, but I was wondering if you have seen anything odd in your flock. Maybe point us in the right direction? Has anyone been acting strange? Maybe someone showed up, created some problems, and vanished?"

"Naw, not that I reckon. Just the usual folk comin' and goin'. Mostly farmers from the countryside. But Keith, look here, I know what you think of my ways. But you got to believe me, I'd do anything to sort this for you, if I could. I reckon ain't no man you got on yer hands. A monster, preyin' on young'uns, that's what you have there. I'll ask around. I'd sure love to see that sucker hang."

"I sure appreciate it. We are working our butts off to try to solve this one. Maybe give some peace to those families. Anything you can think of which could help out would be appreciated." Keith handed him his business card and drained the last of his lemonade. He made his way back to his truck, happy to be leaving Daily's company. One of three down, a big goose egg for Keith on his first outing. He just hoped Dirk or Victor was having more luck.

The next church was closer into town, and the pastor was an old acquaintance of Keith's. He was generally an amiable person and more importantly, a pacifist who was unlikely to point a gun at him. The tires of his truck made a crunching noise as he pulled into the parking lot of a small church backing up against a state park. It was the congregation led by Reverend Jeff Peters.

Shutting off the car engine, he could see an old man in front of the church, tending to a flower bed of carnations. The church was an old Baptist church whose congregation had gone bankrupt, and the building had been auctioned off. Jeff Peters bought it and moved a congregation in that he had grown out of his house.

The old man weeding the flower bed struck Keith as thin and frail. He wore an old blue dress shirt, a pair of worn denim jeans, an apron looking like it might have come from a local gardening supply store, gardening gloves, and a straw hat. Keith knew from meeting the man before that the elderly gentleman tending the flowers was the Reverend Peters.

When he'd purchased the building, he created a local sensation by chopping down the cross on the roof with a hand axe, claiming it was a symbol and therefore against Christ, as they shouldn't worship any idols. During the stunt, he fell off the building and spent three weeks in a hospital getting his leg repaired. He got sympathy points from his congregation, and the other churches left him alone because they didn't want to be seen as picking on the poor reverend in the hospital.

He'd cut down that cross fifteen years ago though, and he'd mellowed considerably since then. The miracle cure for his notorious crankiness came in the form of moonshine. Both drinking and selling.

As Keith stepped out of the car, the old gentleman walked over, taking off his gardening gloves and extending his hand. "Well, as I live and breathe. How the heavens are you, Keith?"

"I'm good, Jeff. You look well. Keeping out of the papers, I see. How is the shine business?" His extracurricular activities were common knowledge, and Keith wasn't breaching any protocols by asking him directly.

"Ahhh, publicity is a young man's game. Shinin' is an older man's prerogative, though. Been brisk lately. You want to try some of the new apple pie? Fresh off the still. Gardening sure does work up a powerful thirst." Jeff motioned to the front door of the church.

"Sure, I'll have a snort. I still need to drive though. Got a couple of questions I need to ask you. Not about you, more about your congregants. Has to do with a murder investigation." Keith had known Jeff for years, so Jeff was familiar with Keith's many different hats.

"C'mon in, Keith. I'll help you if I can." The two men walked into the church and back to the pastor's office, where Jeff poured two glasses of his latest moonshine. Keith took the glass and toasted his good health. Based on Jeff's labored breathing, he could use all the toasting and praying he could get. The old man seemed to have aged twenty years since the last time Keith saw him.

"Wow, I think you get better and better at the corn juice with every batch. Nice and smooth, and it almost tastes like it should have a dollop of whipped cream or something. Amazing."

"You didn't come here to sample the local elixir though. What is on your mind, Keith?"

"Right. Have you have had anyone here acting weird or maybe leaving your little group under odd circumstances? Any other movements in the area giving you trouble?"

Jeff scratched his whiskery chin as he pondered Keith's question. "Let me see, not any I can think of offhand. Well, wait, not necessarily true. You know … we did have this one fellow. A fundamentalist type but very odd."

Keith thought it was funny he'd put his response in those terms. Years ago, Jeff would spend the day on the street corner outside of Woolworths screaming at passing patrons they were going to hell because Woolworths was run by the devil. He'd chant it was because wool came from sheep, and Jesus was the shepherd, and no one could measure the "worth" of Jesus's flock. It represented commercialism, which would send them all to hell.

The stunt, made for the local papers, was slightly insane, but it got him in the press and brought in more parishioners. Back in his heyday, Jeff was a true showman.

"What do you mean *a fundamentalist type?*" Keith asked.

"You know how sometimes people are overcome by the spirit? Well, he'd lie down in the middle of the aisle and scream and speak in tongues. Now, I don't mind a good Tower of Babel kind of day, but he spoke in Latin. Been a long time since I studied Latin, but I could tell he wasn't saying anything nice. He went too far one day when he was quoting out of some book he brought in with him. I had to have a talk with him. I never saw him after that." Jeff was recounting the event as if was happening right in front of him all over again.

"Do you remember the book?" Keith asked.

"The name, no. I do remember what ruffled my feathers though. It had something to do with the weight of a human soul and capturing it. The thing looked like he had written it himself. Ain't gonna fly in this house of worship. I reckon he was committing some sort of chicanery."

"Why do you think he was up to no good?"

"He talked about branching off and leading a congregation in what he called 'the truth.' He carried on with taking the soul of a person and putting it into other people or things. He claimed he could do it and had done it before." Jeff's face turned red as he recalled the heated conversation.

The old man leaned forward and looked him straight in the eye. "Keith, I don't much get along with the folks in town or the other pastors, but you came out to see me on honest terms, and I appreciate the visit. So, I'll give you somethin' straight. If you think he's involved, you're going to want to be very careful. I know dangerous people when I see em', and I can tell you, he's dangerous. There was just something about him. Hard to put my finger on it."

"Do you remember his name? Anything I could use to find him?"

"Yeah, I think he called himself Mr. Harmon. Don't recall his first name, but I am pretty sure that was it. I kept after him for more contact information, but he never gave me anything else."

"Think that was his real name?"

"Unsure. Lots of people come and go around here. You would be surprised at how many aliases I get in the register. But you there was something else peculiar about this guy. He was really interested in the theater. Seemed to know a lot about it. Oh yeah, one other thing. I think he was a doctor of some sort."

Keith was scribbling down notes in his small notebook. "That is very interesting, Jeff. Thanks for that. Do you mean an actual doctor or he worked in the medical field?"

"No, no, not a doctor or a nurse. Curse this old brain! What'd he tell me?" Jeff made some facial gyrations as his mind wandered down a mental path to access the information he was looking for. He brightened, and his brow relaxed. "Oh yeah, horses. That's right, he was a veterinary doctor." Satisfied with his accomplishment, he took another swig of his concoction.

"Okay, that's something at least. Hey, by the way, have you heard of a place called the First Transformational Church?" Keith asked.

"Not that I can recall. You think they are part of these murders somehow? You wouldn't be out here asking pastors about the murders if you didn't reckon a church could be involved in some way."

"Too soon to tell really, but a piece of scratch paper was found at one of the scenes. It was from their office. It might not mean anything." Keith stood and set his glass down on the desk. "Jeff, thank you very much for the information. I'm not sure where it'll lead, but if we find out, I'll let you know." He handed the old man his business card. "And you give me a call if you think of anything else."

"Okay, will do, Keith. Here, take one for home." Jeff handed Keith a full jar of the moonshine. "Tell your friends and neighbors. I could always use more customers. And please, don't be a stranger. I don't get a lot of social calls out here from folks in town, so feel free to drop by and see this old man." The way he said it made him sound very lonely.

"I'll be sure to stop by from time to time." Keith felt sorry for the aged minister. Once he'd been a powerful pastor, and now he was just an elderly man on the fringes of society, doing the only thing he knew how to do. He'd likely die out here in his church. But Jeff greeted him as a friend, and he'd helped him when he could have just stayed quiet. Keith would come back again, if only to sit and talk.

Keith had one more appointment. He was glad it was his last because it was potentially the most annoying. The person he was going to see was Jackson Taylor. Born into an old Southern family, he was raised in the Baptist tradition and was forced into seminary. When he'd started out, it looked like he had a promising career ahead of him, but it was short-lived. He began dabbling in some of the stranger Southern religious practices. He'd once tried to introduce snake-handling as part of the religious ceremony of his parish. He was lucky in that his parishioners had gotten him to the hospital before he'd died.

Keith had met Jackson only once. He reminded him a little of the unholy love child of a used car salesman and the pastor from the movie *Poltergeist*. Jackson was self-serving, making him evil and a dangerous pastor. He mainly preyed on the old and infirm. He'd spent the better part of the last ten years in trouble with the IRS. One year, he had claimed he had ten dependents and his car counted as both a business vehicle and a second office. The IRS was less than amused.

He had a way with the elderly, and by serving the ones with questionable mental faculties, he could essentially just take their money. He especially loved Alzheimer's patients. Keith knew Taylor had a famous gambling problem, and he was partial to blonde hookers and cocaine. Poor attributes as a pastor, perfect for an informant. He understood the sad underbelly of the inner city, and he might know something about what was going on.

As Keith pulled into the parking lot of Jackson's "church", a no-tell motel on the highway, Keith saw several squad cars surrounding the building. To his surprise, Carrie was standing there with a clipboard in her hand, looking at some paperwork. He also saw the words "U.S. MARSHAL" emblazoned across the back of another car. It looked like maybe the IRS had finally caught up with Jackson.

Carrie glanced up from the paperwork and smiled at Keith as he climbed out of his car. "Hey, I hope you're not here to save his soul, because right now his soul is going to be communing in a federal prison."

"Actually, I was here to ask him if he knew anything about the murders," Keith replied. "But it looks like you may be bagging and tagging him for something else?"

Carrie smirked, "Tax evasion. Seems they eventually caught up with this fine fellow. The U.S. government wants their money, or they want you. Either way they're going to get something. Do you have any solid evidence he's connected with the murders? Please tell me you do. That would make my day."

"No, nothing to hold him on. This is really a shot in the dark. Just a cold call to see if he knew anything substantial."

"Okay, well, maybe I can buy you a few moments with the honorable Reverend Taylor. That piece of shit gives me the creeps." Carrie winced as she said it.

"I'll be fast. I have just a few questions."

"Hey, Marshal Thomas," Carrie yelled to a man in a dress shirt and western-style hat with a badge around his neck. "Keith is a PI on another case. Can he have about five minutes?"

"I suppose, but not too long, huh? I need to escort this fine, upstanding gentleman to the county lockup for some soul searching,'" the marshal said.

"Get bent," Taylor said.

"See, preaching the word of the lord already." The marshal laughed at his own joke.

"Keep it brief, Keith. It is getting kind of late," Carrie whispered to him.

"Reverend Taylor, do you remember me? We met sometime before."

Jackson was wearing a stained pair of sweatpants, a ripped AC/DC concert shirt, and a shiny pair of handcuffs. He looked like he'd been roughed up a bit during his discussions with the police officers. A little bead of blood was coming out of his nose. Obviously resisting arrest would be another charge added to his rap sheet.

"Oh yes, I remember you," he grumbled. "You're the Methodist, right? Never understood Methodists. They're sorta like Lutherans, just less religious. Anyway, I suppose I can give you a few minutes. But I'm in sort of a hurry. I seem to have an appointment which positively can't wait. They even sent a car. Can you imagine that? How can I help you?"

Keith made a scowl at the obvious crack at Methodists but instantly let it go, considering Jackson was in handcuffs. "I need to ask you if you've had anyone come into your flock recently who was a little suspicious? Maybe someone you thought was a little dangerous?"

"Well, I know a lot of dangerous people, they need churchin' too, but no one really comes to mind. But that could be because of the concussion." Taylor shot a glance at the marshal, who simply nodded back. "I can't think of a person in particular."

"How about a place called the First Transformational Church?" Keith asked.

Taylor looked at Keith with an air of suspicion. "Now that's an interesting question. Why would you ask about them?"

"We're investigating the murders of the girls. Do you remember something that could help?"

"Well, maybe I do and maybe I don't. What's in it for me?"

"Your eternal soul? How about doing the right thing? Or simply just helping bring peace to some families? C'mon, Reverend, spill it," Keith said.

"I really see no advantage for me to get involved." Taylor shrugged.

"Hey, shithead, tell him what you know. Or do you want me to let it slip to the prosecutor you have information on a murder case and wouldn't help?" The marshal barked from where he was leaning on his car.

"Or we can also drop the hint to the prosecutor how you helped out in a murder investigation even as you were being arrested." Carrie added her two cents' worth, ever the diplomat.

"Fine." Taylor sneered back at the marshal. "So, a few weeks ago I call up one of my normal girls. My local girlfriends. She's a real snow queen. You know, liked the blow. I went over to her place, and she was high as a kite. She went on about this church called the First Transformational Church. It's in some coffee shop or something over on the North side. She said the pastor told her she could be saved and how he had the power to take someone's soul and put it into something else. It was insane. She just rambled on. Here's the crazy thing, she said the pastor gave her the coke. Can you believe that, paid her in cocaine for a blow job."

"Does your snow queen have a name?" Carrie asked.

"Yeah, Julia Severs, goes by Stardust." Taylor smiled at a memory.

Carrie sighed and put away her notebook, "Great, her current address is a drawer at the medical examiner's office. We fished her out of the river two days ago. She had enough powder in her system to kill an elephant."

"Oh well, if you think of anything, or you hear from anyone who sounds like they could help, let us know." Keith handed a business card to the marshal to be given to Jackson at processing.

The marshal loaded Jackson into the squad car. Keith stood by as Carrie finished up a form she was working on. She tore off the top copy and handed it to the marshal. "Congrats, you are the proud owner of one of my biggest problems."

"Sheesh, thanks, Carrie. Nice to meet you, Keith. I am outta here." The marshal and Taylor disappeared into the evening.

She then turned her attention to Keith. "How's the investigation coming?"

"Well, okay, I guess. Not too much on my side. One of my guys thinks he remembers someone who might have been a veterinarian or something. Possibly named Harmon, but that could be an alias. Harmon acted all crazy and was quoting out of a book or something and then disappeared and no one has seen him in a while. And that thing Taylor said about the First Transformational Church was interesting, but with the girl dead, it's going to be hard to get any more information. I'm not sure what to make of any of this yet, but that's Dirk's job. Have you talked to him today?"

"No," she said. "We found out about Taylor this morning and had to get ready for the raid. Sounds like the feds have him good. He may be going off to one of those special prisons. You know … in a spiritual way, involving rape by your cellmate. Maybe he'll find religion in there." She chuckled. "The federal prosecutor isn't happy with him, but I we've said the same thing before. He'll probably be back. It's just a matter of time."

Keith nodded, rubbing his temples, "Okay, I think I'm going to head home. Kinda tired, and I need to do some work before I go to bed tonight. Those sermons don't sound wonderful all by themselves."

"Wait, you mean you actually write those? I figured you just belong to a sermon-of-the-week club, and they were e-mailed to you on Saturday." Carrie laughed at her own joke.

"Very funny," Keith said as he turned.

"Alright, I'll see you tomorrow then," Carrie said.

Keith waved and headed toward his car. His growing headache was less a manifestation of his interaction with Taylor than the stress of knowing that if they did not catch a break soon, the killer could just as easily add to their impressive tally.

CHAPTER 8
THE TEACHER

Victor materialized in the back of the shop and snuck out of his quiet corner. There were only two people still working. The rest had cut out early. He came through the wall to see Claire sitting in the office, watching television. She was normally in the shop tinkering with motorcycles, so someone must have told her to wait.

"Claire, can't you convince your uncle to throw out that stupid old TV and get me something nicer?" Victor popped his head through a wall. "I mean, it's bad enough he makes me do things for him, but I have to watch television on the confounded old thing." She always thought it was amusing to see him do this nifty trick. She smiled at him and hit the power button on the remote, snapping the TV off.

"Vic, just the spectral, paranormal, afterlife-livin' goofball I need to see. My uncle sent me over here to relay a message to you. Maybe it's something or maybe not, but he needs you to run back across the River Styx and see if anyone can tell you about a guy named Arthur Tenebris. I know he's a teacher at the school. I don't have anything to do with him, since he teaches theater. It could be a lead of some sort."

"Hmmm, okay. Arthur Tenebris, I'll check him out." Victor sailed across the room and floated over Dirk's desk. "I'll ask, but Heather hasn't gotten back her memories. They're all still pretty scrambled. Maybe the other victims can tell me something if I can find them. Harder to locate any single person in the afterlife after they've been there for a while."

Claire picked up her backpack and slung it over her shoulder. "Well, my work is done here for today. I have some homework to do. This would all be easier if you had a cell phone or something."

Victor scoffed. "Sheesh, a cell phone. What would I want with one of those things? I see you, the living, spending all yer time talking, texting, or surfing your lives away. Try reading a book or taking a stroll."

"Awww Vic, you're really cute in an antiquated ghostly sort of way. Seriously, Victor, you boys be careful with this one."

"What's this guy gonna do, kill me?" Victor suddenly changed into a giant eye and rolled it at her. "I already killed me many years ago."

"Well, you know what Tenebris is in Latin, right?" She raised her eyebrows like a schoolteacher only half expecting the student to answer correctly.

"Sorry, kiddo, my last Latin class was like a hundred and sixty years ago. I'm a bit rusty."

"Darkness. In Latin, it means darkness. If this is our bad guy, he could be dangerous." She waved goodbye as she stepped right through him.

"Confound it all," he yelled after Claire. "Told you not to do that."

"Bye, Vic." Claire disappeared out of the door of the shop.

"Interesting. Mr. Darkness," Victor said out loud to no one. He dissolved into a vapor trail, starting his trip back to the spirit world.

The return to the spirit world was always a mystery to Victor, since he seemed to emerge in exactly the spot he needed to be, as if someone was purposely directing him. Coming out of the tunnel into the afterlife, he materialized on the green of the park where he had left Heather. He knew instinctively she had to be around there somewhere.

As he looked for her, Victor asked around to see if anyone had heard anything about the other girls. Unfortunately, he came up with nothing.

The living assumed it was easy to locate someone in the afterlife, like there was some sort of heavenly directory where you could just ask for the person and they would magically appear. Victor thought the living had some absurd notions about heaven and hell.

It didn't take Victor long to find Heather. She was out on the ball field, playing with a bunch of other kids. They all looked like they were having a great time, and Victor was pleased to see she had found some friends. This would assist in a smoother transition, and the familiarity of an activity would also help her regain some of her memories.

He felt bad about interrupting the game, but this was important. The name Claire had given him could dislodge a recollection or two. The girls appeared to be playing some version of soccer, but they were laughing more than they were kicking the ball. It made him smile to see them happy.

"Hey, Victor!" Heather shouted, noticing him walking up to the group. "I found some people to hang out with. One girl died in like the 1300s! Another died of the plague." She excitedly pointed at her new teammates.

"See, what did I tell you? In the afterlife you're pretty much never alone. There's almost always someone within earshot of you. Can be downright noisy sometimes." Victor took a seat on a set of bleachers on the side of the field, and Heather joined him.

"So, why are you back so soon?" Although it was highly likely she was unaware how long he'd actually been gone for.

"I need to ask you if you remember a man." Victor leaned back on the bleachers. "The guys on the other side are looking into the circumstances of your death. They want to know if you remember a guy by the name of Arthur Tenebris."

"Not that I recall. It does sound familiar to me in some way." She contorted her face as she tried to force a recollection. "Not sure why, though. I think he was a leader or something. Uuuugh, sorry, Victor, I just don't remember."

"It's okay, honey. I've seen many others in your situation, and I can promise it'll come back to you after a while. Just takes time. So don't worry about it and return to your game." Victor patted her shoulder reassuringly and stood up to leave. "Experience is the best teacher. I can tell you that the harder you try, the longer it'll take. So, relax."

"I know, you keep saying that, but what if it never comes back? What if I see people that I should have remembered and just can't?"

Victor nodded to her. "I understand. But think about it. Did you recall how to play soccer, or football, or whatever you want to call it?"

"I suppose."

"And you like playing soccer, right?"

Heather let a small smile escape. "Well, I should. I mean I have been in leagues since I was five and—"

"Ah, see. A memory. That's the start. That's what we needed. Like a key to unlock the door, that will help open the floodgates a little. It'll come easier after this. I've coached many people through here, and teaching people how to find what they have lost is kind of a specialty."

"That's it, Victor. A teacher! He's a teacher. And I didn't like him at all. Something about him. I can't recall what it was exactly. Still, I know the guy is a teacher of some sort." She was struggling, but at least there was some sort of recognition. "But wait."

Victor sat back down on the bleachers. "What? Do you remember something else?"

"Yes, there was another person. Something to do with an office. I can see him, kind of. But I can't remember a name. Mr. Tenebris was evil. I hated him, Victor. I think he was also a doctor of some sort. No, not a doctor, but he did something with medicine… maybe?" Heather looked exhausted. "That's all I have right now, I'm sorry."

"Oh, Heather, don't worry about it." Victor smiled reassuringly. "You did great. Every bit can help us. Just relax, and eventually more blanks will fill in, I promise you."

Not much to bring back to the guys, but it was possible they were dealing with two people, not just the one. If he had no luck finding the other girls, at least Heather was starting to get back something of her memory. A girl not liking one of her teachers wasn't unusual, but mentioning the other guy might be important. They had to get a look at Tenebris's office.

Victor knew she required more time to sort things out on her own. Forcing her to remember might have the opposite effect of what he was looking for. He needed to rest before he headed back to the world of the living; all this trans-dimensional travel was exhausting. But he wondered to himself, *how much time do we really have before the murderer claims another victim?*

CHAPTER 9
PAIN WILL HEAL YOU

People filed into a small coffee shop sitting unceremoniously in the middle of an old parking lot next to a long-forgotten mini mall, where most of the stores sat shuttered against the economy. People walking in were a little more dressed-up than the rundown coffee shop would warrant. The store was the only business still open in the remains of this forgotten commercial enterprise. Today it was closed, as it always was on Sundays, but they leased their space out to a small independent church, which had recently been established.

As the people walked down the stairs to the basement, it was like they were taking a journey through the history of the building. At the top of the stairs were boxes of cups and bags for to-go coffee and baked goods. At the bottom, there was a long hallway lined with several large boxes of advertisements and a few dusty racks from when the space was used as a travel agency. Further down the corridor were some pamphlets, bottles of expired lotion, and a skeleton wearing a lab coat left over from when the space was leased by a chiropractor, whose office had closed in the early 90s.

The hallway ended in a large conference room that once was used as a small dance studio. One wall was mirrored and still featured a barre that the ballerinas practice with. Today the space was the home of the First Transformational Church.

The entire room looked like it might have fallen out of some company photo taken back in the 80s. The floor was made of the cheap tan industrial tile popular at the time, and the walls were painted with a shade to match. Walls were partially draped with mustard-yellow cloth, put there to hide the marks leftover from the previous tenants.

Sitting on top of a platform, in the front of the room, was a makeshift altar. In reality, it was two sawhorses purchased at the local hardware store and then repurposed into a semi-permanent table. It was covered by a large tablecloth, not quite long enough to reach the floor. If someone looked at the bottom of the table, they would see the bare legs of the sawhorses. A makeshift altar for a makeshift congregation.

Stage left held a small electric piano, which was wired into some old stereo speakers purchased at a used electronics store. The faux wood had been painted black to help the audio equipment blend in.

As the people took their seats in the folding chairs, a young woman walked to the front and lit two candles on the altar. She then sat down on the piano bench and opened a yellow folder with sheet music. She started playing "Nearer My God to Thee". What she lacked in technical skills, she made up for in enthusiasm. The parishioners just smiled at her passionate efforts.

Halfway through the hymn, a door at the back of the room opened, revealing a figure clad in black. He stepped out of the darkness and walked slowly down the center aisle facing the front. As he progressed toward the altar, he touched the shoulders of the parishioners sitting beside the center aisle. The women he touched swooned, and the men nodded their heads in reverence.

The man stepped up onto the homemade platform. "Friends, I'd like to start by thanking you for joining us today. You could have been anywhere today, but you came here. You could have been at any church, synagogue, or mosque, but you are here. Friends, I don't claim to have all the answers, but I know together we can undertake the search for the truth. A truth that will set you free. And if you let me, I can set you *free*!" The final word came out of his mouth with a shout loud enough that someone upstairs could have heard it. The piano player followed along with a melody.

"The man sitting in Washington wants something from you. The man in the tax offices of the county wants somethin' from you, yes he does! The man sitting in the state capital, yes, he wants something from you too. Don't they? What do they want?" As he spoke, he gyrated around the altar, and his face became flush with exertion or perhaps the heat of the shoddily-erected spotlights hanging from the ceiling. Sweat formed on his brow, and he perspired through his shirt.

The reverend worked his congregants into a lather with his words. These were people who were low-level wage earners and pensioners. These were his flock, and he spoke their language. He could entice them to open up to him. He understood they wanted to believe in something.

"Well, I'll tell you what. All those people want your money, but more importantly they want your soul. They need you to keep working so they can take more and more of you. And when you can't work anymore, do you think they're going to give any of your earnings back? Do you think they're going to turn to you and say, 'Well sir, well ma'am, here's some of your money. You need it more than we do.'" The reverend simulated throwing money into the air as he walked halfway up the aisle. "Do you think they're going to do that, my friends?"

Several in the congregation were shouting answers to his questions now. The woman at the piano had gotten up and brought in a tumbler of water from a small table offstage. She was so fast and so smooth that no one even noticed it until the refreshment just seemed to appear. The reverend took a little sip of the water and put the glass back down on the altar.

"Well, my friends. God wants something from you." The reverend looked up to the ceiling of the church and pointed as if he had discovered something new and unique about the nature of God. "He wants something indeed. But He doesn't want what is yours, He wants what's His. He wants the very thing he gave you at the moment you were created in His image. He wants your very souls!"

A few minutes later, the congregants sang a hymn while the pastor stood at the altar table, drinking water from the glass. Two selected readings were read. The first was from the book of Solomon and the second from the book of Mark.

After the reading had concluded, the man in black turned to face his flock again. "Friends, it isn't a simple matter of living and dying. Some people die without ever having lived. Yes, they most certainly do! They just don't understand the true nature of their own souls. We go on daily as if the accumulation of wealth will heal us, but does it, friends? I say no!"

Some of the congregants shouted out to him as he worked the crowd. Two men in overalls were nodding along with him as he spoke. A black woman dressed in a pink dress and a white hat fanned herself while he preached. An overweight woman dabbed sweat off her neck.

"But we could die tomorrow, friends. We could, just as easy as snapping my fingers." The man paused and grabbed his chest for dramatic effect. Looking at one of the teenage girls up front, he continued, "Your soul is pure, child. Pure as white laundry hung out to dry. Are you ready to give up your soul, right here, right now?"

He moved to her brother, sitting next to her. "How about you, young man? Are you ready to commit your soul to a more divine purpose?" The way he said "purpose" came out as a sibilant, snake-like hiss. The crowd was putty in his hands. At this moment, they would have killed for him.

Both the boy and the girl, brother and sister, were spellbound by the minister. Unable to speak, they simply moved their heads up and down in synchronized display of adoration. Their parents, sitting next to them, nodded their approval.

"Good, your time will come soon enough, children. It doesn't matter if you live to be fifteen or a hundred and fifteen, it will seem to have gone by too quickly. But it's alright. The soul is a commodity in many ways. The Bible tells us we are just the physical vessels for our very souls. You can transfer it to others. You can literally leave your soul with someone else! Can you not give your soul to the devil? Sure you can. Then why couldn't you commit your soul to me?

"You can make it so you live in the very heart of another. I can show you how, brothers and sisters. These children before you are pure of heart. Their souls are perfect. In many ways, at the end of childhood, we are at our most unblemished. Willing to believe with the faith of a mustard seed but able to understand what giving it all up really means. But let me bring it down for you, ladies and gentlemen. I want you to hear me, and I want you to understand me. More importantly, I want you to feel me."

As if to illustrate his point, the reverend sat down on the end of the platform making up his pulpit. He leaned on the wall, like he just physically couldn't go on. He undid his collar and wiped the sweat off his brow with the handkerchief from his pocket, the microphone dangling loosely in his other hand. He was a master of the stage, and this was his audience.

He sat, focusing on the floor as if something on it had caught his immediate interest. He brought the microphone up close to his lips. Whispering into the microphone, he said, "The man sitting before you is a simple man. I'm but a man who went through his own trials. You know that already. I led a life of debauchery and shame. I used and abused myself. Feel sorry for my experiences if you like, but please save your pity. I rose from the ground and dusted myself off. Interesting, no? And yet, none of this tells you anything about my soul. It doesn't give you a glimpse of whether I have licentiousness in my heart or godliness in my veins. Ladies and gentlemen, I can take any one of you and get you to eternal life … if you let me."

He drew a ragged breath, as if delivering his message was taking every last bit of energy from his body. "Many years ago, I started with the soul of someone pure of heart, one young precious child, and tonight I have assisted many. But I remain steadfast in my need to help more … but it isn't everything, my friends. Not at all the end."

As if a spring had been installed into the floor, the reverend jumped up into the air and landed in front of the platform. He was yelling into the microphone now like a raving lunatic. "I can't tell you how much it hurts me to know the pain in the world!" He slammed his fist down on the pulpit for emphasis, the impact making a hollow noise that echoed throughout the room.

"It burns my soul to know some of you aren't pure of heart … ain't ready to accept this new teaching, no, sir! No, ma'am! There will come a time when I must stop teaching and take up my scythe and bring down the infertile weed! I'll have to remove the ones who actively work against us."

He shook his head, as if he had walked through a spiderweb. He froze for a moment and returned to a more reserved volume, speaking calmly. "I will have to move from my peaceful nature and put on the mantle of a warrior. It will happen sooner than any of us likes." Looking down at the girl and her brother, he continued, "Someday, friends, I may even have to raise my hand to the children I adore, because they are as the asp in the garden trying to poison my very heel."

Pleading with his congregation, he yelled, "Do you want to strike my heel, friends? Do you want to strike the very heel of Jesus himself?" The crowd screamed back a resounding "no." Women, who were previously standing, had to sit back down in their chairs. The men clapped as if his raving was a song, which whipped them into a frenzy.

The preacher looked down into his flock and was satisfied with what he saw. They were ready to eat out of his hands. They would do anything for him. He glanced at the brother and sister, who were now crying with joy. *Good,* he thought, *the time will indeed come soon enough, young ones.*

After services concluded and the last parishioner had left, Rigby locked the entrance to the coffee shop and headed down to the basement. Although the owner had offered to close up the building, Rigby said he had some unfinished work to tend to before next week's service.

He walked through his makeshift sanctuary and back to the room he had first come out from. Opening the door, his hand found a switch which brought the fluorescent lights to life, which blinked on with a buzzing sound. The revealed space, which had been used to store tools and other maintenance items, had been covered in heavy plastic sheeting. In the center, gagged and bound, was a bloody, weeping man.

The preacher pulled the door closed behind him and stood in front of the unfortunate victim.

He grabbed the tape covering the man's mouth and gave it a quick yank. "Well, I'm sorry for the interruption, I surely am. The Lord's work is truly something having to be tended to. Thank you for remaining so quiet while the good people of this congregation heard the word of God. But I suppose we have medical science and 3M duct tape to thank for your compliance." He sat down in another chair, a few feet away from the bound man, nodding to the syringe on the table.

"You fucking drugged me." The man's body, severely beaten, streamed blood from open wounds on his head. His left eye was swollen shut, and his right earlobe looked like it had been torn slightly.

"Only a little. I could not have you interrupting services, now can I? And, by the way, I needn't have to remind you, sir, this is a house of worship, and I would ask you to watch your language." He took off his clerical collar and tucked it into the pocket of his trousers. "Where were we? Oh yes, you were going to explain why you tried to break into my house. I want us to get off on the right foot, so to speak. The truth will set you free. A chance to confess your sins, if you will."

"I'm not going to tell you anything!"

"Fair enough. That is your choice. Not all will willingly go to salvation. A few are dragged there kicking and screaming." The kidnapper reached into a red leather bag sitting on a table near the door. After rummaging through it, he pulled out a small metal punch generally used to put holes through leather. "You know, the human body was designed by God in a very specific way. It's a wonder. It can withstand quite a bit of pain. For example, if I inserted this behind your kneecap, it would hurt. Not kill you."

"What do you think you're going to make me talk? You're not a reverend, you're a fraud. You're nothing more than a murderer of innocent children." The man raised his head as best he could. He tried to puff out his chest slightly, his final moment of bravado. His outward appearance aside, he couldn't take his eyes off the menacing tool held before him.

For the next hour, the man tied to the chair suffered more than any one human should. His assailant extracted pieces of flesh, removed parts which never should be removed, and even cut out his eyelids so he wouldn't have the satisfaction of closing them against the horror.

Eventually the man stopped screaming, wandering in and out of consciousness. An occasional whimper issued from the chair, noise signifying that although he was failing, Rigby still hadn't taken his final breath from him. Blood pooled around his feet of the chair and dripped from the plastic taped to the walls.

"Well, I think we've had enough, don't you, Mr. Chambers?" The minister stood, wiping blood from a steel mallet he'd used with cruel effectiveness.

"You seem a little surprised," the torturer continued his monologue. "I knew who you were before you tried to break into my house. You're Rodrigo's father. Good student. He was an amazing actor too, as I recall. Before tonight, you both looked very similar." He turned to the man incredulously. "Don't be surprised you got caught. You don't get to where I am in life without being a little smart.

"Pity really. Had you played by the rules and just come to me, I would have let you join him in my heavenly of heavenlies. But you are a wicked man, and I just cannot abide by wickedness, Mr. Chambers."

"What the hell is the matter with you?" Mr. Chambers drew in each breath with deliberate intention. Every exhalation being used to make words. Tortured beyond reason, he lived now to try to exact even a fraction of revenge against the man who had killed his son. Revenge which would never come. "Why didn't you just kill me?"

The assailant pulled a screwdriver out of his red bag. He walked over to Rodrigo's father and without warning, shoved it deep into the center of his chest. Blood stained the front of his already bloodstained shirt. As the light went out in Mr. Chamber's eyes, the minister turned murderer leaned in close and whispered, "Because I wanted to watch you suffer."

Mr. Chambers exhaled his dying breath, and his head slumped to his chest.

The executioner picked up a towel from a table in the back of the room and started cleaning his tools while singing the hymn "The Old Rugged Cross".

CHAPTER 10
A LESSON IN THE ARTS

Dirk woke to the sound of his alarm going off to the song "Walking on Sunshine" by Katrina and the Waves. They were his salvation against a nightmare he was having about being on stage in a theater. A wicked magician made him do a series of nonsensical magic tricks while the audience of cadavers periodically let out roars of laughter and applause, although no hand or lips moved in the effort.

In the dream, pike poles were arrayed at the end of the stage. On top of each pole sat the head of every victim the police knew about so far. Their faces were caught in a variety of expressions. One appeared happy, another sad, one in anguish, and another glared at him angrily.

Although their faces were frozen in expression, they all stared at Dirk. Their eyes occasionally blinked in defiance of their own deaths.

Dirk sat upright in bed, shaking himself from the odd nocturnal vision. Some dreams you hated to have interrupted, others you were just glad when they were over.

Although thankful to be rescued from his nightmare, morning seemed to come earlier than he wanted it to.

Fighting the thought that he could easily lay down and get a few more hours of sleep, he stood and stretched. It was going to be a long day. He had work to do at the shop, and he needed to talk with Keith and Victor to compare notes.

As he drove there, he called Carrie to see about dinner. She filled him in on her meeting with Keith the other day, which explained why neither of them had answered their cell phones. She told him about Taylor's run-in with the coked-out hooker who had been "saved" at the First Transformational Church, only to end up dead a few days later. It sounded like an unfortunate overdose rather than a concrete lead to be followed. Especially with a witness who was no longer counted among the living.

At the shop, Dirk pulled the engine out of an old Vespa someone had bought at a rummage sale and needed a rebuild, a small but therapeutic job. Working with his hands helped focus his mind. The little scooters were vintage, cool way before such a category of thing existed.

He started thinking about the families and the theater tie-in again. He needed to get a look at the building. There was a danger, however, in just showing up at the school and starting to talk about murder. A man Dirk's age hanging around a high school was likely to attract unwanted attention. He'd either look suspicious, creepy, or both. The worst thing he could do was shut the kids down from giving him information. He couldn't show up as a private detective and start asking questions. One false move, and he'd spook Tenebris into running. He needed an ally on the inside.

As a student, Claire had unfettered access to the school. Dirk was her emergency contact, and he could legally come on school grounds to speak to his niece. Dirk and his sister had always been close, and he'd been a father figure to Claire. Perhaps he could orchestrate a reason to visit the school and nose around a bit.

The Vespa was in bad shape but not too far gone. The owner had found it in his deceased uncle's garage. Dirk would need to order some new parts, which would be shipped from Italy, so the rest of the restoration work would have to wait until the delivery guy could bring them or a domestic source could be found.

Sitting in his office, he flipped open his laptop. The question of the morning was Mr. Arthur Tenebris. Who was this guy who seemed to be universally feared and respected by the students? A quick search of the school's website showed a staff listing, with short bios and a photo attached to each.

Clicking on the bio for Mr. Tenebris revealed relatively little. He'd been with the school for the last two years, and he had two degrees in theater arts and a minor in divinity. The short missive also mentioned he'd once worked on Broadway, but the posted information was thin on details.

Claire said that Mr. Tenebris, in her limited interactions with him, would go on about his life as a star along the Great White Way. Dirk confirmed that he had indeed been on Broadway, but he wasn't as famous as he led most people to believe. Dirk found mention of him in a few places but always in a supporting role or as a choreographer.

Dirk developed a good sense for when something in writing didn't look quite right, and there were definitely things in his bio which didn't meet the logic test. The abrupt manner of his coming to the school and sparse details about his past were a sore thumb. To make matters more confusing, the lack of anything on the internet that pointed to the darling of the New York theater scene that he proposed to be was puzzling.

Dirk also thought it a little surprising there was no connection between Tenebris and the church. That didn't really fit the other bits of evidence. Ritualistic serial killers didn't worry about keeping up appearances as they wrote their crazy manifestos. If Tenebris was a serial killer, there should have been crazier spoutings on the internet by him. Or at least there should have been some suggestion the guy had a screw loose.

Everything Dirk found gave him the impression of someone who'd had a small measure of success in the theater. He was no Hammerstein, but he had a fairly decent career up till two years ago, and then he woke up one morning and decided to go to work for Central High School. Another thread that made no sense. From what

Dirk understood of actors, they would live under a bridge and eat garbage from a dumpster before giving up on their love of the applause.

Newspapers from New York mentioned Tenebris in a few instances. One nationally syndicated magazine indicated he had done a few well-received Broadway musicals and had even won a few awards. Most of what he read gave the impression the man's star seemed to be rising in theater circles. At the very least, he'd been working and likely making a living at it. So, why give it up to come here?

During his internet research, he found an abandoned web page for the First Transformational Church. The only article posted, posted years ago, was written by a Reverend H. R. but no additional names. In the article, the reverend thanked "Brother Tenebris" for his contributions to the church and his services during a medical emergency. The article suggested that Tenebris had medical training in the military and his efforts saved a woman's life.

So, Tenebris has some medical training. That's interesting.

Carrie was able to run the name Arthur Tenebris through the police and state databases, and she also found surprisingly little information about him. His official record was bare. As far as the state of Virginia was concerned, he was cleaner than most. She did find that he carried a veteran's card and had served in the army.

While he was finishing up his searches, Keith walked into the office carrying a box of bagels and a container of olive-flavored cream cheese. "So, how'd yesterday go?"

"It was certainly an enlightening day. Not one of the girls really liked Tenebris, but that isn't what was so interesting. The girls were all heavily involved in the theater. Plus, every single one of them had a connection to the First Transformational Church." Dirk selected an onion bagel from the box.

"If being a hated teacher makes you a murder suspect, then the police would have their hands full. The things about the theater and the church are potentially good leads though. I know Carrie told you about the dead hooker. You didn't come across any clues pointing you to anyone who was maybe a little unbalanced, did you?" Keith opened the container of cream cheese.

"No, why?" Dirk answered.

He selected one of the plain bagels from the box. "Well, I visited a few of the local fringe pastors. The only thing interesting was a guy who had shown up at a church and apparently caused quite a scene. Jeff Peters thought he was around a few months and then vanished."

Dirk pondered Keith's words. "Jeff Peters? Isn't that the guy who cut the cross off the church?"

"Yep, that's the guy." Keith stabbed a dollop of spread and put it on a plain bagel.

"Kind of old to be hanging around a psycho, isn't he??" Dirk said, almost more for himself than for Keith.

Keith rolled his eyes. "Not really, you would be amazed at how many different types of people cross the threshold of a church. Besides, we don't have any solid evidence that this guy Tenebris is some sort of psycho." Keith swallowed and added. "Oh yeah, and this character was possibly a vet."

"You mean, he was in the military?"

"No, the animal kind, veterinary doctor."

"Okay, so I found out Tenebris was in the military and has had some medical training." Dirk shook his head. "Too much of a coincidence for my tastes. "Wonder where Victor has gone off to?"

On command, a voice boomed out from the corner of the room, "Nowhere and everywhere! I'm like a wraith or a demon specter from beyond!"

"Seriously, a demon specter?" Dirk yelled toward the voice. "You're going with demonic today? Kind of boring."

"Yeah, really pedestrian." Keith laughed, almost choking on his coffee.

"Well, it's been a long day, and I'm tired. Don't worry, I'm listening to the conversation." Victor's voice went from booming to its normal timbre as he materialized in the room. He'd given up his spooky entrance altogether.

He continued, "Heather didn't like Tenebris either, but she didn't have any more info on him. She said he's a teacher or something. She thought he was maybe a doctor of some sort. Also said she remembers someone else, eviler than Tenebris."

"I suppose it is possible that when people say vet, meaning veteran, they could mean a former military member." Keith turned toward Dirk.

"Medics have medical training, and if you saw combat, you may have more experience than you care to admit to." Dirk cocked his head toward Keith and then back to Victor. "Any connection between Tenebris and Peters's church? Maybe check that angle out. So, what else you got?"

Victor nodded. "She thought she recalled an office. Still remembering things slowly though. I don't want to push her too hard.

I'll keep on it and let you know what I find out. Where would you guys be without me?"

"Well, it would be tons quieter around here," Keith said with a smirk.

"Go suck a cannonball, Friar Tuck!" Victor yelled in response.

"Friar Tuck? Is that the best you got? At least I wasn't killed with my own rifle!" Keith shot back.

"Hey, I'm a veteran of a proud army. Show some respect, you have no right–"

Well, I guess we're done here for now, Dirk thought to himself. He grabbed his bagel and ducked out of the office so the two could argue in acrimonious joy. They seemed to need it like the desert needed a good occasional rain.

Time to visit the school.

The "new high school", as it was colloquially called, had been built on the edge of town. People had complained to the town council that it was too far from the center of the local population. After years of development, those same people argued it was too small and they needed a new one built farther away from the town center.

The campus was laid out more like a college campus than a traditional high school, with buildings set around campus for different disciplines. They now had twelve buildings surrounding a park in the middle. Officially, the high school had the nondescript name of Central High School. The kids called it Goober High.

The main office was in a large administrative complex, which looked more at home on the set of the next *Batman* movie than on a high school campus. The "admin building," as it was unceremoniously known, was an unnecessarily tall behemoth meant to instill a feeling of regality, but it just ended up giving the impression of a castle deserving of gargoyles on the corners of the structure. The kids joked it intentionally looked scary to instill fear in the hearts of the school's inmates.

Dirk was given a yellow "Visitor" tag as he waited for Claire to come get him, which didn't take long.

"Hi, Uncle Dirk." She smiled at him.

"Hi, kiddo. I'm not interrupting anything, am I?"

"Just my formative years where I should be enriching my brain and drinking in new knowledge." She stood with her hands on her hips. "Let me guess, you want to see the theater arts building?" She understood he was there on a case and this wasn't just a social call.

"You know me so well."

"I was wondering when you'd come sniffing around."

As they walked, Dirk took in the enormity of the campus. It lacked for nothing. Near the center of the immense courtyard the town's local coffee chain, the Beanapse, even had a place. The sign had a coffee bean jumping the synaptic gap in a brain cell.

Dirk tried to remember what the school had looked like when he went here. Back then, it truly was the "new high school." He was pretty sure it hadn't had a coffee shop in the courtyard. The buildings around the center were the grandchildren of the ones Dirk remembered, but years of renovations had changed them from anything recognizable. Cost aside, the renovations made it a beautiful campus.

Most of the kids walking around appeared perfectly normal. Dirk wondered why anyone would want to hurt them. What was the motive? He hated working murder cases where children were involved because there was no way he could possibly comprehend the motives of the killer. *How am I to defeat an enemy I can't fundamentally understand?*

Dirk had never wanted offspring of his own, but he loved his niece like she was his daughter. In this regard, he understood the bond between adults and their children. He'd do anything to keep his niece safe, just like any biological parent would risk their lives to protect their child.

At the end of the courtyard, opposite the admin building, stood the main theater. The newest building on campus, Claire explained that it was actually three theaters in one. There was the main theater in the middle and two on either side that served as small performance theaters.

The new construction was thanks to a contribution from the Jennings family. It was a modern theater where the back opened, allowing sets into the building. The old theater had been renovated and refitted as a set design shop, complete with a large pull-barn style door to move around larger pieces. Another smaller structure held the administrative offices of the theater arts teachers and the program director.

Claire opened the door to the Jennings Theater and waved Dirk inside. It still had a new-building smell reeking of busted deadlines and blown budgets. A poster was on the marquee, indicating a new production opening that night.

Each door into the theater had a round portal-style window trimmed in brass and door handles featuring the laughing and crying masks traditionally associated with the theater.

Seeing the wheels spinning in Dirk's head, Claire offered, "Thalia and Melpomene. The Greek muses. Honestly, Uncle Dirk, didn't you pay any attention in high school?"

"Only to the things really mattering to me. Like science, math, and shop. They help me catch bad guys. Oh, and Laurie Wheaton, but you're way too young to hear about her. Speaking of bad guys; shall we?" Dirk motioned toward the stage.

Claire commented that it was theater in the round style and would seat 1500 people. The cushioned seats doubled as small writing desks, which came out of the side of the chairs for classes.

Today the overly-indulgent high school theater was pressed into service on a more mundane pursuit, theater practice. Several students were rehearsing lines on stage while another man sat in the audience, watching them and occasionally giving them direction.

In the background, a crew of students were hammering and painting a scene for that night's performance. Their labors, not nearly complete, were occasionally interrupted by the man in the audience telling them to alternately work more quietly and then to hurry up and quit loafing around.

"Mr. Tenebris," Claire offered.

"Real charmer. Seems like kind of an ass," Dirk said.

"Not seems, he is. Everyone says he's a tyrant on the stage. Loves nothing more than to nitpick the cast and crew. But he is a theater director. They're all asses. You don't get to be a director without being one. Prove you can be more of a jerk than the last guy who directed a play."

"Is he any good though?"

"Some of the kids have acted in the local and regional plays, and they say he's the real deal. Kids who take his special classes say he's pushed them to a whole new level of acting."

"Wonder what the dead actors say?" Dirk glibly asked.

"Sorry Unkie D, that's Victor's department."

"So it is." Dirk wondered, not for the first time, what Victor was up to right then.

Dirk watched Mr. Tenebris run the two through their paces. He'd yell at them about not putting enough passion into the scene. Then he'd tell them they were overacting. Occasionally he'd bark at the stagehands building the set. He seemed to do a lot of screaming.

If there was any method to his madness, it was lost on Dirk. He wasn't entirely sure what the man was hoping to accomplish.

After having the two on stage do their scene three more times, Mr. Tenebris finally said, "Perfect, just perfect. Do it just like that tonight if you can. Remember, it's my reputation at stake. Now, I need to go take an aspirin. You two have literally given me an aneurysm."

Yeah, what an ass.

Dirk wasn't ready to talk to Tenebris just yet, but he was glad he'd watched him at work. He might have a different persona when he spoke with parents and guardians about the kids.

Plus, at this point, he was prime suspect number one, and Dirk didn't want to spook him. This was a time to be careful. The kids on stage might be able to provide some insight into Mr. Tenebris. Better to find a couple of the actors and ask them. It'd be important to get some background information before Dirk let any hint of suspicion out. Tenebris left the stage and walked out the back door toward the building Claire said held the offices.

"Do you recognize either of the kids acting on stage?" Dirk asked Claire.

"Yeah, I know both of them. The girl is the one you want to speak with. She hates Tenebris but respects him. She'd be willing to talk. The boy acts because his mom makes him do something cultural. He has no opinion of Tenebris. You'd like him, a real motorhead." She grabbed him by the arm. "C'mon, I'll introduce you."

Claire and Dirk made their way down to the stage, where the two continued to work on their scene. Both the boy and girl were sweating from the overhead lights providing the illumination.

The girl looked deep into the boy's eyes and said, "But I don't love you, Jake. You don't understand my heart, my soul, and my mind."

The way she said this to the other boy made Dirk embarrassed he was intruding on some lover's conversation rather than two actors working on dialogue of the play.

"But Caroline, I would die for you." The boy pulled her close and got right up to her face, "I would kill for you." He delivered his line with a sneer, which seemed to be a little over-the-top.

Then the boy recoiled from his partner and brought his script back up to his eye level. "Sorry, Melissa, that really was bad for me. Can we try again? You were great, but I still suck."

"Hold!" Claire yelled an interrupt. "Can we have a minute before the two of you get back to practicing your Tony acceptance speeches? And by the way, Melissa, you were fantastic. Daryl, you're an overacting hack, but I love you anyway." She gestured to Dirk. "By the way, this is my uncle, Dirk Bentley. He's getting the fifty-cent tour today."

The girl gave a curtsy and said, "Melissa Barlo. I'm honored."

Dirk bowed in response to her curtsy.

Daryl shook Dirk's hand and said, "Daryl Tubee. Nice to meet you."

"Are you guys done for now? I'd like to talk with Melissa for a few minutes. Girl talk, you understand, right, Daryl?" Claire asked.

"Sure, perfect for a break. I've gotta run to ask Mrs. Shepard about science anyway. You guys have fun. It was nice to meet you, Mr. Bentley," Daryl said. "See you later, Claire," he said, giving her a kiss on the cheek. "Melissa, if I could only be as half as good an actor as you, my mom might let me play football this season." Daryl gave Melissa an exaggerated bow as he exited the stage.

Dirk watched Daryl walk offstage and growled at the boy as he walked away. He was not ready for his little Claire to grow up.

Melissa rolled her eyes at the flourish of romanticism and shrugged. "Actors, what are you gonna do? Daryl would much rather be playing sports or taking apart car engines if he could. Too bad, he's actually pretty good on stage." She pulled a bottle of water from her backpack sitting nearby and opened it. "So, what do you think of our fair school?"

"Nice, this place has changed a lot since I went here. This theater is huge. I saw you working with your director earlier." Dirk hoped to bait her in a conversation about Tenebris.

"Yeah, don't let what you saw color your opinion of him. He is pretty tough on us, but he's a brilliant director, and we're lucky to have him. At least that is what he reminds us of all the time. I think he's a bit of a jerk." Melissa flashed an ironic smirk.

"What's his story, anyway?" Dirk asked.

"Well, he'd undoubtedly tell you within five minutes of meeting him that he's a Broadway choreographer. He's personally studied under or taught the greats and has been involved in many of the Tony award winning performances of the Broadway's past. Naturally, they did not recognize his genius," she said.

"Seemed like he was riding you two pretty hard a few minutes ago. Is he always that much of a taskmaster?" Dirk said.

"Yes, well I guess you could say that. He'll admit it too. But he's good at what he does. If the final performance looks great on opening night, that's what he cares about. His God-like reputation must be maintained. At least in his own mind. I'm not sure the audiences we draw would even notice. Most people sit behind their cell phones and don't even bother to watch the stage."

"How'd you decide to become a part of this? I mean, it seems like a lot of work, and with the yelling, it makes me wonder if it's really worth it."

She shrugged slightly. "Well, I like acting. Mr. Tenebris is right about one thing. It's pretty magical when the lights come up and you nail a performance. I mean, when you play your role exactly right and it goes off without a hitch, there is no better feeling in the world. Drama queen or not, everyone, including Mr. Tenebris, is in this for the rush of a perfect performance."

"Does he actually like any of the actors? Or does he just go through the motions?" Dirk asked.

"It's tough to say for sure. There are some who are more gifted at acting than others, and he spends more time with them. The guys working on the set, he barely even notices. He regards them the same way a homeowner does the rodents scurrying around their basement."

Off to his right, Dirk saw movement in the theater seating. A few people milling around. Although there were no performances or classes going on, one person sat behind a column. Dirk wasn't sure, but the figure appeared to be watching them.

"Can you think of anyone he was giving undue attention to?" Dirk asked.

Melissa's eyes narrowed, and her forehead furrowed with sudden suspicion. She hesitated to answer the question. "Are you a cop? These sound like cop questions. Claire, is your uncle a cop?" Dirk had struck some sort of nerve.

"Uhhh, well–" Claire stammered, looking toward Dirk for any kind of support.

Dirk figured it was better to just come clean with Melissa rather than try to string her along. He had more questions he needed to answer, and if Claire trusted her, then he could too. "Okay, Melissa, I'm not a cop, but I am a private detective, and I'm looking into the girls who were murdered. I was hoping to find out more about the theater here to see if anyone had any additional information."

"You don't think Mr. Tenebris had anything to do with this?" Melissa was visibly shaken by the idea.

"I'm not really sure, Melissa. I need to know the details. Can you answer a few questions? I swear they'll be quick and painless."

Glancing out into the audience, Dirk noticed the figure in the audience leaning forward in the seat, still apparently watching the three of them talk at the stage. Maybe it was time for Dirk to take a walk up there.

"If it will help you figure out who killed the girls, then I'm in. I'm still not sure I know anything." Melissa shrugged nervously. "I wasn't familiar with any of them outside of theater."

Claire took Melissa's hand reassuringly. "You might have seen or heard something useful to us. With the right questions, you may recall something that you had forgotten."

"Anything you tell me will be completely between us, I promise," Dirk said.

Melissa nodded to Claire. Dirk was glad his niece was there. She had a way with people, and he doubted the girl would have talked to him alone. Claire would make a hell of an investigator in her own right.

Dirk pulled out a pen and paper. "Melissa, do you remember seeing or hearing anything strange before the girls disappeared? I mean, anything at all which seemed unusual?"

"What do you mean?" Melissa asked.

"Well, changes in Mr. Tenebris's behavior. Did you meet anyone new, or were any of the kids acting strange around him?"

"Not really. Everyone seemed fairly normal to me. Mr. Tenebris got here shortly before I did. The old theater arts teacher retired kind of suddenly, and Mr. Tenebris just happened to show up to take his place. I heard someone with connections to the school board got him in."

"Did you notice him spending more time with some of the kids than others?"

"A few are singled out for special classes. They call themselves the Children of Dionysus. Most of them are the pretty kids."

"You say *pretty kids*, what do you mean?" Dirk asked. He was scribbling notes furiously.

"You know the ones. Nice hair, high cheekbones, athletic build. The kids who look good on stage or are naturally talented actors. They aren't all like that, but most of them are. Some of them aren't exceptionally good-looking, but they had already acted in regional theater, so they came into the program with skills. I don't think he had a weird teen fetish or anything like that."

"All girls?" Dirk asked. He was thinking it could have been some sort of odd grooming machine Tenebris had set up for his sick plans.

"Nope, a mix of boys and girls. Daryl is one of them." Melissa looked at Claire with a sudden flash of panic. "You don't think he's in any danger, do you?" She instantly communicated Claire's unspoken question.

"I really don't believe so, not at this point." Dirk was really trying to calm her fears. The reality was that if a serial killer was on the loose and they were intentionally targeting the theater, none of the kids were safe. He'd be damned if he would voice those concerns to Melissa.

Until this point, the victims he was aware of had been girls, but Dirk suspected this fact was more of a coincidence than anything else. In his research into the case, he had come across one similar incident three years before, where a boy named Rodrigo had been found murdered in Portland. His body had been drained of blood, and several surgical-style incisions were discovered on his body, similar to the other victims. But the incisions had been far less precise.

Melissa continued to talk, almost to herself at this point. "Come to think of it, the girls killed were Children of Dionysus."

Until then, Dirk hadn't been completely convinced of Tenebris's guilt. Although he hated jumping to conclusions, Tenebris most certainly looked like a prime suspect. Glancing back into the audience, the man sitting in the chair was gone. Was it his imagination, or had the man really been watching them? His intuition flew into overdrive.

"What can you tell me about these Children of Diplopods?" Dirk asked.

"Dionysus," Claire corrected.

"Yeah, them." Dirk motioned to Melissa to continue.

"They meet on Wednesday nights. They have extra fees because of their special training with Mr. Tenebris, but he also brought in other acting coaches too. He asked me to join, but we don't have enough money to put toward acting classes. My mom said maybe next year," Melissa explained.

Melissa's eyes had glossed over. It had obviously occurred to her that anyone connected with the group could possibly be the next victim.

Dirk took Melissa's hand and looked into her eyes, trying to bring her back from where her mind had drifted. "Thank you, Melissa. You've been very brave. I greatly appreciate all the information you've given me." He placed a business card in her hand and added, "If you think of anything else, let me know. But please, for now, can you keep our conversation to yourself? I would like to continue my investigation without too many people getting wind of it." Dirk knew he should really have contacted the girl's family before he had spoken with her, but Claire and Melissa were clearly friends, so he had a little wiggle room. And perhaps more importantly, Dirk felt like time was running out before another student could be in danger.

Why would Tenebris be creating his own group of students? Were they all special somehow? These questions ran through his brain as he left the stage area.

As they made their way out of the theater, something else was bothering him, and it had nothing to do with the case.

"So, Claire?" Dirk said.

"So, Uncle?" Claire answered.

"I couldn't help but notice you and Daryl were, what's the best way to say this? Familiar," Dirk said.

"We're just friends, Uncle Dirk." She rolled her eyes.

Dirk gave her a paternal look. "Okay, so you're kissing friends then? Have you become French all of a sudden? You know they like to kiss."

Claire couldn't hide her embarrassment. She was turning red in the face, and her shoulders were hunched over. He'd busted her, and she knew it.

Dirk looked at her and smirked. "That's what I thought. Now I officially hate him."

"Oh, Uncle Dirk, where would I be without you?" Claire grabbed his hand as they walked out of the theater.

CHAPTER 11
DEEPER CONVERSATIONS

Dirk's chat with Melissa had been helpful. Walking back across campus, Daryl caught up with them and handed them two tickets to the opening performance, set to begin a few hours later. *Hmmm ... maybe I don't hate this kid after all.*

Although he was worried about being away from the shop the whole day, not to mention the rest of the evening, perhaps there would be a benefit to watching Tenebris in his natural environment. Besides, Keith would be around the shop to keep an eye on things.

During the intermission, he could potentially find a way into the theater arts offices to poke around Tenebris's office for anything suspicious. And maybe he would be fortunate enough to catch the mysterious stranger who'd been listening in on their conversation in the theater.

Returning to the school in the evening, it seemed like an entirely different world. The windows of the classrooms and offices were dark, and the people milling around were dressed up a little more than they would be during the day. The inner courtyard of the school was lit with pathway lights , the illumination reflected on the surface of the duck pond. Two ducks were silhouetted against the evening, heads tucked beneath their wings in obvious slumber. A light breeze rippled the water across the pond.

Claire had changed into a new dress. Dirk chuckled at the idea of his tomboy niece wearing a dress. He most often saw her in the shop's overalls, covered in grease. He gave her some grief over it. "You know, you are really pretty when you don't have grease under your fingernails. There may be hope for you yet."

"Stop," she chided him gruffly.

Claire was a beautiful, smaller version of her mother, and he'd loved her since the moment he laid eyes on her in the nursery room of the hospital. Her father, Mike, had died in Afghanistan when she was just a baby, and Dirk, who'd been fond of his brother-in-law, stepped in as surrogate dad. He and Claire had been thick as thieves since then. He'd have to remember to ask Victor, not for the first time, to relay a message to Mike on how she was doing.

They climbed the stairs to the theater, which had been magically transformed into something straight out of old Broadway. The lights in the entryway were on with several students serving as ticket collectors, concessionaires, and salespeople working behind the small counters. The construction materials, previously lying in the entrance earlier in the day, had also been removed.

"M'lady, would you care to indulge in some pop of the corn?" Dirk said, grabbing Claire's hand.

"Why, my good sir, I thought you would never ask, I would love some pop of the corn. Oh, but light on the butter, okay?" Claire said. "And a large soda. I want to be able to swim in that cup, Uncle Dirk, I mean measured in gallons, not in just liters."

"Medium soda it is," Dirk said as Claire just frowned at him. "Hey, I have to answer to your mother. You know, the lady claiming to be my sister? She gets mean."

Dirk steered his way into line behind two women who were waiting their turn. Both of them were talking about the night's performance in hushed serious tones. If he had to take a guess, he would have thought they were waiting to see a performance at the Majestic Theater on Broadway.

"… are you kidding me? Alice, this show is going to be amazing, first-night jitters or not," the woman in the flowered hat said.

"Well, Mr. Bellamy told me the amount of time they'd been spending on practice was really over-the-top," the other woman added, "like they were all trying to get an Academy Award or something. If you ask me, Tenebris is wasting money, which should be spent elsewhere."

"Well, they have had to put in some extra rehearsal time because of the murders," Flowered Hat Lady continued. "If you want my opinion, this production should've been stopped and the theater arts program locked down until this whole mess is over."

"And you know, the rumors are probably true,"—the other lady jumped in—"even if there is only a kernel of truth to it. Those Broadway actors are all drug addicts, pedophiles, and boozers. It won't surprise me when we see him on the news being carried away in handcuffs."

Dirk had heard enough of their idle gossip. "Excuse me for butting in ladies, but if you suspect all of this, why don't you talk to the police about it?"

"Me, go to the police?" The lady in the flowered hat looked at Dirk incredulously. "The police most certainly must have this information by now. I mean, really, how incompetent can they be?"

Not incompetent but incredibly hamstrung by people not willing to come forward with information, even if it's rumor.

Flowered hat woman turned back toward the other woman. "And tell me this, why don't you, why does the school need someone like Tenebris? I mean, if he's that good, why isn't he on Broadway or Vegas or even Branson? For heaven's sake."

"Who cares? We've got him now." The woman with flowered hat said, tossing a lock of hair back over her shoulder.

"I heard the other theaters found out he was straight," the other woman said with a smirk.

"I don't follow. They found out he was straight?" Dirk had no idea what she was referring to.

"You know, not gay. Not a homosexual. Can't have straight guys on Broadway," she continued.

Dirk found himself unusually offended, both at the idea straight men couldn't act in the theater and at the way in which she was sexually profiling men, but he couldn't make up his mind which he hated more. "Oh, come on, you have *got* to be kidding me."

Both women said as they walked away from Dirk, "Dear man, you really don't understand the theater."

Dirk ordered a large popcorn and two medium-sized drinks, hoping to avoid talking to any more theater parents. They'd been right about one thing though; the theater crowd was a mystery to him.

Dirk and Claire located their seats in the back. They were in the far back row and off to one side. The seats had a large support column partially obstructing the view. But the seats were free, and they could wait until the show began and move up to better seats.

As the lights went down, the curtain ascended. Hundreds of cell phones went into the air as parents recorded the performance. Somewhere a cell phone rang, and it was answered by a chorus of "Shhhhh." Under the cover of darkness, Dirk and Claire found far vacant seats only five rows from the stage. They moved through the cover of shadow like a couple of thespian ninjas working their way toward their next victim. Dirk could see Tenebris watching the performance from the orchestra pit.

The first half went off without any problems. Melissa and Daryl played their parts beautifully. They were as convincing as ever. It was almost as if they weren't simply acting but really living the lives of the characters on stage.

Dirk kept a close eye on his watch as he planned his surreptitious reconnaissance of the offices just before intermission. This way he allowed himself as much time as needed while ensuring his absence would go unnoticed. As he got up to leave, he handed Claire the popcorn and said, "Showtime." She grabbed his hand and mouthed, *be careful.*

Dirk exited the side door of the theater and jogged down the little path connecting the theater with the department's administrative building. He did his best to stay out of sight, ducking out of the beams of light being cast down the sidewalks and heading back into the bushes. He waited in silence, listening for the slightest of noises.

As soon as he was sure no one had noticed his hasty exit from the theater, he tried the doors to the administration building, which was locked as anyone would expect them to be after dark.

Dirk made his way behind the bushes and along the building, hoping to locate another opening to get inside but found no luck.

He was trying the last unchecked door to the building when a baritone voice came echoing from inside the building. "Look, Carl, buddy, you know I would do anything for you, but Michelle isn't really into you, my friend. She just doesn't like you that way."

Dirk jumped back behind the bushes just as the door was shoved open. A young man walked out of the building, pausing briefly at the door. "Okay, tell you what. I'll ask Heather to ask Michelle. But this is a complete dead-end, my friend."

The young man shoved the door open the rest of the way and walked clear of the entrance, giving Dirk just enough time to slink into the building before it closed. He waited in the dark along the wall until the teen had vanished from the building. The last thing he wanted to have to do was explain why he was wandering around in the hallways of a high school building at night.

Surely it's not breaking and entering if the door was ajar when I walked in?

The main corridor was half-lit, with only the emergency lights giving the place an eerie glow. He remembered these halls from when he was in high school. They'd done a great job renovating the buildings since then. The hallways were an off-white glossy finish popular with public buildings, and the walls were covered with playbills from long-past performances. One older poster was from the theater adaptation of Stephen King's *Carrie*. The blood-covered girl gave Dirk a start in the dimly-lit hallway.

Each of the doors had a small placard next to it with the room number and the name of a faculty member. It didn't take long to find the one marked Tenebris. The office was locked.

As he stood in the cavernous space, trying to work out his next move, Dirk was startled by the handle of a door jiggling at the end of the hallway and the voices of two men billowing through the cavernous spaces. Too close for comfort. He'd have a hard time explaining his presence.

Dirk tried the door on the other side of the hallway, but it was locked as well. He pulled on another, with the same result. The voices grew louder and louder as they walked up the stairs. Dirk needed to hide and quick.

At the last possible moment, Dirk jumped into a narrow passageway leading to a small cubbyhole of a janitor's closet. He backed into the mops hanging on the wall to blend in as best he could. A few feet away, in the light of the hallway, he saw two men pass his hiding place. One of the voices he recognized as Tenebris, but the other one was unfamiliar.

"Reverend, I'm in kind of a hurry. I have a performance in intermission right now, and I'm expected back on stage in five minutes. I just have to to grab something out of my office." Tenebris spoke quickly and somewhat meekly. To Dirk, it appeared to be more like he was trying to placate the man and get back to the play as quickly as he could. He said it the way someone at home would lie to a door-to-door evangelist that they have a cake in the oven and have to pull it out. Dirk heard the door to the office open.

"I understand, I won't take but a moment of your time." The other man spoke out in a conciliatory tone. The empty hallways echoed with the sounds of their voices. "The stage, those kids, they need you. But, Arthur, I need you too. I count on you to help fulfill our plans. Without you we can't proceed, and I know you share my goals and God's mission."

"I have to be straight with you, Reverend, I'm not sure I want to be a part of this anymore."

Dirk crept closer to the corridor to better hear the conversation. The men's voices suddenly became muffled as the entrance to the office closed.

Are they working together? Maybe they are both pastors at the same church? How does this fit in with the school? Does it have anything to do with the murders?

Dirk reentered the hallway to try to listen in as best he could. The other man spoke in a more hushed tone, but based on the timbre of the conversation, it reminded him of an argument. Behind the closed office, the words were impossible to discern.

The office door was pulled open, making a swooshing sound sending Dirk scrambling back to his hiding place among the custodial supplies. Dirk heard the other man say, "Alright, tonight then. I shall meet you after the performance. You need to understand this is a sign from God, and we have a responsibility here. Remember what happened to Jonah and the whale."

"All right, Reverend, after the performance." Tenebris let out a lengthy sigh. "This hurts, and I think this is a bad idea."

"You're tired of helping me, and I get that. I promise you, we're almost done. Almost there, Arthur, and then you can say you were part of something great. Your own flock will rise up to applaud your great accomplishments." The deep-voiced man struck a positive tone as if he was trying to convince a young child to do something they most assuredly did not want to do.

"Sure, almost there," Tenebris murmured in a sullen tone.

Of course, for all Dirk knew, this conversation could simply be Tenebris's preacher reminding the teacher of his promised tithe. Although the reference to Jonah and the whale was interesting. Was Tenebris or the other man Jonah? Maybe, more significantly, who was the whale?

He followed the men out into the night, leaving by another door on the opposite side of the building, but by the time Dirk made his way back to the front, they were both gone from view. He had really hoped he could get a better look at the man with the deep voice. They'd presumably both reentered the theater, but he couldn't tell.

Dirk returned to his seat, and Claire handed him the mostly-empty box of popcorn. "Anything interesting?"

"Definitely. How was the play?" Dirk replied.

"Let me put it to you this way, you got the more entertaining job tonight. The acting is good, but the play itself is *boooring*," Claire said, with sarcasm only a teen could muster.

From behind her, a voice whispered loudly, "Shhhhh."

"Oh, shhhh yourself," Claire shot back at the people behind them.

"You wanna leave early, maybe go get a couple of burgers?" Dirk whispered over some dialogue which seemed needlessly long and rambling.

"Are cats inherently evil?" Claire stood up from her chair and stepped out into the aisle.

"Yes, they most certainly are." Dirk chuckled as he followed.

CHAPTER 12
WHERE AM I

Melissa Barlo woke in a daze. She had the sensation of looking at the world through a pair of ill-fitting, very dirty glasses. She tried to move but couldn't. Her brain was reaching out for anything to make sense of life before waking up. All she could remember was the applause from last night's performance.

She tried to move her hands and then her feet, but they wouldn't cooperate. At first, she thought they felt heavy and then realized she was restrained. As she tried in vain to shift her limbs, she could hear the sound of leather creaking under the strain.

With some effort, she was able to bend her knees slightly, but her feet were held firmly in place. She no longer wore the clothes she had on the night before and rather was covered by a coarse fabric. Maybe a cheap blanket or material, but she could not bend her head down low enough to see what it was. Across her chest and hips, leather straps secured her to a surface. Her backside felt bare and cold. A table, yes, she was strapped to a metal table.

In the air, she smelled the faint odor of medicine and wet dog.

The top of her head was being held in place, but she was still able to turn it around slightly. It felt like a belt on her forehead was keeping her from looking around. Panic washed over her as the reality of her situation sank in. Melissa tried to let out a scream but was met with only a muffled moan as a gag in her mouth made any loud noise impossible. She was trapped.

She lay inclined at a forty-five-degree angle, with her head above her feet. Her eyesight sharpened, slowly at first but then quicker, like someone had pressed a button on her eyes. The walls came into focus;

they were blue, covered in a shiny gloss paint which reminded her of her little brother's room. Looking down, she made out a concrete floor with a drain at her feet, like the floor in their garage.

Melissa tried again to move against the restraints. They squeaked under the pressure but wouldn't budge. She worked to pull her head out of whatever was holding it in place, but she couldn't. She managed only a short squeak from her dry throat that simply echoed through the room.

Her mind raced. Where was she? How'd she get there? Where were her parents? Was she in a hospital? Had they been in a car accident, and she was now stuck on an operating table? Had no one noticed she was awake? Where had she been before this?

A snippet of a memory flashed before her. She was being called to Mr. Tenebris's office after the play. She figured he was going to tell her what a great performance it had been. Or, more likely, what she'd done wrong. It was the last clear image she recalled before she woke up in this room.

Why was she on this table? She could feel the cool air against the exposed parts of her skin. A single fluorescent bulb was the room's solitary light source, its constant buzz the only sound aside from the leather straps straining against her movements. She cried.

From behind her, a door made a heavy metallic thud as it opened, and Melissa heard the footfalls of someone entering the room, the door closing with a loud bang behind her. She was both terrified and relieved anyone was coming to her aid. Perhaps they were there to release her or explain what was going on.

Maybe the situation isn't as bad as it appears.

She saw the figure of a man in a tan trench coat enter her field of vision. He was shaking off his coat and hat, which were covered in rain. With his back still to her, he donned a facemask and a plastic visor. The bald man reminded her of a 1970s television detective she'd once watched reruns of with her parents.

Turning toward her, he said, "Ahhh, I see, Miss Melissa is awake now." He reached over and undid her gag. His voice sounded familiar to her, but through the mask and her foggy mind, it was impossible to put the speech with a face.

"I'm sorry for it being so cold. You can't imagine how expensive it is to warm concrete and keep it reasonable in here. I turned the heat up, so it should be better soon. When I'm not using this room, I usually shut it down. I didn't have time to prepare it like I usually do. No matter, you'll only be in here for a short while." His mind seemed to drift off. "Perhaps it is better to say that you will be with us forever?"

Melissa was confused by his last statement *forever*. What did he mean? "I really need to get out of here. My parents will be concerned."

"Oh, don't worry about them," the man said, performing some task on a nearby table. "They've been told what they should know for now. You'll be made quite comfortable. I'm a good host. They wouldn't have it any other way,"

"They? Who are they? Do you mean my parents? When can I see them? What's going on?" His inability to answer her questions only served to send her heart racing. At once she felt sweat forming on her brow and at the same time she could not shake the unescapable cold of just being in his presence.

"My dear, no, *they* are the rest of my little family here," the man continued. "Have no fear, you'll be meeting them soon enough. They're always watching. Not sure how they see in here, but they do. Those little scamps are always watching. I love them so." His voice was like that of a grandfather or beloved teacher introducing her to a new idea or concept. It was simultaneously melodic and aggravating.

"And as for your parents, I guess it depends on your views on religion and the afterlife, Miss Melissa. But let's not worry about such matters now." He pressed a button on the wall, and music flooded the room. Melissa recognized it as a Mozart waltz.

"I love Mozart, don't you? So soothing, so wonderful. There's just something about the masters we've never been able to recreate in modern times." The bald man swayed to the music as it came out of the speakers in the corner of the room. He held his arms up as if he held an invisible dance partner in his arms as he waltzed across the room.

Is he insane? What the hell is he doing?

He flicked on the light above the table where he was standing, illuminating a collection of shiny medical equipment.

Melissa had become more and more convinced this wasn't a hospital at all. She even doubted her parents had any idea where she was. His answers were strange and detached to her pointed questions, like he was being purposely vague.

Or maybe he was just plain out of his fucking mind.

"So, my parents know where I am, and they're coming to get me?" Melissa said.

"Oh no, no, dear. That wouldn't do. Not at all." He turned and stood in front of her, admiring her helpless figure strapped to the table. He took the back of his hand and touched her cheek, "You and I have a date with destiny."

"You're going to rape me, aren't you?" Melissa asked, her voice shaky with terror and tears streaming down the sides of her face, along her neck, and onto the metal table she was strapped to. The acrid taste of fear overwhelmed her. In another instant, she pulled and strained against the leather belts holding her in place. Melissa resolved to fight like hell before she would let this man do anything to her.

He turned back to face her, and his eyes grew wide as saucers. "Heavens no! What would've ever given you that idea? Kids these days. What do you think I am? Some sort of monster? Why would I ever hurt you in any way? It wouldn't to provide a defiled tribute! The very idea, young lady! I have half a mind to punish you for leveling such insults. I would never do such a thing. I am hurt, positively hurt."

Looking at the back of his hand for a moment, he said, "Oh, now I see. You thought that... Ha Ha Ha! Ho Ho Ho! He He He! I understand the confusion, I apologize." He seemed embarrassed and slightly amused at having given her the wrong impression. "No, Melissa dear, I'm not going to rape you. I appreciate your beauty; not only in body but in spirit. If my dearly departed wife and I had been able to conceive, I would have liked to have someone like you as my daughter. You have such fair hair, such beautiful skin. Your body is as yet untouched by the ravages of time, pollution, and excess. In your heart resides the soul of someone with resolve and vigor. Your age is the perfect for tribute you know. You are pure light. Yes, pure indeed."

Melissa's mind raced to process everything she had heard. A different feeling of panic replaced her earlier terror. If he did not intend to rape her, then what did he have in mind? Suddenly the prospect of knowing what he was going to do to her was just as unsettling as not knowing at all.

He turned back to the table and resumed dancing, seemingly satisfied that his words had cleared all her questions right up and he should go back to his work.

"I don't understand! Why am I tied up? Why can't I leave? Where are my clothes?"

"Silly naïve thing. Okay, I'm a gracious host, and I suppose you deserve some answers. You can't leave because you are my guest, and manners would dictate you stay until we're done. The clothes are no longer a concern. They are now part of the ash in my firepit."

The man reached into a drawer and pulled out a pair of surgical gloves. "You know, I used to do this with my bare hands, but with diseases and all, you really can't be too careful. I hope you're not offended. The ritual has lost some of its personalization these last few years or so. Oh, that reminds me, do you have a latex allergy?"

"A what?" Melissa was more concerned about the syringe the man was looking at than the latex gloves he had pulled on.

"If you really don't know, then we can safely assume you don't. Even so, this is just a small injection shot." He picked up the needle from the table.

"Wait a minute. Who are you? What are you doing to me?" Melissa tried to interject, anything to keep him talking and buy herself some additional time.

His eyes widened, as if he realized he'd forgotten something important. "Really, where are my manners? I'm seriously slipping in my old age. This is a little something to help you sleep so that I can clean you. Don't worry, it doesn't last very long. A few hours at the most. Probably longer for you, because you are slight of frame, you see. I am known by a lot of names. For the time being, you may simply call me Harmon. We will, after all, be achieving perfection together." He slid the needle into her neck with alarming precision.

Melissa let out the loudest scream she could possibly manage.

"Oh, scream, child. No one can hear you outside. I made sure of it," Harmon whispered in her ear through his surgical mask. The way he said it was less in his normal soothing manner and something approaching a deep growl. "Soon you will understand. They will all know the sum of genius."

"No, please don't. Let me go, I'll tell no one. I promise." Melissa struggled through her tears.

The drugs worked fast, and the room blurred and dissolved around her. The lights, the walls, the face of her abductor faded into darkness as she slipped into unconsciousness.

CHAPTER 13
A GIRL NAMED MELISSA

Dirk pulled into the driveway of the Sleepaway Diner and Inn, parking in a space next to Keith's motorcycle. The Sleepaway was where they had all their meetings during a case. The booths offered them a quiet place to work, the coffee was always plentiful and fresh, and they made a mean pot roast sandwich. A lunch fit for a meeting of the Bentley Detective Agency; cheap and a lot of it.

He pushed open the door to see Keith haunting their regular booth. His bible was open on the table in front of him, and he was making notes on a pad of paper. Sermon-writing was an ongoing thing for Keith. He started working on the next one even before he gave his last.

"Hey, Keith," Dirk said. "Coffee and the special please, Gail!" Dirk motioned to the waitress who was well acquainted with the pair. She was already on her way over to the table with a cup and the pot of coffee.

"So, Keith, anything new on your end?" Dirk asked.

"Not really. I've been doing a little research. Everything seems to be a dead end. Funny thing is, Anything I find is generic. Even the First Transformational Church website gives us nothing, and they're no longer at the location listed on the website or the pieces of paper you gave me. So, since the papers were found mixed in with theater stuff mainly, we can infer the link is maybe not the church but Tenebris himself. Maybe he is a member of that church?

"Your boy Tenebris seems to have been born only two years ago. Even in New York he's as good as nonexistent. No records at all. How about you?" Keith started to cut into his roast beef sandwich.

"Awfully tall for a two-year-old," Dirk quipped. "The girls seemed to be part of a group called the Children of Dinosaurs or Diplopods or something. The god of theater or something or other."

"Do you mean Dionysus?" Keith asked chuckling, obviously amused by his friend's inability to remember his high school Greek mythology class.

"Oh yeah, the theater dude."

Gail brought over a plate heaped with a roast beef sandwich and mashed potatoes that were swimming in brown gravy. "Here you go, Dirk."

"Oooh, thanks, Gail." Dirk gave the cook a wave. He went extra heavy on the meat today.

"So, we know there is some sort of connection to the theater. What'd you find out last night?" Keith took a bite of his club sandwich.

"The kids think Mr. Tenebris is a bit of a jerk, but they also seem to respect him too," Dirk said. "He was some sort of big shot on Broadway back in the day, or at least that's what he tells everyone. Makes me wonder what you have to do to get thrown out of a high-paying gig like that and take your talents to a public high school. Probably not the exorbitant salary of a teacher or devotion to the craft. I don't know, maybe he got caught slapping around a hooker; it's New York, after all. But some of the parents think he has a drug problem. Usual rumor mill stuff."

"Not too much on the Internet about him. I wonder if it's his real name. Was it an interesting show at least?" Keith asked.

"Well, not exactly, but I found my way into the administrative building, and it seems our friend Tenebris was having a heated discussion with someone. I couldn't tell exactly who, but the guy he was talking to seemed to want Tenebris to do something specific. Tenebris kept calling him 'Reverend,' but I never got a last name. Tenebris agreed to meet him after the show was over."

"Did you crash their party?"

"No, I had Claire with me. My sister would have me tarred and feathered if she knew I was taking her to a stakeout."

Keith held up his index finger. "Well, you pretty much were."

"Let's stay on point here." Dirk deflected Keith's observation. "I think it's time you and I have a chat with our friend Arthur Tenebris. Maybe we can rattle his cage, and he'll give us more information. Gotta start slow. We don't want to let on that he's our prime suspect. Let's tail him first, find out what he knows. Perhaps he'll do something so amazingly stupid we can wrap this up quickly."

Keith nodded in agreement. "These theater types are curious cats, that's for sure. He could be a pretty strange bird, but you're right, he might make a mistake."

Dirk's phone vibrated its way across the top of the table as he started on the second half of his sandwich. He picked it up and looked at the caller ID.

"It's Carrie." Dirk tapped the phone icon to answer the call.

"Hey, babe, how—wait, what? Slow down," Dirk implored. His eyebrows furrowed, and all the color drained from his face. Whatever news Dirk was getting on the other end of his receiver, it was not good.

Keith knew Dirk better than almost anyone on the planet. An unspoken command passed between the two, and Keith immediately put his fork down and motioned over to Gail. They'd be leaving without eating.

"Okay, we're on our way." Dirk said to Carrie and hit the end call button on the phone. "Keith, we have to go."

Gail came around the corner, and Keith said to her, "Okay if we settle up later?" Gail nodded in response. She was familiar with them enough that if they were leaving in such a hurry, there was some reason behind it.

Dirk grabbed Keith by the sleeve of his coat and pulled him out of the restaurant.

"Wait, Dirk, what's going on?" Keith said.

"We've got to run, Keith. We're needed at the police station."

Keith left his motorcycle in the restaurant parking lot, only stopping long enough to grab a few things out of his saddlebags.

They made it to the city building in record time. The structure was an unusually large building for a mid-sized city. It housed the police, fire, the HAZMAT team, dispatch, the National Guard Unit, and the city's municipal hockey rink. The product of a grant given after 9/11. Some would argue the project had been unnecessarily large, but the community center was always a busy place.

Dirk and Keith ran up the stairs and made their way into the squad room. They were both well-known figures around the station, but this was the first time either of them had been summoned there for a briefing.

As they entered the room, Police Chief Dixon was talking. "…
and I know I don't have to tell you the importance of turning over
every rock we can to find this girl. I've called in everyone on this case,
including Mr. Bentley here." She motioned to Dirk and Keith,
"Bentley Detective Agency was retained by the family of the recently
deceased girl to find answers. Remember, no body means we don't
have a murder yet, and we're going to do our best to keep it that way."

Behind the chief was a large briefing board. On it were posted
pictures of a home, a school, and a photo of a young girl, smiling for
the camera.

To Dirk, it looked like an overwhelming indictment of him
personally. He should have been more careful. The face staring back at
him was the same face who, less than a day before, stood on a stage
and performed for hundreds. Underneath the photo was a simple piece
of paper, onto which was scribbled the name "Melissa Barlo."

Dirk read the name over and over again. Some part of him hoped
that by doing so she would magically walk through the door and say,
"Just kidding." He felt like someone had kicked him in the gut and
then shoved a knife into his forehead for good measure. He'd spoken
to her about Tenebris. He could see her face and hear her words.

The man in the audience had been watching them. Could it have
been the other person Victor had mentioned? Was it possible Dirk had
been *this* close to the murderer and had simply let him slip through his
fingers?

 Melissa's selection and abduction could have been random, but
his instincts told him better. Dirk's heart melted into a lump of lead in
his chest.

The chief continued, "Ms. Barlo was last seen at Central High
School after a performance. She was supposed to come home after the
show was over, but she never made it. According to school officials,

her student ID was used to badge out of the school property, so we think she was abducted somewhere in between the school and home. A local homeless man came forward and said he saw someone loading the trunk of a car outside the school. He thought it looked like they were carrying a rolled-up carpet or something, but he couldn't give us any details."

Oh, sweet Jesus, they were planning the next abduction.

"Chief, may I add something?" Dirk was never in the habit of interrupting the police, but time might be of the essence.

"Mr. Bentley, the floor is yours." The chief stepped to the side.

"Yesterday, I actually talked to Melissa Barlo as part of my investigation." There was an audible gasp in the room. Several of the detectives' eyes grew big as saucers as the enormity of his words sank in.

Dirk continued walking through the details of his investigation so far. He even included the information from Victor, steering clear of telling everyone it had come from a ghost. Dirk had gotten enough grief over the years from the department about the paranormal part of his methods, so he left it out.

Detective Peterson, who had been sitting silently in the corner, stood up. "Well, great and all, but what do you have in the way of proof? We don't have enough to get a warrant here, Bentley."

Dirk knew the detective wasn't trying to necessarily be a jerk, just pointing out that what Dirk saw would never hold up in court.

"Understood. I'm planning on watching Tenebris tonight. He may just give us some more information. Maybe he will make a mistake." The police couldn't authorize a stakeout against Tenebris without anything more solid, but Dirk could observe Tenebris all he wanted to under the auspices of his own investigation.

The chief spoke up. "Okay. Dirk will stake out Tenebris tonight and report back in the morning. The rest of you invest some shoe leather in this. Canvas the neighborhoods. See what you can find out. Someone besides a drunk homeless guy had to have seen something. Guys, I can't stress this enough, I want her alive. Bentley has been retained by the department as private consultant on the case. Dirk and Keith have full access." Dirk had known the chief for years. She was normally as cool as they came, but she wore the enormity of the task on her face.

The squad room jumped into a frenzy of activity. Everyone knew what would happen if they didn't get to Melissa fast enough. Statistics of missing children indicated they had days, if not hours, before the girl could be killed, but there was no way to be completely sure. Dirk and Keith grabbed an unused desk, and Carrie brought them the case files. Dirk wanted to refresh his memory on all aspects of the case before the stakeout.

As personally as he thought the chief was taking this, Dirk viewed this as his own mistake. Like he was solely responsible for Melissa's abduction. He tore through the case files, looking for any clue to point him in the right direction. Internally, he chastised himself for putting the girl's life in danger. This was no longer about simply performing the work of a private investigator; this was about saving Melissa.

After combing over the case files, Dirk made his way to Melissa's house. This time he'd get a crack at the room before the police walked all over anything interesting.

Upon entering the house, the crime scene investigator standing at the door made him put on booties and rubber gloves, not wanting to run the risk of him contaminating any DNA evidence on the premises.

But Dirk was sure there'd be no DNA evidence to find, since she hadn't been abducted from the house. He doubted she'd even made it home that night.

His search revealed very little. Just like the others, Melissa had a ton of theater-related books lying around. Like the other girls' bedrooms, the rest of the room was fairly typical for a teenage girl. On her desk were a collection of phone numbers and her day planner. The script of the play he had seen the night before was sitting on the desk. Notes in the margin told her where to stand and when to move from one mark to another.

The family had no connection to the First Transformational Church. The lack of evidence or any tie to the church confirmed, at least in Dirk's mind, that she'd been a spur-of-the-moment kidnapping. She'd been taken because she'd talked to Dirk, or perhaps this was a copycat. The sudden welling up of his stomach acid told him that it didn't matter who had done the kidnapping. Her blood was on his hands.

Pulling off the booties and gloves, he made a quick phone call to Keith, who was still at the station. Given the circumstances, Dirk thought it better to start the stakeout immediately. He'd sleep when the girl was safe.

"Keith, I have no right to ask you to do this, but I really need a favor."

"Want me to spend a little time with our buddy Tenebris tonight?"

"You can say no." Dirk hated requesting this of him.

"I wouldn't let you do this by yourself. How about I take the two-to-eight shift?"

"Thanks, man you're awesome. Can you fill Carrie in? I have a bad guy to go watch." Dirk hung up the phone and breathed a sigh of relief. It was good to have friends.

CHAPTER 14
IN THE MOONGLOW

Dirk sat alone in his car. He considered himself an old pro at stakeouts, but he always hated them. Next to him was a thermos of coffee, a pair of top-of-the-line binoculars, a small cooler with snacks, and a portable police-band radio with one earbud stuck firmly in his ear. If something went wrong, he could listen to the cars responding to wherever he was.

The night was potentially going to be a long one. Thankfully, the weather was mild and cloudless, and he could leave his windows open and let the fresh air in without having to run the engine. The moon was full and bright and looked close enough to the ground to touch. He could've easily read a book by it. This made it easier to watch Tenebris, but it offered Tenebris the same opportunity to spot Dirk.

Staying up all night didn't bother him; the boredom coupled with the constant worry someone might see him was the bigger issue. Normally, he have Keith take the night shifts since he was more of a night owl than Dirk was. This time was different. Melissa reminded him too much of Claire, which made this personal. Worse yet, he felt responsible for Melissa's abduction. Whoever was doing this had to be stopped, and Dirk had to admit, at this point, there was a part of him that wasn't above vigilante justice. He wouldn't lose any sleep if this guy mysteriously showed up dead in an alley somewhere.

Dirk chose a spot under a tree to shade him from the moonlight. The car was as close to invisible as it would get.

Attempts at invisibility aside, it didn't matter that much; most people were blissfully unaware of their surroundings. Cell phones, personal electronics, computers, and e-readers made the job of a private detective much simpler by ensuring people were always distracted. He could've likely sat outside Tenebris's office and followed him to his car, and Tenebris wouldn't have noticed.

When Dirk had first arrived at the school, he'd seen teachers leaving in groups from the front door, visibly thrilled to be going home. Then they came out in smaller groups, and now individually, as the evening trudged along.

Carrie had called him earlier and gave him the description of Tenebris's car. Dirk had no problems finding it in the parking lot. She joined him for a couple of hours and even brought dinner. Eventually, she had to leave. Once again, Dirk had tried to say "I love you" but failed to spit the words out. She just frowned at him and gave him a kiss goodbye.

His phone said it was 10:30 when Tenebris finally exited the small security gate at the side of the school. He carried a large attaché case and a lunchbox, the normal trappings of a high school teacher. Dirk waited for his quarry to get into his car before starting his, not wanting to spook the thespian.

Dirk was good at following people. He knew when to get closer and when to back off. Granted, he'd had his close calls, and once or twice he'd blown it, but tailing a tired schoolteacher should be relatively easy.

The drive started out routinely enough. Tenebris stopped at a fast-food drive-thru, then at a post office to drop off some letters. They made their way down Mayfield Avenue, the main thoroughfare in town. As they approached the intersection where Dirk figured Tenebris would turn down, heading toward the address Carrie had given him, he was surprised when Tenebris's car stopped along the side of the road.

Dirk passed Tenebris to avoid arousing suspicion and then allowed his car to slow in time to watch Tenebris make an erratic left turn and plunge into a residential area. "Shit!" Dirk yelled as he swung the car around in the middle of the intersection.

Dirk headed in the direction Tenebris had gone. Driving past the first block, he shot a quick glance toward the empty street. He went up one more street and thought he just caught the tail end of his target. Dirk flew up to the next intersection in time to see Tenebris make another right and was now coming directly toward him. Dirk yanked the steering wheel, pulling his car into an empty space on the side of the road to let Tenebris pass. To his surprise, the car parked in a space on the opposite side of the street about a half-block away. He prayed he hadn't been discovered.

He couldn't see what Tenebris was doing, but he could tell he was still inside his car. He began to second-guess himself. Maybe he had been given the slip?

All his questions were put to rest when the car's courtesy light came on, illuminating the profile of Tenebris as he stepped into the street. Through his binoculars, Dirk watched him tuck something into his belt while taking a furtive look around, like he was deliberately checking for something.

Tenebris walked down the street, straight toward Dirk. He ducked down, so he could just barely see above the dashboard. After a few steps, Tenebris broke into a jog. Dirk grabbed his pistol out of its holster.

Showtime.

He was closing fast. One hundred feet, seventy-five feet, fifty feet away from Dirk's car.

Without warning or seeming to even slow down, Tenebris turned to his right and ran across the pavement, shifting into a walk as he entered a small path leading to a back alley barely noticeable under the cover of night.

Shit, now I have to chase him in the dark. Dirk got out and ran as quickly as he could to cover Tenebris's lead. Even at a walker's pace, Tenebris was surprisingly fast. As Dirk got to the alley, he could just make out the teacher's form turning left behind a row of houses.

Dirk watched as his quarry looked around him, checking to see if anyone was following him.

A bit paranoid, are we? Although, maybe it isn't paranoia if you really are being watched.

Dirk slunk into the alley as soon as Tenebris had put some distance between them. Not quite an alley in the city sense, these were community walking paths crisscrossing the neighborhoods. Slinking through the Rotary-maintained flowers and the park benches donated by the local Boy Scout troop, Dirk stayed close to the shadow of the tree line, the moon still emitting a haunting glow.

Dirk picked his way from cover to cover, trying to remain as stealthy as possible. It began to feel like he'd lost Tenebris completely.

Maybe he is behind me?

It didn't seem likely. Dirk would have heard the footsteps moving past him. The alley was only about twenty feet across at its widest, and even in the dark it would've been difficult to pass each other without noticing another person. It might have been possible that Dirk moved past some recess Tenebris had turned into, but doing that without making any noise would be difficult. Yet, none of that accounted for the suddenly missing educator on a midnight run. Not knowing where the suspect he was following went made Dirk feel especially vulnerable.

Carefully creeping back, he found a gate that was partially ajar. He hadn't noticed it because the night shade of an oak tree kept it hidden. He carefully slipped around it. Technically this amounted to trespassing, but the gate was open, and he was on the trail of a murder suspect, so maybe this transgression would be forgiven.

Ahead of him, the rear porch light pierced the darkness. Two men carried on a heated discussion. One of the men was Tenebris and the other, a bald man, was someone Dirk hadn't seen before.

Dirk picked his way along a hedge and under some flowering bushes. He was just beginning to make out the conversation as Tenebris reached into his waistband, pulled a weapon, and pointed it at the other man.

Dirk's own hand instinctively grasped the butt of his pistol, just as he had practiced hundreds of times before. He undid the leather strap holding it in place and drew it out. He thought about his firearms instructor telling him that as a private investigator, Dirk was statistically more likely to suffer a fatal heart attack on a stakeout than draw his pistol during an investigation. Dirk hated being an anomaly.

For a moment, indecision held him tight. He couldn't just let Tenebris shoot the other man, but he also didn't want to jump in quite yet. Thankfully, before he had a chance to work out his next course of action, the matter resolved itself. The unidentified man rushed Tenebris, and a minor scuffle ensued. The commotion gave Dirk enough cover to get in closer.

The other man grabbed the weapon out of the teacher's hand and punched him in the mouth. Tenebris fell back on his ass, as if he were a sack of grain that had been pushed over. It looked like he was out cold, but after a second, he tried to scramble to his feet.

For a moment, neither one of the men spoke. Tenebris interrupted the silence.

"I never signed on for this. I never wanted any part of this." Tenebris's voice broke as he rasped through sobs.

"Arthur, don't be stupid, you knew what you were getting yourself into the first time we established our joint venture. You understood perfectly what you were doing. Perhaps it is better to say that you understood what I needed," the man said.

Who the hell is he talking to? Could this have anything to do with the murders?

"The kids, yes, but I didn't know this was going to happen. A police officer came by the theater the other day. This is all too risky."

"Do you think I'm some sort of idiot?" The other man sounded incredulous. "I was there. I watched the exchange. He's likely not a police officer, though; I think he was a private investigator of some sort. The last gasp of desperate parents, I assure you. And now we don't have to worry about her either." His face took on a very condescending look. "You still don't get it, do you? This is perfect. It tells me that they have nothing, and we are free to make perfection."

Dirk realized this other man was talking about his conversation with Melissa in the theater. The silhouetted man must have been the figure he saw. *Damn it, I had the guy and let him go.* Anger welled up inside of him as he tamped down the urge to jump up and rush both of them. At the same time, he realized it would be a foolish to rush in.

"Why don't you just let me handle things? One private investigator makes no difference to me. I can take care of him. All you need to do is agree to meet with them when they call, and they will, and you just let old Reverend Rigby see to the rest."

"Have you lost your fucking mind, Harmon? We can't kill a cop or a private investigator!" Tenebris was standing up again, and the two men were only a few feet apart now.

Harmon. Dirk's mind suddenly went ablaze with details of the case, an epiphany setting off alarm bells in his mind. The librarian in charge of filing facts and figures in his brain was jumping up and down to get his attention. Harmon was the religious zealot from one of the churches Keith had visited. The papers from the girls' rooms with address and the name of the church. Keith's guy had it wrong, Dr. Harmon wasn't his last name, it was his first. Reverend Harmon Rigby? Could he be connected to the First Transformational Church?

This is the same guy!

"You are a pathetic little tool." Rigby leaned forward slightly, hovering over Tenebris. "You'll do what I tell you when I tell you to. Do you think I'll put up with such insolence? Just remember I own you. I own your soul. You'd be wise to remember that."

"But I don't want to hurt anyone!"

As if turning on a switch, Harmon's demeanor changed from confrontational to conciliatory, almost as if another personality had completely taken over. "My dear boy, you haven't injured a soul. No one has. Remember the divine purpose we are undertaking here." Harmon threw back his shoulders and launched into an eerily deep voice he likely reserved for sermons. "The beloved, wonderful, divine order we are trying to put the world in. I don't think you appreciate how much I've done for you. But no matter, if you want out, then we are done. I no longer need to burden you. Obviously, this yoke is too heavy for you to bear."

"What do you mean?" Tenebris said warily.

Rigby waved his hand at Tenebris as casually as if he was politely dismissing a waiter. "I release you, Arthur. You owe me nothing, and I owe you nothing. Your debt has been paid. You're out, my friend. No hard feelings. Of course, I'll need a new job at the school for someone else to replace you. Maybe an opening will come available. Perhaps in the theater department? Do you know how often those positions change hands? It's shocking, really. People leave their jobs, resign, and some simply disappear. No, my brother, I will take care of everything."

"Are you threatening me?" Tenebris asked shakily, moving a few pensive steps back from Harmon.

"No, no, of course not." Rigby dismissed the sentiment with a sarcastic flair. "I just mean sometimes things happen to people. And replacements are made. I just happen to know a few possible candidates who would do nicely to fill your shoes. Oh, did I say your shoes? Slip of the tongue, really."

Although a threat like this would never hold up in court, Harmon's intimation was received. Either Tenebris would wise up or he'd be out, and in the permanent sense. Dirk desperately wanted to make a recording of this encounter, but his cell phone was in the car. And yet, he didn't dare move a muscle. Every syllable of this exchange was gold in his mind. They might even let slip where Melissa was being held, and that was the most important thing now.

"Wait, now, let's not be hasty." Tenebris put his hands up as if he was trying to stop an imaginary object from hitting him. "I'm sorry, Harmon, I don't know what got into me. I … I'll keep working with you. It's just been a lot of pressure, Harmon … I mean Reverend Rigby … and I'm just a little overworked, and finals are coming up, and you can certainly sympathize." Tenebris stepped back down the stairs as he said this. Whether he'd done it on purpose or not, he'd lowered himself in relation to Harmon, as if begging.

Dirk watched with fascination. The turn of the confrontation to reconciliation spoke volumes about the relationship between the two men. Tenebris wasn't the steel-backed, hard-nosed criminal Dirk had taken him for. He appeared to be more of a spineless weasel. Rigby was in control, which meant Tenebris was the weak link in the relationship. Useful information he could exploit.

"I'm so glad you see it my way." Rigby threw the gun back at Tenebris's feet. Wordlessly, Tenebris picked it up and put it in the pocket of his windbreaker.

Good God, why would you give your would-be assailant back his weapon?

"I know you have been a loyal servant. And after tonight's little performance, I was going to hold this for another time." He drew out a package from his bathrobe the size of two decks of cards. "But I want you to understand, I still have faith in you. A little present so you know I don't take any of this personally."

Whatever he handed Tenebris was rounded on the edges and appeared gray in the night. Tenebris accepted it and appeared to sniff the package. "Oh, thank you, Reverend."

Dirk was reminded of the family dog when he was a boy, just after you gave it a rawhide to chew on.

"There, now all is forgiven. See, isn't this better? You help me, and I give you what you want or perhaps what you need?" Rigby stood there in his bathrobe, considering Tenebris. "But Arthur, if you ever pull a stunt like this again, I will sadly have to remove your heart with my bare hands. You do understand, don't you?" The coldness with which he said these words reminded Dirk of a sociopath talking to a potential victim.

Either way, Dirk didn't think it mattered to Tenebris. Since he'd received the package from Harmon, he was only paying minimal attention, the same way the dog would lose interest in its owner after receiving a treat.

Dirk had a bad feeling about Harmon. Something about his voice bothered him. The way he spoke was cold, calculating, unfeeling, but the man was capable of pouring on the sympathy if needed. Like a psychopath with delusions of grandeur thrown in for flavoring. He didn't have to get any closer to the man to know this guy Harmon was bad news. A cold shiver went up Dirk's spine. He was looking at evil.

Dirk had another epiphany about the case. From the start, he'd had it all wrong. Tenebris was not the aggressor here. Too many things just didn't add up. The way Rigby punched Tenebris, the little package, the throwing back of the gun. Dirk finally understood this tragic comedy playing out before him. This was more like an interaction between an addict and a dealer, where the addict was trying to get clean and sober, and the dealer would hear nothing of it.

The package must have been something Tenebris was addicted to. Dirk thought back to the teacher's words. "Didn't want to hurt anyone" … *could he mean the girls*?

Drugs of some sort? Something he needed to live or that he thought he needed to live. *Oh my god*, Dirk thought. *Tenebris is being controlled through his addiction.*

But what of it? All he knew for sure was that Tenebris, his number one suspect, was not only a kidnapper but a drug addict. That told him nothing. Worse yet, it made the situation far more dangerous than before.

If he just came in over-the-top, guns blazing, there always was the risk he would push Tenebris into a gunfight, leaving someone dead. There was a good chance that person would be Tenebris himself.

They would not only lose the opportunity to interrogate the man, but it would also cut their chances of finding Melissa to almost nil. That was a risk he couldn't take. No matter how bitter the bile was creeping up the inside of the throat, this was not the time for rash decisions.

Still, Dirk had no evidence, nothing solid to go off. The compulsion to jump up and place Tenebris under arrest was palpable but also the wrong move. He'd have to follow him.

And how did this other guy fit into the equation? This whole situation was getting weirder all the time.

"Now, Arthur, go home. Enjoy what I gave you. Go easy on the stuff. I'll call you tomorrow." And he added, with no small amount of disdain, "The next time you go to kill someone, you may want to load the gun." Harmon turned from Tenebris and disappeared into the house.

Tenebris, still holding the package up to his face as if it were a cherished treasure, pivoted from the house and walked back toward where Dirk was hiding. Under normal circumstances, any man passing this close to Dirk would have seen him. Tenebris was off in his own world.

Dirk knew the type. With the package in his hand, a hooker could have offered him her services for free, and he wouldn't have noticed. Harmon had likely only given him enough to keep his addiction going but not enough to let him completely string himself out. This Harmon guy needed Tenebris just on the verge of searching for his next fix. Tenebris was his tool, just as Harmon had said.

Tenebris made his way back to his car, with Dirk following at a discreet distance. Both men returned to their vehicles and soon were on the road. A short drive back to Tenebris's small duplex, it was all Tenebris could do to keep his car on the road. He'd periodically swerve from one side of the road to the other and then back again.

Thankfully, at this late hour, most of these streets were abandoned anyway.

Arthur Tenebris, one-time rising Broadway star, theater arts director of Central High School, and apparent drug addict, got out of his car, walked up his three steps and into his house. Dirk didn't even think he had bothered locking his car, as whatever was in that package had a complete hold on him. Soon the door opened, and the lights from what appeared to be a kitchen snapped on.

Dirk sat outside in the street, watching Tenebris through his binoculars. He could just make out Tenebris sitting at his kitchen table. The lace curtains did nothing to hide the interior for the prying eyes of the world.

Although he couldn't make out every detail, he could just see Tenebris cut the package spilled a substance onto the table. Tenebris was making little lines in whatever white powder he could see. He then leaned over, and although Dirk couldn't see it, he imagined Tenebris was snorting the material up his nose. Dirk had no way to confirm if the powder was cocaine, but it sure wasn't baby powder. Tenebris was a junkie, and Harmon was his supplier. What was the currency he was using to pay for the drugs?

Before heading home for the night, Dirk stopped off at the house where Tenebris and Harmon had their altercation. He remained in the shadows for a while, hoping to catch anything of interest that might give the police an excuse to bust the front door open and conduct a thorough search. Not finding anything useful, he wrote down the address from the front of the house, which belonged to Dr. Harmon Rigby. He texted the address to Carrie and updated her on what he had found. She could do some digging into this new information.

Exhaustion him like a locomotive. Although he wanted more than anything to continue on watching for anything that might help, he knew the lack of appreciable sleep made it more likely than not he would make some sort of error. And errors had already made one person a kidnap victim.

It killed him to think that Melissa was out there some place, scared and possibly in pain. He quickly spoke with the night commander of the task force and gave him the short version of what he'd seen. The next morning, he could put together a more formal report, but right now he was too tired to keep going. Looking through blurry eyes at his radio, he saw the night had slipped into early morning.

Dirk still wasn't sure what the connection was between Rigby and Tenebris, but he was certain the relationship was more than just drug dealer and addict. There was something deeper, he was sure of it. He'd track down more information on Harmon after catching some sleep. He only hoped his efforts were enough to bring her home safe.

Turning the corner onto his street, Dirk called Carrie. "Hey, sexy, you ever get the chance to check up on Tenebris?"

Dirk knew Carrie was likely sitting behind her computer at the station, staring at the screen with all the information she had compiled on Tenebris. She loved data and went at it with the efficiency of an accountant. "Awww, you are so complimentary when you need something. Silly boy. Yep, took some digging, but I sure did. Odd fellow. You need to start hanging out with a better class of people."

"Interesting comment from the person I hang out with the most but continue." Dirk let out a chuckle.

"Remember how we couldn't find anything in the Virginia database? I expanded my search out to the federal level. Still, there was nothing. However, get this, I did see where he transferred his driver's license from New York to Virginia. I called a friend in New York, and you'll never guess what I discovered about your new best friend?"

"I'll bet you breakfast at my place I already know what you are going to say," Dirk said as he turned the car onto his street.

Dirk never made a bet unless he was sure he'd win. "Okay, hotshot, deal. What's your guess?" Carrie said.

"Tenebris had some drug problems, cocaine most likely. Bad enough to get him bounced from the limelight in New York." He was guessing his sudden move to Virginia was likely related to the performance he had just observed at his house.

"Dammit! Eggs or French toast?" Carrie said, sounding a little dejected. "Just tell me, is it enough for a warrant?"

"Possibly. I would like to talk to him in the morning though. Oddly enough, Tenebris seems to be wrapped up with another guy."

Carrie let out a dejected sigh on the phone. "Crap. That complicates things."

"Maybe. Depends how closely linked they are, I suppose. We just need some more evidence. There is another person involved, but if we move too quickly, they might kill the girl, if they have her. If we're wrong about where he's keeping her, then he'll walk." Dirk knew busting onto a guy's property with no evidence was a professional mistake he couldn't afford to make. The fallout would land him in hot water and Melissa in the morgue.

"Did they find the info on Tenebris in the regular records?" Dirk asked. "It strikes me as a little odd that a drug conviction would be a good point on a resume for someone looking to teach schoolkids."

"Here's where it gets interesting," Carrie continued. "There's nothing in his file. No record of any drug conviction at all. Turns out he went to a court-ordered program called 'Clean and Sober.' The deal was if he completed the program his record would be expunged. No one in Virginia would know because the record was as white as snow on Christmas morning."

"How did you figure this out then?" Dirk wasn't surprised by his girlfriend's resourcefulness.

"I have a friend on New York's narcotics squad." Carrie sounded pleased with herself. "He arrested your buddy personally. Followed his case till the end."

"Funny how these things work themselves out. I need some more syrup, can you pick some up too?"

"Sure, after I get off. You know, if you gave me a key, it might be a little easier. Trust me, there are plenty of benefits for the both of us."

Dirk sensed where she was going with this, and he agreed with her more than he could say. "We'll talk. I'll leave a key under the mat for the morning," Dirk said.

"Score! That is not a no. See you later Mr. Private *Dick*." Carrie hung up the phone with a giggle. She had a few more hours of the night shift and then she'd be over.

Before climbing into bed, he sent Keith a text.

Buddy,

Never mind tonight. Clear the deck for late morning. You got out of stakeout duty, but I need you when I go visit Tenebris. We move on him now. I'll explain later. Let's meet at 11:00 at the school.

BTW, found crazy Harmon guy. Interesting character. Talk to you in the morning.

CHAPTER 15
THE KEY TO A GIRL'S HEART

Dirk woke up to the sounds of pans rustling around in the kitchen. The scent of coffee and bacon drew him to his feet and pulled him into the kitchen. Stakeouts always left him exhausted, no matter how much sleep he managed to get.

Turning from the hall into the kitchen, he half expected to see Carrie dressed in one of his T-shirts, but to his surprise, she was fully dressed and ready to go for the morning. He could never figure out how she survived on as little sleep as she did.

"So, sleepyhead, how'd the stakeout go?" she asked.

"The night was certainly eye-opening. I watched him get some drugs from a guy in an alley," Dirk said, kissing a greeting and taking a cup of coffee from her hands. "Not really a drug neighborhood though. I followed him back to his house and saw him snorting the stuff. But what I can't figure is the relationship between the two."

"No way, you actually observed him snorting? Describe it to me," she said.

Dirk led her through a description of the events at the house. Seeing someone snort cocaine was underwhelming, but he told her everything he witnessed. Ever the police officer, she seemed satisfied with his description. While it was not as good as being there, if Dirk would swear out testimony, it would be enough to proceed with getting a search warrant. He was considered a reliable witness.

"I really don't peg Tenebris as the murderer type. I think I can break him, Carrie. He's weak, and I mean paper-thin," Dirk said.

"How so?" Carrie abandoning her girlfriend voice for her detective voice.

Pouring syrup over the French toast, he continued, "You know what a junkie and dealer relationship normally looks like? Well, this isn't it. Their relationship is more like Tenebris is truly deathly afraid of this Harmon character."

"Lots of users are scared of their dealers." Carrie shrugged.

"Not like this, though. Tenebris said he wanted to stop doing something, but I am sure he was not referring to drugs. And he was begging this other guy, Harmon Rigby. But Harmon just kept stringing him along."

"Hmmm," Carrie muttered through a piece of French toast. Dirk watched her think about what he had told her. Occasionally she would furrow her eyebrows and point to imaginary objects she was seeing in the air. He often commented on how cute she looked when she was deep in thought.

"Before you ask, let me answer. I am totally sure this is Keith's Harmon." Dirk anticipated her next question. "Tenebris said he never wanted anyone to get hurt. But the words were less important than the body language. I'm not exactly sure how to describe it." Dirk searched through his recollections of the night before. There was something about their interaction that screamed volumes and was also really hard to qualify.

"I've got it." Dirk put his fork down and stared directly at Carrie. "Tenebris was kowtowing to him, like he was treating him with reverence. That's it. He was being reverent. Tenebris looked at this guy with a mix of fear and respect."

A tingle in Dirk's scalp turned into a shiver, which rushed down the down his spine. It was all there, if only he took the time to put the puzzle pieces together. Jumping to his feet from his "eureka" moment, he leaned across his chair and kissed Carrie on the cheek. "Harmon has an almost cult-type of hold on Tenebris. Oh, Carrie, I think I know the connection. Tenebris is supplying the girls in exchange for drugs, and Tenebris wants out!" He fished a paper from the pile of evidence he had collected. The single sheet was the thank-you note from the Pastor to Brother Tenebris from The First Transformational Church. "Harmon is his dealer *and* his pastor!"

"You got this by watching him from your car?" Carrie, the consummate professional, always worried about little things like a grand jury, admissibility in court, and other detective stuff.

"Oh, well, things become a little tricky. The car would've been too far away to see any of this, but it turns out the bushes in his backyard are the perfect spot to listen. I swear, I didn't set out to listen from the bushes, but I saw Tenebris draw a gun, and I needed to get closer to him to make sure he didn't kill anyone."

"So, you moved closer to the guy with the gun? I should arrest you for trespassing and for being an idiot. Instead, I'll just get you some more breakfast." Carrie pointed her spatula at him menacingly.

"You can tie me up and interrogate me later. I want to go talk with Tenebris. This time we'll make it official. Don't worry, I'll leave out the part about lurking in the bushes. Can you arrange to have one of the guys from the station accompany Keith and me?"

"Why not me?" Carrie looked a little hurt.

Doing his best Sam Spade impression, Dirk said, "Sorry, dollface, but this is a guys-only party." Returning to a more conciliatory tone, he continued, "Seriously, you're normally my first choice, but I want someone tall and built like a brick shithouse. Tenebris is a paper tiger, and I need a physically intimidating presence in the room to get the interview off on the right foot." Dirk and Keith were smart and cunning, but they weren't a scary pair. They could handle themselves in a fight, but they preferred the more cerebral approach.

"Tell the chief I'd be willing to testify on seeing the cocaine. I did see it from the street, so they can't claim I was bending the law to get evidence. I'm thinking we can break him. We've got all the levers we need to throw." Dirk glanced at his watch. He had to speed things up if he was going meet Keith at the garage.

Carrie called the station and found out which of the sergeants were on duty and arranged to have someone meet them at the school. Then she filled in the chief and got clearance to go ahead with the operation.

Dirk leaned over and gave her a kiss. As they kissed, he slipped her own house key into her pocket. "Thank you," he said.

Carrie reached into her pocket and looked at him with surprise, "What's this?" She knitted her eyebrows together in a look of confusion. "Shit, you didn't steal someone's house key too, did you? I really would have to arrest you then."

Dirk smiled at her. "No, sweetie, try the lock on the front door."

"What? Why are you giving—" Carrie stopped herself. "A key to your house? Really? My own key?" Dirk saw her eyes welling up with tears as she held it in front of her.

"I know I can be a real pain in the ass sometimes." Dirk slid his arms around her.

He had a devil of a time trying to say the words *I love you*, but it didn't mean he didn't show it in other ways.

Dirk headed to the shop. He'd texted Keith and told him he would pick him up there. As he pulled up to the building, Keith jumped into the passenger seat.

"Turns out Tenebris and Harmon are really close friends."

"Oh yeah? This could get interesting," Keith said.

CHAPTER 16
AN INTERVIEW WITH AN ADDICT

Keith and Dirk pulled into the Central High school parking lot right next to an easily recognizable unmarked squad car. Out of the car stepped Officer Andrews, who'd been assigned to work with Keith and Dirk.

Officer Andrews was one of the nicest officers on the department. Unless, of course, you happened to be a criminal. Then the police sergeant likely wouldn't be the person you'd want to meet. If you weren't in a confessing mood before he entered the room, you would be shortly after. Not only was he exceptionally tall, but he also held the police record for fitness and was an amateur bodybuilder. He was precisely the look Dirk needed.

His instructions were to let Dirk and Keith do the questioning, at least until there was enough to make an arrest in the case. Tenebris was to leave in cuffs no matter what the outcome of the interview was.

The three of them made their way to the second floor of the theater arts building. Stopping at Tenebris's door, Dirk pointed to the small hallway he had hidden in only a few nights before. Keith smiled, shaking his head at his friend as he knocked on the door.

"If this is a student and you don't have an appointment, I will boil you in your own pudding!" A gruff voice barked from inside the office.

"No sir, not a student," Dirk responded. "My name is Dirk Bentley, and I'm an investigator. May I have a word with you?"

"All right, wait a moment. I'm coming."

Dirk could hear movement inside the room. It sounded like some shuffling of papers and a desk chair. There was a dull thud of what could be a knocked over wastebasket.

The door to the room flew open, and Tenebris stood there. He was slightly sweaty, and his nose was red and irritated. "An investigator, you say? If this is about the girls, I've told the police about all I know."

"I understand, sir, if I can just have a moment of your time," Dirk said calmly. "I only have a few questions, and we'll be out of your hair. Really, I'm just trying to tie up some loose ends." He took a half-step forward. "As I said, my name is Dirk Bentley, this is my associate Keith, and this is Sergeant Andrews, our police liaison. They already told us you were cooperating fully, but I just want to make sure my investigation is complete."

Tenebris's gaze shifted to the massive Sergeant Andrews who stood mute for the moment. "Please come in and have a seat. I apologize for only having the two chairs. I can get one more if you like."

"That won't be necessary. We won't be long," Keith said.

The room was well-furnished. More than what you would expect from a high school theater arts teacher. The office was large, with one side converted to a small stage that had a few props lying around. It looked like a miniature theater. Eight chairs faced the stage.

Shelves overflowed with books on theater theory and stage design. He had several awards hanging on the walls, thanking him for his participation in some performance or other. On one table a collection of statuettes for his work in the theater. One was recognizable as a Tony Award. On the floor, a large Persian rug dominated the space. Behind the desk was a door that Dirk thought might lead out into the back hall.

Tenebris remarked. "I'm just glad you're not students. They love to play pranks on the faculty here from time to time. The interruptions can get a little frustrating, if you ask me."

"I can certainly understand. I imagine a teacher's time is precious." Dirk took a seat.

"Wow, these are nice chairs," Keith remarked. They were made of leather and had thick padding on them. "The school must be doing well to furnish your office like this."

"Ha! Hardly." Tenebris laughed at the suggestion. "You think they could furnish this room on what a school makes? Please. It just so happens that those two chairs are famous. They were from a Broadway adaptation of the life of Harry Houdini. I played the lead role of Harry, probably the performance I'm proudest of. The whole thing takes place in a psychiatrist's office. The shrink's office was my idea. Won a bunch of awards. The director gave me those chairs after the show had run its course, as a thank you. But I'm guessing you didn't come to here to talk about my furniture, did you?"

"Exactly right," Dirk said. "We're investigating the murder of Heather Smithfield, on behalf of her family."

Andrews stood behind Dirk and Keith. Dirk had specifically told him to stay quiet until the law absolutely required him to jump in. He wanted the mountain of a man that was Sergeant Andrews to be the scary, strong, silent type and to remain out of the picture to allow the fiction that Tenebris was not in trouble to persist as long as possible. His part in this performance was critical.

Sergeant Andrews, normally would never take orders from a private detective. However, he agreed because either way, he would be bringing back a suspect today. He only needed to let Dirk bait the trap and watch Tenebris walk into it.

"Yes, sad thing to befall this school," Tenebris said. "Heather Smithfield was a great kid. Talented actress too. She had a lot of potential. Working with me, she could've been one of the greats. A young life snuffed out too early."

Dirk sensed all the world was Tenebris's stage, and they were his audience. His responses rolled off his tongue as if reading a part in a play. He'd spent a considerable amount of time thinking through this exact situation, perhaps had even been coached.

"Do you remember where you were the night she was murdered?" Dirk asked.

"You certainly don't think *I* killed her, do you?" Tenebris looked appalled.

"Just routine. I have a gap, and I want to make sure I know where everyone was at the time. It's important to have a complete picture. Plus, after a few days, sometimes additional details emerge that people did not remember before." Dirk saw a flash of something across Tenebris's face. A bead of sweat had formed on his temple.

"I'm incapable of such a thing," he retorted. "I'm a man of the arts. Refined in my nature, I'd never do anything to hurt any person, let alone one of my students."

"You didn't answer my question," Dirk said.

"Let me check my calendar." Tenebris opened the calendar on his computer. He immediately pulled up the entry to the day Heather died. "Let's see. I worked late and then I had dinner with my mother. She's getting old, and she likes the company. Then I went home and read for a while. Nothing more, nothing less."

Dirk thought it odd he remembered the exact date without any further prompting.

"Did you see or talk to Heather that day?" From their vantage point, both Dirk and Keith already knew the answer. The bookcase behind Tenebris reflected the screen of the computer perfectly. In it they could both clearly make out a notation which read "6:30 – Smithfield".

"Well, I just don't recall. It was weeks ago, gentlemen. I really don't remember that far back, and I have a lot of students." Tenebris clicked on the entry for that day and hit the delete key while trying to shield his keyboard, not knowing his furtive movements were already irrelevant. Then he snapped off his computer screen quickly. "Nope, nothing on the computer. I am sorry, gentlemen."

Dirk, and likely Keith and Sgt. Andrews, picked up on the change in Tenebris's demeanor right away. His previous answers were immediate and succinct. This time he hesitated, and his eyelids fluttered a little. He may have won a Tony for work on Broadway, but he was a terrible liar.

"Did you rehearse or maybe meet with her the day she disappeared?" Keith continued.

"You can't imagine how hard it is to recollect the actions of one student out of so many. Everyone fades into the background after a while, you know. I'm not sure if I worked specifically with her before she vanished. Although it is certainly a possibility." Tenebris's shirt started to show small blotches of perspiration. His shaking hand pulled out a handkerchief from his pocket, and he dabbed at his brow.

"Wait a moment. Something just occurred to me." Keith held up a finger in interruption. "You said she 'could've been one of the greats.' I would think you'd remember one of your stars coming to your office."

Tenebris started to say something in his defense when Dirk cut him off. "Did she ever object to being in the theater? Anything about being here she specifically didn't like?"

"No, she loved the theater. She loved acting." Tenebris's voice had changed modulation now. He spoke low and stared off into space, as if he was suddenly talking to just himself. The tone was different from his previously rehearsed answers. This story came from his heart. "She was a good actress. She had real talent, could've been great. Why would he take her? Why was she so special? I mean, whoever did this, of course."

Dirk leapt back into the interrogation. "You said *he*. Do you know something you're not sharing with us? It seems interesting the girls were here, meeting with you, on the precise day they disappeared. The only thing they have in common is you, Tenebris."

Tenebris just stared at the three men. His skin had gone from red to an ashen gray. They had him cornered, and everyone in the room recognized it. Sergeant Andrews remained stoically behind them, still as a statue. Dirk would owe him a pitcher of beer after all this was over.

Dirk leaned forward in his chair. "Sergeant Andrews here can get a search warrant, and we can keep this room sealed until he does so. All it will take is a hair on the floor, a fingerprint, a simple notation in a notebook, or maybe an entry on the computer of yours, and we're in business. You can either answer our questions, or we can do this the hard way. Isn't that right, Officer Andrews?"

"Nothing would bring me greater pleasure, Mr. Bentley," the mountain of a man said in reply.

Keith added in his own personal observation. "Even if an entry were to be deleted, the cybercrime investigators can find it. Nothing ever vanishes from a networked computer."

Tenebris had now turned from ashen gray to green in color. He sat back in his chair and appeared to be on the verge of a heart attack. He picked up a small handheld fan and started fanning himself. "I watch enough television, gentlemen, to acknowledge when I need a lawyer."

Sergeant Andrews's reaction to Tenebris's acclamation was so quick it caught Dirk and Keith off guard. The giant of a man slammed his fist down on the table in front of Tenebris, knocking over the cup holding his pencils and pens. "You'll need a mortician!"

Dirk and Keith recovered from the sudden outburst quickly, but the flare of emotion had its intended effect. Dirk couldn't have asked for better timing.

"Don't hit me, you can't hit me," Tenebris screamed as he cowered in his chair. His hands covered his face.

Sergeant Andrews nodded to Dirk. Technically, Tenebris had yet to lawyer up. He had not said specifically "I want a lawyer." But Dirk sensed he was nearing that point.

Dirk had heard of people who were complete cowards, but he had never met one. Tenebris had folded far quicker than Dirk ever would've imagined. They had him right where they wanted him. *Time to reel in this fishy,* Dirk thought.

Picking up the cup and putting the pens and pencils back in, Dirk said, "Mr. Tenebris … Arthur, may I call you Arthur? No one is going to hurt you. At least, not if you start telling us the truth. We just want to understand what happened."

"I don't have any idea, I swear." Tenebris was now half on the floor and half on the chair. Dirk's gut feeling told him Tenebris lacked the intestinal fortitude to commit this kind of crime. If he could fold this quickly and be led around like a puppy by a brick of cocaine, then murder was out of his wheelhouse. That left another interesting possibility. Harmon Rigby was now suspect number one. While that suggested a different direction to their investigation, Tenebris was still the gatekeeper.

"Now, Arthur, if you remember, I was only asking about Ms. Smithfield." Dirk found himself enjoying watching the man squirm. "Again, I inquire about your interesting word choice. You just said 'girls.' That is the plural form of girl. That makes me think you're not telling us the entire truth. What do you know about the 'girls?'" He paused for a moment for dramatic affect. "Better yet, let's wait on that answer for a moment. I'll give you time to think a bit. I have some other questions."

Dirk got up from the chair and walked the length of the room. He purposely avoided any eye contact with Tenebris as he made a show of inspecting the titles of the books. He found several by famous actors on Broadway and even a few scripts which were signed by the cast of the play. He could feel Tenebris's eyes on him.

"Seems to me," continued Dirk, "you like being the mighty Broadway choreographer. You like yelling at these kids. But I don't think it tells the whole story. I hear you charged a few kids some special fees for acting lessons. Where does the money go? Do you pocket the cash? Oh yes, I know about the extra dollars on the side."

Tenebris had composed himself a little. "Those are fees the families pay to the program. There's no budget in school theater. It allows us to buy lights, scenery, paint, and other things. Yes, I'm hard on the kids, but it makes them better actors. If they are serious, they must get used to it. You think I'm difficult, then try the big stages in New York. It will break you in no time flat. I just want the kids to be great, to have their shot. Even if they only find their bit of heaven at a local theater, there is joy in the stage."

"So, if I go to the administration and ask about these things, they'd validate it all?" Dirk was still leafing through books on the shelf. The money probably was for the program, but he figured it would rile Tenebris enough to move him to the defensive, which was where Dirk needed him. "Okay, Keith, that's on our 'to do' list."

Dirk turned around again to face Tenebris. "Let's go back to the 'girls' remark earlier. You said 'girls', which is plural, not singular. I never said anything about girls. That strikes me as a little odd." Dirk held a finger up in the air as if he were about to make a point but then opened his hand up in a more conciliary gesture. "Now, Tenebris, I love the arts. I'd hate to see someone like you fall for something like murder. Do you have any idea what they would do to you in a maximum security prison? People with such a delicate constitution like you shouldn't be in a place like that. Not good for them, you know. I personally see you become someone's bitch. Unfortunately for you, I have a case to solve, and someone's going to go down for murder. So, what do you think, Mr. Tenebris? Do you really want to find out if what I am saying is true or not? 'Bout prison, I mean?"

Tenebris sat in silence. Dirk didn't expect an answer.

Dirk leaned in, staring directly into his eyes. "I'm going to get paid either way. I can either send you to a prison where you're going to be someone's little boy toy, or you can work with me, and we can see what kind of deal the prosecutor will give you. Better yet, let's try this. You want out from under Harmon's thumb? Maybe get clean?" Dirk paused for dramatic effect. "Yes, I know about Harmon Rigby and the cocaine. We can help you, but you have to be straight with us."

"Okay, okay, I—" Tenebris held his head in his hands. His hair was wet with sweat, and his shirt looked like he had run a marathon in it. He'd finally broken under the weight of questioning. "I'll tell you, but you have to believe me. I didn't kill those girls."

Dirk stepped away from Tenebris and sat down in the chair. "Okay, hotshot, for argument's sake, let's assume I believe you. You have my full attention. I am willing to accept, for the moment, you didn't kill those girls. But I'm pretty sure you know who did. Let's hear the whole story from the beginning."

Tenebris sat back in his chair. For a moment, he looked up at the ceiling and took a deep breath. His gaze then left the ceiling and fixed on Dirk and then Keith, before drifting to a spot off in the distance, affixed on nothing in particular. "I used to live in New York, as you can guess. Life was great at first, and I did some of my best work there." He motioned to the statuettes, awards, and other things around the room. "The theater can be a fickle place though. The stress, the constant pressure. Young kids showing up every year trying to take the spotlight. That place is a meatgrinder for artists who don't keep their wits about them."

"So, you started doing drugs, get on with it," Dirk interrupted.

"It's my story, Mr. Bentley." Tenebris, no longer looking frightened, drilled into Dirk with a forceful but resigned gaze. "We both understand how this day ends for me, so at least let me tell it my way. For the record, you're correct. I got involved with some people who gave me something to take the edge off, at least at first. But the powder, it took ahold of me. I can't explain it to someone who has never lost a fight like this before. It robs you of time, your soul, your money, your sanity, and eventually it takes everything."

Dirk suddenly felt a little twinge of sympathy for the man. He'd seen junkies before. When they lost, it was spectacular. Those who couldn't control it eventually ended up in the gutter or morgue.

"I got rolled by the police in a sting operation." Tenebris cast a glance toward Sergeant Andrews.

"But I was a first-time offender, and the prosecutor gave me a deal."

"The Come Clean Program?" Keith interjected.

"Precisely right, the Come Clean Program. Within two months, I was truly clean and sober." Tenebris looked a little relieved at the memory. "I felt great. I knew I needed to get out of Broadway for a while. A place to begin again, away from what made me into this thing I had become. I wasn't more than a month out of the program before I was approached by a man. He said he represented a school searching for a theater arts coordinator."

"Was this Harmon Rigby?" Dirk guessed.

"Yes, he had some pull with the school board and wanted me for the position. The pay wasn't great, but I could rebuild my life."

"Did he give you the drugs, Mr. Tenebris?" Sgt. Andrews asked, sounding very official.

"Yes, but not right away. I took the job, and he introduced me to people who could mentor me in the life of a schoolteacher. I then found out he was a pastor in a local church, and he invited me to come. Only after I was here for eight months did he offer me the chance to get high."

"And you caved," Dirk said.

"Well, no one's perfect, are they, my dear investigator? Everyone has their own vices."

"Go on," Keith encouraged.

"Well, I came to his office one day, and he was sitting in his chair," Tenebris continued, reliving the scene in his head. "Told me he had a special project. One ordained by God himself. He wanted me to some of my performers in the roles of eternity. A simple favor, something he said would be to help him prepare."

Tenebris was still sweating, but he seemed to be more relaxed now, as if telling his story was taking the stress off his shoulders. "The private lessons were his idea. It helped pay some of the bills for the department. I don't make much, and it defrays my out-of-pocket expenses. The Children of Dionysus was also, essentially, Harmon's suggestion. For the record, Mr. Bentley, the money is completely aboveboard. I also use it to pay a small honorarium to guest lecturers."

Dirk thought it might be fun to string him along some more, but they needed answers and to find the girl. "So, do you select the girls to bring to him, or does he get a say?"

"He does. During the practices for the Children of Dionysus, he sits in the back of the theater and watches, but only when he wants a new victim."

Dirk shuddered at the realization the person in the back of the theater, when he was talking to Melissa, was Rigby himself. The words of an old mentor came back to him about not ignoring that gut instinct. *I should have known.*

"You didn't think it was odd the girls you were giving to him were showing up dead?" Sgt. Andrews asked.

"Well, he can be calming and quite convincing, you know. And then there were the drugs, for which I could lose my job. He said our efforts were for the good of God, and through the haze of my addictions, it all sounded reasonable. You couldn't possibly understand. Certainly, I had my suspicions, but he told me not to worry, that it would all be okay. Seems silly now, since it definitely isn't going to be fine."

Dirk hesitated with the next question. He was afraid of the answer. "Tell me, what happens to the kids after he takes them away? Rape? Murder? Torture? What does he do to them?"

Tenebris was crying and holding his head in his palms. "I don't know! One day they meet with me in the office, and a week later they are found dead. You have to believe me!"

Dirk and Keith exchanged knowing glances. It had been only three days since Melissa had been taken. That meant there was still hope.

"Alright," Dirk said. "Next question: How does he get them out of here? I mean, does he hit them on the head, drug them, how exactly?"

Tenebris said in between his sobs, "He drugs them, carries them out the back door and into his car."

Tenebris was a complete pawn in Rigby's game and didn't even comprehend how in over his head he was. Dirk would've felt sorrier for him if the theater arts teacher turned addict wasn't so completely clueless.

Dirk thought about the drunk who had provided an eyewitness account. "Listen, Tenebris, there is still time. You need to give up Harmon Rigby," Dirk said.

Tenebris folded his arms around himself, much like a child who no longer wanted to eat his veggies. "You haven't been listening to me. There is no way you could possibly understand. He'll kill me. I've seen into his heart, and he will get to me no matter what you do."

"We can protect you," Sergeant Andrews calmly replied in a more conciliatory tone.

Dirk spoke with a calm voice, "If we don't have someone to burn for the murder, we'll always take the next best thing. Tell me, is he worth it to you?" After a few seconds of silence, he added, "C'mon, Tenebris, he can't hurt you after he's been executed."

"Better to give up the real murderer." Sgt. Andrews leaned his large frame forward, driving home Dirk's point.

Dirk had an idea. He'd be stepping out on a limb. If he was right, it could push Tenebris over to their side. Dirk had watched him working with the kids, and he'd heard the other kids talk about him. Tenebris may have been a pretty poor judge of character and a cokehead, but he seemed to genuinely enjoy the kids.

"Look, Arthur, you don't want any more kids to get hurt. You never signed up for murder. As a matter of fact, I'm guessing you like working with the students. Stop me if I'm wrong, but Rigby targeted you because you were an addict on the mend, and he did everything he could to push you off the wagon. You were nothing to him. Just a tool. Sound right so far?"

Once again, Tenebris sat still and mute, like a statue. His shoulders were hunched over, and he stared off at a spot on the rug. Dirk knew he was on the right track, so he continued. "You didn't want to start doing drugs again. I mean, the drugs got you thrown off Broadway, right? Too many drugs? Then you found this job teaching and decided to make a new start in the middle of Virginia where your past wouldn't have followed you. You could be your own man. Maybe claw your way back to the Great White Way someday? But you didn't count on one thing, did you? You enjoyed the little rug rats here at the school. It was fulfilling in a way nothing else ever had been."

Keith picked up for Dirk. "They had youth, enthusiasm. They listened to you. You were a tough teacher, but the kids respected that. At least the true actors did. You loved seeing them succeed on the stage."

"The kids." Tenebris had resumed sobbing. Dirk knew he had hit the right nerve. "The kids are the best thing about this job. It's in a crappy place, in a crappy school, but those kids love it when a performance is perfect. They love the theater."

"But you didn't want to see anyone else hurt, right? So, you went to Rigby and asked him to stop, didn't you?" Sgt. Andrews asked.

Tenebris spoke out loud to no one in particular. "He laughed at me at first. He gave me more cocaine and said I needed to just listen to him. He told me to keep my mouth shut. And the cocaine, I had to. I couldn't make it without the cocaine."

"Help me give you your sanity back." Dirk stared straight into Tenebris's watery eyes. "You are the only one who can stop Rigby from ever hurting another soul."

Keith saw the opportunity to do what he did best. "Look, Rigby isn't in control of you. *You* are in control of you. It isn't going to be easy, and it isn't going to be painless, you know that is true. You can take satisfaction in stopping another murder and regaining your sanity again in the process. Right now, there's another girl missing, and we need you to get her back home where she belongs. She doesn't deserve this."

"Rigby says he's helping the girls find the creator," Tenebris said through his sobs. "I don't know what he's talking about. He scares me. He'll kill me."

"Rigby is hurting them, *killing them*, and you need to stand up and protect them." Dirk felt like he was begging at this point, but he also sensed that a sympathetic ear was what the situation called for.

Tenebris shifted in his seat a little and then sat upright in his chair. He looked straight at Sgt. Andrews. "I want a lawyer. Not another word until I get a lawyer. I've already said way too much."

Dirk watched his opportunity evaporating right in front of his eyes. In the back of his mind, he saw Melissa chained to a wall in a dungeon, and he only sat inches from her location. An invisible hand pushed him back farther and farther from the one thing he truly needed. "What about Melissa Barlo? Where is she? Dammit, Tenebris, we can save her if you just point us in the right direction."

Sgt. Andrews put his hand on Dirk's shoulder and gave him a knowing glance. Their interview was over. Once someone asked for a lawyer, there was nothing they could do but wait for one to show. They were done for now. Maybe a day in detox would help clear Tenebris's mind and he would have more information to provide, but it might be a day too late. They needed a break, and they needed it fast.

CHAPTER 17
"FRIENDS"

Melissa woke with a start. Not so much a diluted, foggy rise to consciousness but more of a sudden awakening, similar to how she felt when she was late for the bus in the morning. She lay, once again, on the table, which had been turned to face the glass window covered by drapes. Leather straps held her in place. With the shades on the other side of the window drawn, she could see her reflection. She was dressed in a red gown, as if she were going to a school dance. She was even wearing makeup.

At first glance, she was reminded of the gimmicky porcelain dolls her mother had brought back from her visit to Korea. She couldn't help but think the liberal coating of eye shadow, foundation, and lipstick made her look clownish.

The distant sounds of a door opening and closing reminded her of the soundtrack in a movie she had once watched where an executioner made their way to where they would administer the lethal injection. She shut her eyes and pretended to still be asleep. Maybe he'd untie her if he thought she was unconscious. Perhaps buy herself enough time to engineer an escape.

Rigby entered the room and turned on the big overhead light. She remained motionless, desperate to avoid another dose of the medicine. He opened the small door next to the window and pulled on what sounded like the cords used to open the drapes.

"Good afternoon, my lovelies. How was my day? Excellent, thank you so much for asking, Mr. Sanchez. You are looking unusually well." Rigby was obviously talking to someone on the phone or in another room.

"No, Mrs. Worthmeyer, right now isn't the ceremony." Rigby answered a question Melissa couldn't hear. "But soon, I promise. My, my, aren't we impatient little ones today? We have to wait for the right moment, you know. It pains you to be like this, I understand, but I need to make sure everything is ready." The sound of a faucet turning on and water splashing around suggested Rigby had turned toward the faucet.

Every fiber of her being told her to scream out as hard as she could. A caricature of the situation sprang up in her conscious mind where the sheer power of her own voice was enough to blow out the walls of the room, killing this man and whomever he was talking to. Perhaps the scream carried with it enough power to propel her from this chair and back home in an instant. Small tears formed in the corner of her eyes.

Shit.

"I have to prepare some instruments to treat a Labrador retriever later with a touch of aphagia." Rigby continued his seemingly one-sided conversation. "Oh, thank you, Princess Sarah, I'll let the doggie know you wish him well. Of course he won't be able to understand you, since he doesn't speak English, and I don't speak dog, my silly one.

"What about the girl? She's not sleeping? How can that be? I see her eyes are still closed. But wait, there is a tear. But she is faking, you say? Ms. Bundy, are you pulling my leg?" Rigby moved to the table and placed his hand on her arm. "Melissa, are you awake? Please wake up, and I'll introduce you. I so hate it when people aren't properly acquainted."

In spite of her utter terror over what he might do to her, Melissa was overcome with curiosity. Who was he talking to? The light from the overhead lamp was bright, and she was temporarily blinded. Looking at the window was hard because of the glare. She could make out figures, which appeared to be seated, but the room in front of her lacked any lighting. The drugs he was using to sedate her made it hard for her to work out precisely what she was seeing.

"Oh, dear me, too bright." Rigby moved to the wall, shut off the large overhead lamp, and flipped on the light in the next room. Melissa could clearly discern six seated figures, all dressed in a variety of what looked like festival costumes. They were seated in two rows, theater-style.

Rigby stood next to the window and appeared to swell with a measure of pride. "It gives me great pleasure to introduce you, Melissa, to my dearest friends. This handsome gentleman is called Mr. Sanchez. As you can imagine, he's Mexican, though he won't tell me precisely where he is from. I think he's a little embarrassed to admit he was born in a small village. No, he's not actually a mariachi band member, as you might assume, but he just likes to dress this way, the little scamp."

Melissa was at once confused and horrified by what she was seeing. Mr. Sanchez, as Rigby called him, was sitting motionless in a chair, with his left arm dangling at his side. He was indeed wearing a mariachi band outfit like she had seen many times at the local Mexican restaurant. He had a painted-on mustache and a head of hair, which looked glued on. His right arm was folded neatly across his lap, save for the hand, which was completely missing at the joint, a stub protruding slightly from the sleeve.

"This lovely creature," Rigby continued, "is the delightful, patient, and kind Mrs. Worthmeyer. She came to us from San Francisco last year. Pretty thing, isn't she? Interesting fact about our missus here, she used to be a veterinary doctor like myself. She gave it up when she got married. She is our matriarch now and looks after all of us."

Mrs. Worthmeyer, seated to Mr. Sanchez's left, was wearing a blue dress which was made entirely out of papier-mâché. Around her neck she wore a pearl necklace which appeared to be painted on with white paint. She had black patent leather shoes similar to what a young girl would wear. One of the straps was missing from the right shoe, and it dangled from her foot. Her head was gone. The neck just ended, like the head had never been there in the first place, and a hat was placed over the stump of the neck.

"You may or may not have heard me chatting to Ms. Bundy. She is related to some noted criminal, but she doesn't like to talk about it. She came to me from out East a few months ago. Such a lovely girl. You see her curls in her hair? I did those. Much the same way I did the ones in your hair."

He crossed the window with a flourish and pointed to the two other bodies. "And then we have Princess Sarah and Queen Azalea. Yes, they are royalty, but not of a land we are familiar with. They came to live with me because the king was a cruel man and hated people, most of all his own family. You could say I rescued them."

Melissa looked at the crowned court of this mad display. Both were wearing fake-looking crowns that were likely made of plastic and missing half their jewels. Melissa remembered having similar ones as a small child.

The queen had only one eye, and the princess was without her hair as well as her left arm, which was completely gone. Both of their heads rested on the back of the chair, since both had lost the ability to hold them up long ago.

"And last, but never least, we have Ms. Tilly. She is the baby of the group. She came to me about six months ago. Pretty, isn't she? She keeps her eyes shut most of the time, as she is terribly shy. Go ahead, Tilly, say hello." Rigby turned to Tilly as if she had done as asked.

satisfied with what he'd heard, he smiled. "Yes, Tilly, Melissa is quite lovely. She will round out our little family nicely."

Tilly was small, the smallest of the grotesque collection appearing in the window. She also was the only one to have all her parts attached to her. Dressed in a pink dress and white socks, she lacked shoes. A butterfly was clipped to her hair, keeping it in place.

Melissa looked over the motley band he had assembled before her. Melissa had tried desperately to keep her own terror in check as he went through his introductions. The pit of her stomach came alive with the horror presented before her. She wanted to vomit but had nothing to produce. Chills ran through every part of her body as she comprehended what she was seeing. She was more afraid of what he might do to her if she started screaming. Most of all, she didn't want to have him drug her again.

Instinctively she pulled at her restraints. Although she realized there was nothing that yanking at them would do except potentially injure herself. She willed herself to calm and tried to bring her own reactions back under her control.

He spoke to them as if they were alive and listened to them as if they could respond to him. He seemed to genuinely care about them. She was part of this and had no idea why. She didn't fit into this particular assemblage. None of them were alive, and none of them had ever been alive. Dr. Rigby's companions were all marionettes.

Melissa had read in her psychology class about how people could slip off the deep end and start talking to dolls and inanimate objects. Until now, she'd never met anyone who actually had lost their mind. She'd figured those kinds of people only existed in books or mental institutions. But here he was, right in front of her. She was going to have to think of something fast, and she knew enough not to get him excited again.

"Ummm, well it is very nice to finally meet you," Melissa forced herself to say. "I'm sure we will have a wonderful time together." Thinking quickly, she added, "Soon, I can be off of this table, and we can go outside or something."

"Oh, silly girl, you still don't understand, do you?" Rigby said. "No, dear, you will become part of them. You see, I'll use my own divine power to merge your soul with theirs. Then we will all be able to play together. You are a gift, my child." Rigby was now right next to Melissa and started stroking her hair the way a father would while explaining something to his daughter. "I'm thinking Tilly would be a good match for you."

"What?" Melissa fought to keep her fear from overwhelming her.

"Oh yes, Melissa, After I have completed the transfer, then we'll be together." Rigby's voice remained irritatingly soft.

"What are you talking about? I don't want to be part of any of this." Melissa quavered, no longer able to hide her fear. Tears started forming in her eyes.

"Hush now, Melissa, I promise you, it won't hurt. In fact, you won't feel a thing." He smiled at her and turned back to the table, pulling another syringe out of the drawer.

"No, please, not again. Please, Mr. Rigby, I mean Harmon, please, no." Melissa resorted to using his first name, hoping to appeal to him on a more intimate level. Maybe she could get him to delay giving her any more of the sedative.

Ignoring her, he said, "What did you say, Tilly? Oh yes, I think you're right. It's time for the ceremony, now that we are properly acquainted." He pushed the plunger into the bottle. She could see the bubbles come out of the end of the needle in the infernal liquid.

"What was that?" Rigby said in response to an unspoken question. "Oh, the doggie with aphasia? Princess Sarah, always so caring. The doggie can wait until a little later."

In slow motion, she watched him draw the mixture into the syringe. "Don't worry, my dear, this is the last, I promise. The next time you wake, you'll be part of our wonderful family."

An alarm bell suddenly rang out from an enunciator panel near the door. With an annoyed expression, he put the syringe down on the table along the wall. Melissa could just make out the corner of a television monitor in the dark corner of the room. "Oh dear, Ms. Melissa, I'm so sorry. There will be a short delay. Please wait here, there is something I must attend to. I'll leave the window open so you all can get better acquainted. When I return, the ceremony can begin. Won't be but a moment."

A thousand considerations ran through her mind. She thought about her parents, her friends, her teachers, and her school. She wasn't ready to be dead. Instinctively she reached up to brush the tear from her eye, but the restraint was still on her wrist. In her sudden frustration, she gave way to anger. Beating the restraints against the table, she strained, just as she had before. Although this time felt different.

She yanked harder, as if the mere act of reaching up would break the leather. As she did, she the buckle slipped under the strain. Craning her neck down, she saw he'd failed to secure it as tightly as before. She strained against the leather again, and it slipped a little more.

She pulled against the leather as hard as she could. It stretched under the pressure. The leather dug into her hand, but she kept at it. The metal clasp sliced her skin, and blood dripped to the floor. Melissa fought through the pain, resigning herself that if she needed to tear her own hand off, she would. Bit by bit, her hand was clearing the strap.

The blood acted as a grim lubricant, making her wrist slide farther along out of the restraint.

Finally, the strap gave way, and the leather strap fell toward the floor. Although the leather burned a little and her hand bore a considerable cut, the sensation was the most wonderful anguish she'd ever felt. One hand was free.

Working at the other restraints, she was soon completely free of the table, and she mentally prepared herself to find her way out of this deranged nightmare. She just hoped whatever was detaining Rigby would take long enough to give her time to put together a plan. She was sure she could outrun him, but he was far likely far stronger than she was.

If she was going to be successful, she would need a distraction.

CHAPTER 18
REVELATION

The afterlife, so far, had been good for Heather. She'd made a few friends. She'd even met a few distant relatives who had died either before she was born or when she was young. Everyone told her memories would come back soon, and she had to admit the blank spaces were gradually filling in. She continued to play with her new friends and allowed the process to continue.

During a break in the game, she sat on the park bench, reveling in the perpetually nice weather, neither too hot nor too chilly. As she relaxed, she tried to make sense of other flashes of recollections coming back to her. Like a secretary dealing with filing, she looked for places in her own timeline where she knew, or maybe just sensed, they fit. Every recollection a glimpse of her life before she passed away. They didn't use the word "died" here.

She remembered her mom and dad. They'd had a great relationship. She loved them both and missed them greatly.

The images of her school also came to mind. Glimpses of her friends, their names, and classrooms floated past her consciousness. She came back to acting, and she recalled loving it. She'd even thought she might like to be a stage actor someday. She remembered Mr. Tenebris asking her to come to his office after the show. As a member of the Children of Dionysus, he was always intensely critical of those students which he held to a much higher standard.

She had walked up the stairs to his office. She'd still been on the high every actor felt after they'd nailed a perfect performance. The roar of applause rang in her ears. The play itself had been a little lame, but she'd crushed her part. Her sweat-covered brow felt cool in the night air as she crossed from the theater to the office building where the theater department had their offices. He'd left the side door open for her, as he always did after the shows so he could talk to the kids after the curtain closed.

She thought about any questions he might have for her. What did she think was the weakest part of her performance? What could she have done better? What went wrong? What went right? He was going to grill her; she was sure of that.

Heather could see the hallway she was walking down, as well as the door to his office. It looked slightly ajar, but she knocked lightly on it anyway. As she did, she heard some sort of shuffling from the inside of the room, like maybe he wasn't alone.

"Yes, who is it?" Tenebris bellowed from the other side of the door.

"It's me, sir. You wanted to see me after I got cleaned up." Heather had run from the show and grabbed her things, making her way to the locker room in a hurry. She didn't want to keep him waiting, so her shower would come later.

"Oh yes, Heather. My star this evening. You can come in now. I was just putting away some testing materials." Tenebris opened the door to the room and beckoned her to enter. He motioned to a seat.

As she moved to sit down, she saw a man standing in the corner of the room. He was tall and bald. "I'm sorry, sir, was I interrupting?"

The moment felt awkward, and she wasn't sure how to respond. The bald man was the first to break the silence, which had become uncomfortable. "No, my child. Please, sit. I'm an associate of Mr. Tenebris."

She took a seat as instructed. Mr. Tenebris sat down in his office chair and leaned forward slightly. He looked like he was going to say something, when suddenly she had an odd sensation in her neck. Not a pain really, more like the prick of a needle. And then nothing.

Heather couldn't remember anything after sitting down. No matter how many times she replayed the sequence of events in her head, she still couldn't see what happened after she felt the pinch in her neck.

This is hopeless, I'm never going to figure this out, Heather thought in disgust, standing up from the bench. Maybe some more time playing the eternal game of soccer would help take her mind off the problem.

As she stepped away from the bench, she sensed an overwhelming force push her down. Like an invisible hand was holding her in place, she found herself unable to get back up. An image of the bald man came back into her head. Then, as if responding to her questions, the name of the man appeared. A memory forced its way to the top, something she'd desperately needed to remember. He introduced himself as Harmon Rigby.

The memories flashed through her mind as if she was a computer and someone had uploaded images into it. The table, the room, the injection, those horrible dolls, every terrifying detail exposed itself. Then that final injection and then she woke up here.

Then her consciousness was driven by something, or someone, beyond her control. Images she didn't own appeared before her like a movie being played. She saw the room again along with the thoughts of another. A girl in a red dress ... the exact red dress Heather remembered wearing before she passed away.

She wasn't sure how she knew this, but she was looking at the next victim. The girl was strapped to the same table that she had been. Heather could see Rigby standing next to his dolls, talking to the girl.

Although she appeared to be saying nothing, Heather could feel the other girl's terror.

Heather needed to find Victor, and time was not on her side.

Looking across the soccer field, she could just make out the form of Victor stepping out of the fog slightly down the hill from the soccer pitch. "Victor! I need to talk to you!" She ran directly through the soccer game, earning dirty looks and a few choice barbs from the players. Running up to Victor, she cried, "I don't know how I know this, but he's going to kill again! Please, you must believe me."

* * * *

Victor was overwhelmed by the suddenness of it all. He'd come back to check up on Heather, only to have her jump out at him. He'd heard of things like this happening before and this information was likely being given to her for a reason. "Wait, slow down a moment, child. Are you talking about Tenebris?" Victor asked, looking confused at her sudden insight.

Heather began speaking as fast as she could, running through all the details. "Please, Victor, we have to go, and you have to take me with you. I can't explain how I know this, but if we don't hurry, we're going to be too late to save her. We need to stop this now!"

"What you're asking is no small thing. We don't normally let people who have only been here for a short while make the trip back. Bad things can happen."

The look on her face told Victor she was bracing for him to tell her no. There was something in the way she frowned at him, how the information came to her, and a gut feeling he couldn't shake. "Heather, I believe you. I agree, we need to do something, but do you know how many people in Virginia are named Rigby?"

A sensation came over him, one he'd felt only once before on a case; a sudden urgency to move. Instinct told him Heather was no longer acting on her own memories, but divine intervention was now at play. That kind of intervention was ignored at considerable risk.

"Okay, we'll have to have more than what you saw to go on, but we've got to move fast." Victor understood he likely had the heavenly approval he really needed bring her back in the land of the living, but he also felt strongly that Dirk had a role to play in all of this.

"Grab hold of my hand and don't let go."

Heather did as instructed, and they both were sucked into the vortex between the land of the living and the dead. This unsettling sensation morphed into the familiar tunnel he was used to. In the distance, the tunnel bunched up into bursts of light surrounding a portal of darkness. Above the humming and clatter around them, he yelled, "Hold on, here we go!"

With little fanfare, Heather and Victor found herself floating slightly above the well-worn carpeting of a small office. "Pugh, what is that smell?"

"Oil and grease. We need to find someone to call Dirk.," Victor said.

"Who's Dirk?" Heather asked.

"Don't worry about that right now, kiddo. We can make introductions later. Just try to think of everything you can tell us about Rigby. Anything you can remember. Leave no detail out. I'm going to get someone. I'll be right back." Victor turned to enter the garage area, where he hoped to find anyone working. As he moved, he heard the familiar sound of rubber car tires crunching on the gravel of the parking lot outside.

An unmarked squad car pulled into the driveway. "Crap, not her. Anyone but her," Victor remarked, running his hand over his scalp.

"Oh good, the police." Heather said matter-of-factly.

"Not, 'oh good.' I've been avoiding her for a long time." Victor huffed.

"Victor, for an old dead guy, you sure do have some funny quirks." Heather looked with satisfaction at her ability to sit, maybe only float, on a faux-leather chair.

"You know, for a newly dead girl, you are a bit of a smart-mouth!" Victor retorted.

"Well, I may be dead, but I am still a teenager. It is kind of our thing."

As Carrie stepped out of her squad car, Victor watched her through the window. He really had no reason to like or dislike Carrie. He knew she was terrified of him, and it made him automatically wary of her. Although she was a normal fixture at the shop, in the past, Victor had found a way to vanish before she came in. Once or twice, he'd hung around and listened to them talk. She never believed Dirk when he'd said the shop was haunted, and he'd always been offended by her lack of faith in him. Then again, Victor had never done anything to disabuse her of that idea.

Carrie pushed open the door and said, "Hello, it's just me, Carrie. Anyone here?"

She stepped inside with a perplexed look on her face. "I could have sworn someone was in the office."

"So, this is a bit strange." Victor said from the corner of the office, trying to sound as nonthreatening as possible.

Carrie spun around, instinctively putting her hand on her weapon.

He laughed. "Carrie, you should know that you can't really shoot me. I shot myself many years ago, and now here we are. Reckon we've this very awkward situation to contend with."

In a different corner of the room, another voice manifested from the shadows. "Oh, she's pretty, Victor. She's a cop, and she can help us."

She swung around to the other voice. Sitting, in front of her, on a chair, was a ghostly teenager. Although Carrie couldn't put her finger on it, she was sure she'd seen the girl's face before. She could only respond to the girl's statement with a quiet, "Ahhh, yeah, cop."

Victor continued, "Carrie, I know, this isn't how I imagined we'd resolve this situation either, but you gotta to focus. The missing girl, the one y'all are looking for, is still alive, but you need to hurry. Time is running out." Seeing Carrie still had a vacant stare, which he assumed was the result of her meeting him for the first time, he added, "Snap out of it, kid. Need you to do that cop thing that Dirk says yer so good at."

Again, Carrie turned to the sound of the voice, and where there had been nothing before, now there was a man floated about six inches off the ground. He was shorter than she had imagined, and she could see right through him.

Outside, a truck pulled into a parking stall marked "Owner, Head Biker."

Carrie muttered, "Thank God for that." She jerked back toward the girl in the chair. "There is something oddly familiar about you. Why do I know you? Wait, you're the girl. The one who was murdered."

"You don't miss a beat, do you, Columbo? Victor, I like her," Heather said.

Dirk opened the door. "Vic, oh good." Suddenly seeing his stunned girlfriend, he said, "Carrie?" Then, noticing Heather, now floating slightly above the chair, he asked, "Who are you?"

"I'm Heather, I'm dead," she said with a smile.

"Well, this is different. Hey, wait a minute. I know you." Dirk pointed at Heather. "You're the Smithfield girl. I'm sorry you're um… for your… well, I'm sorry."

"Interesting friends you got here, Victor, but we don't have much time. Victor?" Heather said, motioning for him to hurry it up.

"Right. Look, everyone. Carrie, snap out of it. Dirk, sit down." Victor could hardly believe he was suddenly the voice of reason in the room.

Dirk took his usual place behind the desk, "Okay, Vic, the floor is yours."

Victor had Heather recount her story to Dirk and Carrie. They sat there and listened. Carrie finally got it together enough to take notes, but she kept one wary eye on Victor. Trust didn't come easily to Carrie, and when it came to the dead, it was even harder. Although Victor didn't say so, the feelings were not mutual. He liked her, for some reason. She seemed like a perfect match for Dirk.

"We know where Rigby is. Heather, do you remember what the inside of the room looked like?" Dirk asked.

Heather described what sounded like a surgical suite. Instruments everywhere, a large cylinder she told him was an "auto plaze" he put utensils into, which Dirk guessed would be an autoclave that doctors routinely used to sterilize instruments. These were all the hallmarks of a doctor's office but also very similar to the things one would find in a veterinary clinic. Harmon Rigby was a veterinary doctor. Therefore, the girl must be at his house somewhere.

"Wait, I remember too there were a couple of metal tracks on the ceiling."

"Like a crane?" Carrie suggested.

"No, my dad had the same ones in his garage."

"Maybe for a garage door?" Carrie said.

"Yes, that's it." Heather stood from the chair.

Dirk shook his head. "Damn. The garage behind the house. I was literally only twenty feet from her. Okay, Victor, I hate to ask you this because I know it's hard on you, but if I show you a map, can you go there?" Dirk rarely requested this kind of help. For Victor, this was such an expenditure of energy, and it often left him weak and potentially vulnerable. He would need to recharge before doing anything else after he arrived. This was how some of his spirit colleagues found themselves stuck in the world of the living for a time.

"We'll do it. If I bring Heather, she can help. I'll be exhausted, but she'll have energy left to do... something," Victor said.

"Heather, honey, are you okay with this?" Carrie suddenly spoke up, sounding surprisingly maternal.

"Well, why wouldn't she be?" Victor asked.

"You'd be putting her in danger," Carrie said.

"Um, Carrie, they're dead. What is he going to do to them?" Dirk said.

Carrie's eyes narrowed. "We really have no idea what he is capable of. Not knowing is what bothers me."

CHAPTER 19
I'D BET MY BADGE

While the police department waited on a warrant to search Rigby's home and property, the chief sent Detective Hodges and Officer White to Rigby's house. Both seasoned officers, they could talk to him and maybe get him to give them probable cause, which would provide a reason to enter the premises without the legal authority.

The pair walked up the footpath from the street and past a little sign reading "Dr. Harmon Rigby, D.V.S." It had a silhouette of a cat and dog with their tails intertwined in the shape of a heart.

Officer White rang the doorbell, but there was no immediate answer. However, the pair were certain they'd heard noises from the back of the house, perhaps the garage area. As they waited, they could see a figure come in through the rear door of the house and make his way to the front.

A man they knew from a photo to be Rigby answered the door with a friendly smile. "Yes, officers, can I be of assistance?" He looked Officer White up and down, the only one of the two in uniform.

"I hope so," Detective Hodges said. "We're working on a case in the area, and we are trying to generate some leads."

"Well, I always like to help the police if I can." Rigby responded in a calm voice, charming and irritating at the same time.

Officer White continued, "Can you tell me how long you've been at this residence?"

"Why yes, I have been here for a little over two years. I moved here from Portland, if it matters."

"Never been to Portland," Officer White replied.

"Well, Virginia takes some getting used to," Rigby continued. "You have to learn to live without so much rain all of the time."

Detective Hodges gave a polite laugh. "I saw the sign saying you're a vet. Do you work out of your home, or do you have an office?"

"I work here, no office," Rigby answered. "I'm a bit of a homebody, I must confess. But I do make the occasional house call."

"How well would you say you notice people walking up and down the street in your neighborhood?" Officer White asked. While he had Rigby's attention, Detective Hodges peeked into the interior of the house, looking for any possible signs of the girl's presence. It killed them to know that she might be there, but without a warrant or any probable cause, they couldn't lift a finger to help. They needed to play their roles and hope the evidence led them to where they needed to go.

"Oh, as well as someone can, I suppose." Rigby sounded slightly agitated. "What's this about, officers? I hate to rush you, but I'm in the middle of an appointment right now. I have a full schedule today. You understand."

"Where do you do your surgery, Dr. Rigby?" Detective Hodges asked, dismissing the comment.

Although the detective couldn't be sure, he could have sworn he saw a flash of uneasiness across Rigby's face.

"Out back, in my garage," Rigby said. "I had it converted into a small surgery. Nothing major, just minor stuff. For the larger surgeries, I contract with another clinic."

"May we see inside it?" Officer White asked.

"No, I'm sorry." Rigby shifted his weight back and forth nervously. "I am prepped for surgery, and all the instruments have been sterilized. Maybe if you come back tomorrow I'll give you the grand tour, as it were."

"We may just take you up on your offer. One more thing before we go, and the reason we're here." Officer White pulled out a picture of Melissa. The photo was from the high school yearbook. "Have you seen this girl?"

Rigby looked over the photo for a suspiciously long time. "No, I'm sorry. I can't say I recognize her. Is something wrong?"

"She's missing, Doctor, and we're trying to find anyone who might have information on the case," Officer White said, extending a business card. "If you think of something, can you call the department? We would be grateful."

"Anything to help the police," Rigby said, letting out an almost imperceptible sigh. Almost imperceptible to anyone but a trained detective, that was.

"Her parents are devastated," Detective Hodges said, eying Rigby with renewed suspicion.

"Well for their sake, I hope you find Melissa."

"How did you know her name was Melissa, Dr. Rigby?" Officer White jumped on Rigby's obvious slipup.

Rigby, unrattled, composed himself. "The papers, of course. Her mother has been worried sick. I hate to be rude, officers, but I really do have a busy day ahead of me. Surgery waits for no one. I must get back to my work."

"Thank you, Doctor, have a nice day." Detective Hodges turned from the door, noticing a single bead of sweat rolling down the doctor's cheek. The weather had been relatively cool. Certainly, nowhere near warm enough to cause someone to perspire.

Crossing the street to where they had parked the police cruiser, Officer White turned to his colleague. "You think he was lying?"

"I'd bet my badge on it," Detective Hodges said with steely certainty. "There's a convenience store a few blocks from here. We can get some coffee and call the chief. We'll stay nearby and wait for the warrant. And most of all, I want a good look at that garage."

CHAPTER 20
FLEEING THE SCENE

Melissa took her first steps away from the table. She tried out her legs with a few cautious steps, which felt stable enough. She was a little stiff from being tied down for so long. *So far so good,* she thought.

She walked to the wall where she'd seen Rigby looking at the video monitor. A closed-circuit television monitor offered several views of the house and the garage. A selector on the box enabled her to switch between camera views. One image was of the front door and the entryway of the house. She saw the black-and-white video feed of Rigby talking to a police officer and another man dressed in a suit.

Melissa knew she had to escape the room, and time was going to run out quickly. Pulling on the door, she heard the latch move slightly. Furiously, she yanked at the door handle with little effect. A deadbolt or something was engaged from the outside, making escape impossible.

Melissa turned to the screen and watched Rigby close the door. He'd be back within moments.

She scanned the room for something she could use to defend herself, determined to fight to the death if it came to it. On the table was the syringe Rigby had filled earlier. The needle contained an unknown liquid, but it was not hard to figure out it was the sedative he had been using on her. She picked up the syringe and searched for a place to hide in the dark and attack him as soon as he entered the room.

At first, she thought her eyes were playing tricks on her. Perhaps it was a side effect of the medicine he'd given her, but she could swear two forms were coming into focus in the corner of the room.

"What?" Melissa said as she wiped her eyes, fearing she was suffering some sort of nervous breakdown. The forms coalesced into an older man and a girl similar to her own age. There was something familiar about the girl, but for the moment she could not place it. Melissa wasn't sure if she should be more terrified of these beings appearing before her or of Rigby, whose return was imminent.

"You're in great danger," a male voice suddenly said. "We need to get you out of here! Time is up."

"Who are you?" Melissa couldn't believe she was talking to these ghostly things standing in front of her. *Have I lost my mind*, she thought? And then it struck her. "Heather? What are you doing here? Wait, you're dead!"

"Yes, I know it's crazy, but you have to listen to us. You need to leave now. He's coming for you. He intends to kill you."

"Yeah, I know, the door is locked, and I can't get out." Although the pair's appearance was sudden and unexpected, now seemed like a bad time to argue with Heather and this other stranger.

Outside the room, there was a loud bang. She distinctly heard whistling moving closer to the room she was in. She pleaded with the two figures in the room. "Help me. He's coming."

"We have to do something fast," Heather said. "We need a plan, and I think I just got one. Hide behind the door." Melissa looked at the spot where Heather indicated. If she stood behind the sweep of the door, he'd walk past her and likely not see her until he realized she was missing. Not perfect, but it could buy her a few precious moments.

Heather continued barking out orders. "Victor, you go over to the other corner and stay there for now. I'll do the rest." She pointed at Melissa's hand. "Do you think you can handle a syringe? You need to knock him out."

Melissa hadn't considered what it would be like to inject Rigby. She'd grabbed it off the counter in her desire for a weapon rather than anything else. However, the more she thought about injecting him with the same stuff he'd been giving her, the more she liked the idea.

"It will be my pleasure." She ran to the corner behind the door, just as the sound of metal scraping against metal resounded through the room. Rigby had reached the outside door of the garage.

"Wait for the right moment," Heather said as she vanished.

Rigby stepped inside the surgery, letting the door close behind him. "I'm sorry I took so long, my charmed one, but I was—" His voice trailed off as he saw the empty table in front of him. "What do we have here?"

"Rigby!" A voice rang out from the direction of the table. Loud and thunderous, it achieved its intended purpose.

Rigby's head jerked in the direction to the corner where the voice came from. "What? Who is there? Identify yourself immediately."

With Rigby distracted, Melissa held the syringe close. She didn't have a clear shot at him, even though he was only about five feet away. He was moving too much, trying to determine the source of the disembodied voice.

"Harmon Rigby, you have been very, very bad. We aren't happy with you at all." Suddenly the drapes covering the marionettes flew closed and then open again. The lights in the room flickered. "You

222

moron! You have hurt innocent lives, and now you'll pay for your crimes." Heather's acting talents on full display, she worked hard to hide the youthfulness of her voice.

Rigby stood there for the briefest of moments, seemingly too thunderstruck to move. "It's working. I can't believe it." He said those words in a drawn-out manner. He ran to the window, unfortunately out of Melissa's reach, and knelt in front of the glass. "I'm sorry, I'll fix what is wrong. I promise. I'm just so glad it's happening." He pressed his palms into the glass. "You are finally coming to life. I love you, my children. I mean, I had my doubts, but I never lost faith. I knew, one day, all my efforts would be worth it. I just knew."

Melissa crept up behind Rigby as he sat on the floor. Seven more feet and she'd be within striking distance. She just needed to get a little closer.

"Rigby, you must fix this. I'm not a boy, and you put me into the Mexican guitar player." Heather was trying to think of something scarier to say to him, but it came out ridiculously wrong. Thankfully, Rigby was either too insane or amazed to reason past it.

Melissa crept closer. There were five more feet between them.

Each footfall felt like her legs weighed a thousand pounds. Four more feet were all she had left to cover now.

Her hands were soaked with sweat. Three and then two more. All she needed to do was lunge at him and then run to freedom. She was convinced the dress was going to make a swooshing noise and Rigby would turn on her.

Rigby looked up at his beloved marionettes. The surface of the glass provided a reflection of the surgical suite. Melissa saw her reflection in the glass and noticed, in the same moment, that Rigby's eyes were now directed at her in the glass as well. A menacing scowl replaced his previous smile. Her opportunity had evaporated.

Swinging his leg around with as much force as he could, he swept her feet from under her, the syringe falling from her hand and rolling out of reach. "You little bitch!" His eyes filled with rage, and his face reddened with anger. She was sure she was going to be beaten to death on the spot.

"You make fun of my friends and insult my hospitality? Do you think these manners can be tolerated?" He grabbed a surgical mallet off the table and approached the fear-struck girl, the hammer raised high above his head. Rigby was foaming slightly at the mouth, spittle flying out as he yelled. His hand was clutching the mallet so tightly his fingers turned white. He stood over the top of Melissa.

Victor materialized out of the corner of the room and flung metal tray off a table at Rigby's head. Not forceful enough to hurt him, but the metal tray hit hard enough to catch him off guard and daze him.

Melissa rolled over to one side, picked up the syringe from where it lay on the floor, and leapt on Rigby. With one fluid motion, she stuck the needle deep into his neck and pushed the plunger down as hard as she could. She held onto him for a few seconds more as she felt his body go limp, sending him crashing to the floor.

Melissa slumped off Rigby's back and leaned against the wall. She was breathing heavy and shook with fear. She was in shock from what she'd just done. The three just stared at Rigby's unconscious body. Still alive but no longer an immediate threat.

"I don't understand. Heather, you are dead, and who is this the old guy?" Melissa shook her head at the odd turn of events.

Victor frowned at Melissa. "Hey, watch who you are calling old. I am a hundred-and-seventy-years young."

Melissa shrugged her shoulders. "Sorry, I did not mean to offend. Still, I owe you both my life."

"Well, kiddo, you aren't out of trouble yet," Victor said. "You need to vamoose. We're going to have to leave, I'm afraid. It's hard for us to stay in the world of the living, and time is running out. Do you know how to get out of here?"

"He has to have a key or something," Melissa fished out a set from his coat pocket. "But how can I find you again? Heather, how are you here right now??"

"Hopefully you won't see us for a long time, kiddo. Not for many years." Victor smiled warmly at her as he started fading from sight.

Heather began to fade as well. "Melissa, can you tell my mom and dad I love them and I'm alright?" Melissa could see tears in the specter's eyes. "I have friends over here, and I even play soccer. I'll be waiting for them. I promise. And ... also ... that ..." A mist, which had been thickening steadily, enveloped Heather, and her voice grew more and more distant until Melissa could only make out mumbling. The fog then abruptly vanished, as if it had never been there in the first place. In a flash, she was alone again with Rigby's prone, unconscious form on the surgery floor.

Melissa shook off the sudden quiet of the room. There was still work to be done. She did some quick mental math and figured the amount of drugs she was given had been enough to knock her out for about four hours. Since Rigby was much larger than she was, she likely only had a little time before he'd begin to stir. As if to confirm this point, she heard Rigby murmur to himself in his drug-induced stupor. She needed to get out.

The key ring she took from him contained four keys, and one fit the lock perfectly. She turned the key and heard the reassuring click, and she pushed the door open.

Two steps away from the outside of the garage, she stopped abruptly. There was something else she felt compelled to do, for all the girls Rigby had abducted, terrorized, and murdered before her. It would only take a few minutes to accomplish, minutes she might not have, but she had to do it, or she'd be haunted by the memories of this room forever.

Her work done, Melissa stepped outside Rigby's chamber of death, letting the door slam shut behind her. Her cheeks were red, and her brow was covered in sweat. She knew she could leave with a clear conscience. She'd done what needed to be done.

The sheer cunningness of Rigby's plan was in its simplicity. His home and office were located in a residential area of the city. No one would think to look here for the missing girls. Rigby had a house, which blended into the bland landscape of suburbia.

Melissa shook away the realization of what had happened to her. Now was not the time to fall to pieces. She needed to find some help. Locking the door of the surgery from the outside, she dropped the keys to the ground by the door for the police to find and ran as fast as she could from Rigby's den of terror. Rounding the corner of the street, she saw the reassuring lights of a convenience store. And parked in one of the stalls, a police car suggested help was only short sprint away.

Melissa staggered through the door and tripped over a rubber floor mat. Upon seeing this, Officer White dropped his coffee cup to the floor, sending its contents everywhere. He ran over and held the young woman by her arms. "Young lady, slow down, where's the fire?"

Melissa pushed a lock of hair from her face. "I'm Melissa Barlo," she blurted out, her voice a mixture of relief, terror, and desperation. "I was kidnapped. I escaped. This guy tried to kill me. He's nuts." And then, spent from her efforts, she fainted into the arms of a very surprised Officer White.

CHAPTER 21
VENGEFUL HEART

Tenebris sat in the corner of a detox cell for the first twenty-four hours after his arrest, navigating through a variety of withdrawal symptoms. One of his jailers told him he'd asked the officer if he wanted to join him on the airplane he had waiting in the alley. He remembered a similar story from his delusions the last time he went through detox. During hour twenty-five, he was over the initial and most severe withdrawal symptoms. Now he thought of Rigby.

Tenebris was angry at Dirk and at the same time could not blame him. Dirk had been telling the truth. Rigby had recruited him, groomed him even. He used his connections to the community as a veterinarian, ensuring the people making the hiring decisions at the school leaned in Tenebris's favor. Rigby had thought this through, and perhaps the most disturbing thing was the realization that this had not been the first city Rigby had set up shop in.

The introductions seemed like a lifetime ago. And now Rigby was somewhere, free to roam the world while Tenebris sat on a cold, hard jail cell floor.

In the neon glow of the booking room he could see from his cell, his anger grew.

Who the hell was Rigby to do this to him?

All he'd wanted was his life back. Maybe work with the kids and stay connected to the theater community he'd loved and had devoted much of his existence to. He knew the chance of getting back to Broadway was slim. To just feel the lights, to hear the music and applause, even on a small stage, would have been more than enough.

Rigby stole that all away from him.

I have no idea how long it will take, but I'm going to kill Harmon Rigby.

He'd be sitting in prison until he rotted because of Rigby. If he was going to prison, his penitential stay would be for something more substantial than conspiracy to commit murder. Tenebris sat back against the metal wall of the cell and started plotting.

* * * *

Heather regained consciousness back in the afterlife. She was exhausted. "Oh crap, I'm tired."

Victor appeared mere moments later. "You never get used to how much energy a trip like that takes."

"Do you think Melissa will be okay?" Heather asked.

"Well, I know this, we gave her as much of a chance as anyone could. We make a good team, you and me." Victor tussled her hair.

"Yeah, our success was mostly due to my brilliance. Admit it, my terrifying voice was really the special awesome sauce that operation needed." Heather laughed at her own joke.

"Yeah, real scary." Victor then said with his best falsetto voice, "'You put me into the Mexican guitar player.' Really, you had to improvise something, and you came up with a Mexican guitar player?" He laughed.

Heather shrugged. "Well, it worked, didn't it?"

"Yeah, kid, it worked, but we've got to up your scariness game if you're gonna go back to the other side with me again," he said with a chuckle.

* * * *

Dirk and Carrie paced around the office while Keith was out finishing up some errands. Neither one of them was nervous by nature, but this felt like a closer call than either of them was comfortable with. It was a waiting game for either the police to get their search warrant or for Victor and Heather to help the girl escape.

Carrie was helping herself to some of the shop's coffee when her cell phone rang, causing her to spill the coffee all over the table. "Officer Pettygrew," she answered. "Wait … what? Hold on, say again." She listened for a moment and then put the receiver to her chest as she looked at Dirk, a relieved smile spreading across her face. "They have the girl, she's alive."

"Alright, Chief, I'll be in shortly." She hit the "end call" button on her cell and looked at Dirk. "Oh my God, Dirk, she's alive! Do you know how tired I get of having to tell people we found the bodies of their loved ones? She's fine, no physical harm done. She's at the hospital, and they're checking her over now. Chief wants me to go there and guard her until Rigby is brought in."

Dirk sat stunned by the news for a few moments. There was always a part of him that steeled himself for the possibility Melissa was going to end up dead. He was responsible for her selection as a target so he, by extension, felt the weight of the world on his shoulders. And now he would never have to find out what a mess it would have made of him if she had wound up dead. He wanted to jump for joy, but another part of him knew the job was only half complete.

She turned toward the door, "If you see Victor, you tell him I owe him a beer." She ran over to Dirk and tackled him around the shoulders and gave him a kiss. "Dirk, she's alive. She is *alive*." Tears of joy streamed down her face as she left the office.

Carrie rarely got emotional about a case she was working. But Dirk had to admit to himself, this one had been hard on him too. They'd managed to stop a serial killer from another score to his macabre tally. They still needed to find him and bring him to justice. A life was saved, and that was worth every moment of stress. Dirk flopped down on his office chair.

Melissa Barlo is alive.

* * * *

Rigby regained consciousness. It felt like he was being pulled out of a dream. Something cold pressed against his cheek. Although he couldn't see or move, he knew he was on the floor of the surgery. The familiar scents forced their way into his nostrils

His eyes began to focus on the world around him. First he could see the floor, the legs of the surgery table, and then the cabinets and the refrigerator on the other side of the room. *What happened?*

Still unable to walk, he dragged his body across the cold concrete floor of the surgery. He pulled himself up to the window where the marionettes, his dearest of friends, were. He had to see them, talk to them, seek their counsel.

Reaching behind the door, he grabbed the rope to raise and lower the drapes. Rigby resolved to start again. He'd find more tributes, another place, and start over. *This time it had to work.*

Although he was still weak from the drugs, the dose was meant for a teenage girl, so its effects were limited and were wearing off quickly. He'd only been asleep for ten minutes.

He looked over his shoulder into the dimly lit room.

"The little bitch!" Rigby yelled. While he was out, she had attacked his friends, viciously and mercilessly. Their chairs were broken, clothing torn from their fragile bodies. Several arms and legs had been ripped off and thrown in every direction. Strings which had once held them up were wrapped around their heads as if they had been strangled to death.

Not one of them had been left unharmed. "She killed them … all of them. A monster, she's a monster!" Rigby sat at the window and sobbed. Melissa had destroyed his friends. She had murdered his very soul.

Standing, he used the wall to steady himself. He struggled to enter the room to see if any part of the dolls had been left untouched. His legs were wobbly, but his strength was returning quickly. He tripped over something as he entered the room. The offending item was the head of Ms. Tilly. A sharp surgical instrument had been stabbed through her eye.

He gently picked up the head from the floor and cradled it in his arms. "My poor… poor Tilly. What did she do to you?" Streaks of tears ran down his cheeks as he stroked the head of the doll. Rigby looked around the room and found the rest of the body torn to shreds. Even the white material used to stuff the dolls had been ripped out.

In a moment of rage, he threw the head of the doll into the glass wall separating the dolls' room and the surgery. The metal handle of the surgical instrument struck and shattered the glass into fragments, spilling them out onto the floor. "Fucking little cunt!"

He'd avenge them, oh yes, he'd avenge their deaths. *An eye for an eye was only right*, he thought. How could she kill them? They were innocent, delicate souls. They'd loved her and accepted her as one of their own, and this was how she paid them back? Who did she think she was, attacking a man of God who was clearly inspired and driven by the truth?

"The Lord throws down the wicked from their high places, and I am the hand of God," Rigby shouted to the empty room. Those words were his command to seek her out. Melissa must die.

Grabbing one remaining syringe and quickly loading it with tranquilizer, he threw it into a small doctor's kit bag. Fishing in his pockets for his keys, he realized she must have taken them from him while he was unconscious. "I'll bet she thought she was smart, didn't she, dear ones? That little bitch! Smart, but I am far more cunning."

Marching past the table, he grabbed the surgical mallet and added it to the bag along with a small bone saw and a scalpel. He had a purpose now, and he'd find Melissa no matter what.

He'd cut her up. *No need to make it easy*. It would be his revenge for the innocent blood she'd spilt. He stumbled over the broken pieces of chair and marionettes, making his way to the back of the little room. He shoved a shelf holding a mop bucket and some cleaning supplies. Behind it, there was a small opening designed for a commercial fan that he'd never installed. The space was just big enough for him to fit through. The other side was a dead space between the outer wall of the surgery and the false garage door. Off in the distance, he heard a chorus of police sirens, likely on their way to his house. Outside of the garage, he broke into a run, hoping to put as much space between him and them as he could.

A few blocks away, he dove behind a stand of garbage cans as three squad cars flew past him with their lights on. He glanced down the alley as he saw them stop in front of his garage. His luck was holding out, and he'd escaped just in time. *It's unlikely she told them how she viciously murdered the only ones I've ever cared about,* he thought. *I'll make sure they know, after I make her pay for her crimes.*

CHAPTER 22
WHY DO YOU DO THIS

Carrie sat and talked with Melissa for two hours. Unlike many kidnap victims, Melissa was able to give her important details about where she'd been held prisoner. She even told them where she'd dropped the keys to the garage and where they could find Rigby. Based on her information, it had taken Melissa about fifteen minutes to wander into the convenience store. By the time the entirety of the police department swarmed in on Rigby's residence, he had already escaped.

"I was just so terrified," Melissa said.

"I have to be honest, I would've been terrified too," Carrie replied.

"I thought he was going to rape me or kill me or something." Melissa's voice was raw with emotion.

"Look, this is going to be the hard part for you. You have to learn to come to peace with your escape. You got away from him when others couldn't. You're safe, and Harmon Rigby can't hurt you anymore. And because of you, we're going to find him and make sure he never does this again. There's nowhere he can run to, no place he can hide. He's going to pay dearly for his crimes."

Carrie held Melissa until her parents came. When her mother walked in the room, Carrie rose to leave when Melissa grabbed her hand. "Please don't go."

"I'm not going anywhere, sweetie. I'll be right outside. I want to give you guys some privacy," Carrie said. She nodded to Mrs. Barlo who smiled back in appreciation.

"Okay. Thank you, Carrie," Melissa said, releasing her hand.

Carrie's heart melted like butter. She left the room quickly before Melissa could see her protector's eyes well up with tears.

* * * *

The police searched every corner of the property for Rigby, but they had just missed him. The house was essentially a showroom: impeccably clean, with furniture looking like it still would have the tags on it from the showroom floor. In the basement, they found several kilos of cocaine, packaged in sizes just large enough to wet a hard-core addict's appetite but ensure they would need to come back soon for their next fix.

His clothes were all pressed and hanging in the closet, his bed perfectly made, and his dishes in the cupboard organized as if they were soldiers in formation. One crime scene investigator said it looked "serial killer" clean.

The police found the keys where Melissa left them and had no problems entering Rigby's hardened inner sanctum, which had been constructed inside a garage.

As soon as the medical and psychiatric doctors had a chance to clear her, Melissa was checked out of the hospital. The Barlos had made the decision, on the advice of the police, to leave town for a week or two until the police could track down Rigby. They took their family and headed upstate for some quiet time together. But Carrie had assigned a regular unit to follow them until they passed beyond the city limits. They were not taking the chance that Rigby was done with Melissa.

Carrie made her way to the garage-slash-torture-chamber as soon as Melissa had left the hospital, wanting to see the scene for herself. She noticed the garden Dirk had crawled through as she approached. Unconsciously, she glanced down for any sign of his handprints or footprints in the dirt.

Sgt. Andrews, second in seniority only to Carrie, sat behind a makeshift entry control point. He was in charge of the crime scene for the moment, logging everyone in and out. "Hi, Carrie, it's pretty creepy in there," he said, looking up at her.

"What's it like?"

"As crime scenes go, this one is off the charts. We did a quick search, and it reminds me of a mass murder in a toy shop."

"Toy shop?"

"Yeah, you know, there are body parts everywhere. But little body parts from dolls. The ones you can buy at cheap border towns in Mexico." He was making odd hand gestures, which added nothing to his description.

"Do you mean marionettes?" Carrie asked, laughing at his ridiculous display.

"Yeah, yeah, those are the ones." He handed her the clipboard to sign.

"Okay. Maybe it's time you take a vacation, Andrews." She signed her name and set the clipboard back down on the table.

He harrumphed. "Very well, Miss Smartypants, go see for yourself. Don't forget to put on booties and stuff," Sgt. Andrews said, putting the sign-in sheet down.

Entering the garage, Carrie could see a bunch of medical equipment that would have been at home in any hospital. An autoclave, used to sterilize medical equipment, sat on the counter. A surgical light hung from the ceiling, shining down on a table like this feature of the room was the star attraction. She was about to pick up a mysterious medical instrument that lay on the counter near the autoclave when a voice yelled, "Don't touch that, please."

"I'm sorry, what?" Carrie said, a little afraid to turn to the source of the admonition, which she realized reminded her a bit of Victor.

"Please don't touch. I need to photograph it and check it for blood," said the lone crime scene tech in the room.

"What the hell is it?" Carrie looked perplexed.

"It's called a trocar. Used to remove fluids from the body. Normally you only see those at the medical examiner's office or a mortician's shop," the tech said in a way that made him sound incredibly geeky. "To prepare bodies for embalming, it sucks out body fluids."

She shivered a little at the thought of someone inserting something like it into her body. "I think I'll have myself cremated."

"I know, right?" the tech said as he continued taking pictures of the items on the counter.

She walked past the tech and into the room in the back of the surgery, noticing where Rigby had climbed out of the surgery and pushed his way through the false garage door to his temporary freedom. Little pieces of marionettes lay everywhere, strewn over the floor. Sgt. Andrews was right, it looked like a toy store massacre. Carrie instantly pictured Melissa ripping them to shreds. She'd told Carrie she felt compelled to smash them to bits, as payback for every girl Rigby had murdered.

Walking back out to the main part of the room, she focused on the long stainless-steel table, about the size of an adult human being. It had been turned to face the room where the marionettes were positioned. Bending down, Carrie examined the various hinges and joints of the table. It could be adjusted to different angles and positions, and the sides had been added to accommodate arms and legs, complete with leather straps on the ends. The crime scene tech was examining the left arm-strap, lifting a blood sample he'd found there. Carrie was certain it would turn out to be Melissa's.

A wave of fear and emotion overtook her. Melissa had been strapped to this table for three days while Rigby was preparing her for some sort of sick ritual that involved removing her blood. He'd planned to insert some sort of instrument, maybe that trocar, into her to maybe let all her blood flow out of her body until she was simply gone. That sweet, wonderful girl she'd held in her arms at the hospital as she cried into her shoulder. This was the same table he'd likely strapped the other girls to. Their lives ended here, in this very room. Slowly and methodically. They knew they were being murdered every step of the way. She could almost feel the residual fear.

Carrie had worked dozens of homicide scenes over the years. Gangbangers having shootouts in an alley, rape victims brutally disemboweled, and domestic violence cases leaving even the toughest detective in tears. This was different. The disturbed nature of the crime sent a wave of nausea over her.

"I'm gonna get out of here and let you work," Carrie said to the tech as he took swabs of the sink handles.

He just nodded and continued without looking up. "You know, Sergeant, the crime scenes with little or no blood always seem to be the creepiest. I don't blame you for wanting out of here."

"Oh yeah, then why do you keep doing this?" Carrie said, making her way toward the door.

"Oh, that's easy," he said, taking a deep breath. "To catch the fuckers."

To catch the fuckers. Perhaps the best reason of them all, Carrie thought as she stepped out of Rigby's house of horrors.

The most critical task remained left undone. Rigby had given them the slip, and it bothered everyone connected with the case.

Moments later, she dialed Dirk on her cell phone, anxious to hear his voice, and inwardly rejoiced when he answered. "Hey, sweetie. Are we going to meet for dinner later? The girl is safe. I'm in the mood for a celebration. With lots of alcohol."

Hours later Keith, Carrie, and Dirk met for a late dinner at The Roadhouse bar for dinner and a few drinks. Tempered by Rigby's escape, there was still good reason for optimism. With the FBI, county, and local police departments scouring the area for him, his capture was only a matter of time. They raised their beer steins in a toast to Victor and Heather. Dirk suspected Melissa owed her life to them.

Unlike the search for information on Tenebris, there was quite a bit to find on Rigby. As Keith ate his cheeseburger, he told Carrie and Dirk the man had been active in several churches out west. The last one he'd successfully wrestled control from its leadership and brought the congregants to their present location. Keith had indeed found the First Transformational Church, a coffee shop on Fifth Street. Maybe he would drop by and offer counseling to the parishioners once they realized they had been duped.

Carrie pulled his records to find Rigby was not only a licensed veterinarian but also dabbled in poison and antidote research as well.

This was likely what enabled him to sedate his victims. Blood tests on Melissa showed residual traces of etorphine hydrochloride in her system. Rigby obviously knew what he was doing when he mixed the paralytic drug because a higher dose would have killed her.

The girl was alive, and they counted that as a big win. And yet, somewhere in the darkness, a killer lurked. On the run and angry, like a wild animal, this was when he was apt to be the most dangerous.

CHAPTER 23
THE ESCAPE

Deputy Sanjay Kumar's day started the way it always had for the past year; working county transport. He filled his coffee cup and picked up the list of inmates to be transported from dispatch. Normally he had at least two or three, but this morning's list of passengers only featured one name, Arthur Tenebris. Deputy Kumar was to transfer the inmate from county jail to a secure holding facility up north.

The paperwork was all in order and contained a short description of the inmate, which was there to give the deputy an idea of whether he could expect a difficult time with the inmate. *Really, how much trouble could a theater arts teacher be?*

The only information Kumar thought relevant to the amount of work he'd have to put into moving the inmate was listed on the top. *Tenebris/Drug possession/PI.* Kumar knew the "PI" on the paperwork meant he was turning prosecution's informant. *Even better. Far less of a flight risk.* The background page also gave the deputy Mr. Tenebris's height and weight, as well as a picture so he could compare it to the man he'd soon take into custody.

A map was included in the transfer paperwork, prescribing the roads and highways he'd take from the facility. He didn't really need the map, as he'd driven the route countless times and he knew it like the back of his hand. Individual marks indicated where he'd call into dispatch with his progress, which was required with felony transfers of this type.

Normally they didn't let a single driver do the transport, but a series of bad flu outbreaks had left the jail extremely shorthanded, and since Tenebris wasn't considered a threat to anyone but himself, the administration decided to go forward with the transfer.

The drive was three hours long, if everything went as planned, and it almost always did. He'd drop off Tenebris, have some lunch at the pulled pork place next door and then make his way home. Day complete, nice and easy.

After finishing his portion of the paperwork, the deputy neatly put it back in order and placed it into the cellophane envelope he'd present to the intake guards at the Tenebris's new facility. Taking out the bagel he'd brought from home, he ate it on his way to get Tenebris for their trip.

Deputy Kumar walked up to the detention desk. "Hey, gorgeous," he said to the man behind the desk.

"Oh, I'll bet you say that to all the guys. So, my fine chauffeur, what prestigious client hired your services today?"

"Ahhh… Tenebris I think is the name," Kumar said.

"Oh yeah, the DT poster child. You're in luck, he finally broke through a few hours ago. He no longer thinks he's either the King of Spain or Sally Struthers. I have no idea how these guys get this jacked up on blow, but they keep coming through here. Fairly reasonable guy for the most part. He won't give you any bullshit, I think. Real artsy fartsy type."

The deputy was referring to delirium tremens, a condition occurring after withdrawal of narcotics or alcohol sets in. In the early stages of DTs, inmates were at their most unpredictable. They could do almost anything from jumping off a building to their deaths to sneaking into an unintended office, believing they were at a strip club. This was the time the correctional officers watched the inmate closest. To protect the inmates lives and their own.

"All right, here you go. Sign at the bottom, and you are the proud owner of a brand-new shithead."

"Just like I ordered. You guys give the best service here. My compliments!" Kumar feigned a bow.

"See you, Kumar. Be careful out there, eh?" the other deputy said.

"You too. Catch you on the flipside." Deputy Kumar picked up his paperwork and headed over to the cell. The correctional officer working the door was already bringing out Tenebris when he got there.

Kumar scanned at the picture on the paperwork and compared picture with the man. "Yep, you sure do look like yourself."

"Well, don't be absurd, of course I do. I'm me, after all," Tenebris replied.

"Alright, well, we have got about a three-hour drive, so if you have to use the john, this would be the time. I won't stop once we start moving. So, do you need to hit the pisser?"

"My dear man, if you are referring to the latrine, I have already relieved myself. Really, the vocabulary you men utilize around here is deplorable," Tenebris said as if he was insulted by the question. "I'll be fine for the trip. I once held my bladder for an entire stage performance of the *Phantom of the Opera,* including two curtain calls. Let's be on our way."

"Okay, your majesty, the road awaits."

As the door to the vehicle holding area opened, Tenebris felt assaulted by the smells of exhaust fumes mixed with the scent of every inmate who had ever been brought through the garage. *Still, it's better than the holding cell.*

Kumar escorted him over to a van sitting in the far corner of the garage. "Watch your head, Tenebris. Do you want a seatbelt?"

"*Mister* Tenebris, if you please, my dear deputy; I'm a cultured man of stage and a well-respected choreographer."

"You are an inmate being transferred to a different jail. We can make this hard or easy. So, don't be a jerk. You want a belt or not?" Kumar fired back, irritated at his response.

"Yes, please, a seatbelt would be preferred." The seatbelt wouldn't matter. After he was free of these cuffs, one more button would hardly slow him down. It was also possible the seatbelt might give the deputy an extra layer of false security.

Kumar buckled him in and shut the door to the van with a metallic thud. Tenebris looked out the windows as the garage gave way to the streets of Caral city. The weather was supposed to be warm and sunny with low humidity, the perfect Virginian day.

"Hey Tenebris, you want some air back there?" Kumar yelled.

"That would be lovely, thank you," Tenebris said. *And quite noisy too.*

Kumar rolled down the back window, which was still covered by a metal grate to prevent someone from climbing in or out. With the noise of the wind and the relative seclusion of the cavernous vehicle, Tenebris quietly pulled a small metallic object out of the waistband of his underwear. An unfolded paperclip he'd managed to steal off the floor when he was being booked into the cells. He needed something to help him escape, and though he didn't know it at the time, the small piece of metal served as his ticket to freedom.

While preparing for a role as Harry Houdini, he'd studied the art of lock-picking. As a method actor, he put his all into learning the role and became so good at it he could even do it with his eyes closed. This skill allowed him to watch the deputy while he picked the lock on the handcuffs. With his hands free, he made short work of the ankle cuffs.

Deputy Kumar only intermittently glanced up into the rearview mirror. The deputy's lackadaisical approach to his job would make the rest of Tenebris's plan simple. All he had to do was wait for the right moment, or rather the right place, to affect his escape.

The van groaned its way out of the residential areas and into the countryside. Tenebris kept an eye on the time, hoping to be as far away from both the city and the secure facility as possible before making a break for freedom. Too close to either would make it more difficult to disappear. His actor's sense of timing helped to formulate a crude plan.

The van moved through villages and hills. Over small rivers and former Civil and Revolutionary War battlefields. A large stand of trees appeared to rise from the ground and stretch into the distance for miles and miles on either side of the road. *This is my chance*, Tenebris thought.

He waited for Kumar to check on him in his rearview mirror one last time before he carefully moved to the back of the van. There was a bend on a hill coming up, and Kumar would need to slow the van enough so Tenebris would increase his chances of survival while maximizing his chances of escape. Or so he hoped.

The pin system on the door lock was fairly easy to defeat, but there was still the lock on the outside to overcome. Tenebris knew it would be painful, and he steeled himself for the heavy blow. He crouched down in the center of the van.

Deputy Kumar, as predicted, decreased speed. It rocked slightly forward when the brakes were applied, and Tenebris threw all his weight against the van doors. With a burst of pain and a loud crash, the doors gave way. For a brief moment he found himself virtually floating in air before he tucked into a ball and then fell to the pavement.

As he rolled to a stop, he heard Deputy Kumar yell from behind the wheel, "Son of a bitch!"

Dazed for a moment, Tenebris fought through the temporary self-induced fog—there was no time to lose. Although sore and bleeding from a small abrasion on his head that he'd received upon impact, he got up to his feet and ran into the woods. He needed to get some space in between him and the deputy.

It took a few seconds for the deputy to exit the van, which was enough time for Tenebris to vanish into the underbrush along the side of the road. Before disappearing from earshot, however, he'd heard the deputy repeating himself several times as he called in for reinforcements. Kumar had stopped in a dead zone, ensuring his radio and his cell phones were creating more confusion than anything.

Tenebris had always been a good runner. He'd run in high school but was forced to stop when the cocaine habit had burned him out too much. Even so, he was still in decent physical shape. He liked the challenge or deer trails barely noticeable by other people.

Having one more trick up his sleeve, Tenebris remembered to take the handcuffs with him. The deputy likely still thought he was chained and therefore would underestimate how fast he could travel. The reinforcements would show up and concentrate on too small an area. He'd be long gone.

As he ran through the trees and thicket of the Virginia countryside, he steered his course back toward town. His instincts guided his way through the underbrush and away from the road like a rabbit fleeing a fox. Although the crash from the cocaine had sapped his energy, his driving force now was finding the man who had brought him to this point.

His rush of adrenaline helped carry him swiftly. Only one thought ran through his mind as he ducked under half-fallen trees and jumped over logs and small depressions in the forest floor. *I will crush the windpipe of Harmon Rigby.*

* * * *

Dirk and Carrie made their way back to the station. Dirk had promised to testify as to what he'd seen at Tenebris's residence. They wanted Tenebris for accessory to murder, but Dirk was willing to talk to the district attorney and tell them everything he knew about Rigby. This would mean a lighter sentence for Tenebris in exchange for his cooperation.

As a rule, Carrie wasn't permitted to take Dirk's testimony since they were romantically involved, but she was allowed to sit with him while he gave his statement to the detective, as long as she stayed silent.

"State your name for the record."

"Dirk Bentley."

"And you are the owner of Bentley Private Investigations?"

"Yes, I am."

"During the night in question, you were following Mr. Tenebris from his place of employment, is this correct?"

"Yes, it is."

"For what reason?"

"I was surveilling him as part of my investigation into the disappearance of a girl, Melissa Barlo, who had gone missing from the school," Dirk said, sounding very official. "I was watching him to determine his patterns."

"And you drove your vehicle to the residence of Dr. Harmon Rigby?"

"Yes, I did." Dirk was worried about this part. He couldn't let it slip that he'd been trespassing on private property.

The door to the squad room opened. The detective taking Dirk's statement was so shocked by the noise of the door opening he almost fell out of his chair. The Chief of Police knitted her eyebrows, and her skin was ashen in color, like she had just seen a ghost.

"I'm sorry, ma'am, we were just getting Mr. Bentley's testimony. Did you want this room?"

"No, shut the recorder off, detective. We aren't going to need it any longer." The detective did as instructed.

"First I have some good news," the chief said. Addressing Carrie, she continued, "Officer Pettygrew, I know you've done some great work on this case. Effective immediately, I am promoting you to Acting Detective. You will take the place of Detective Robins, who'll soon be going on maternity leave. Congratulations." The chief held out a detective's badge to Carrie, who took it with a gleeful look. "We'll give you a more official ceremony later."

"That's awesome, Carrie!" Dirk grabbed her hand under the table and gave it a squeeze. Reaching the rank of detective was something that she'd wanted for a long time. "But Chief, why do we no longer require my testimony? Did I do something wrong?"

"No, Dirk, that's the bad news. Tenebris is going to be facing charges trumping anything else."

"Such as?" Carrie asked.

"Felony escape," the chief said with a sigh. "About thirty minutes ago, he jumped out the back of a police van. He is at large. Mr. Bentley, your consultation services with this department will be needed a little longer, if you don't mind."

"Anything you want, Chief. You know I am willing to help out." Dirk sat stunned at the thought of Tenebris breaking out of custody.

"Is Kumar okay?" Carrie asked.

"Yes, a little embarrassed but okay," the chief said. "There will be an inquest, but no one blames him. Honestly, we are so shorthanded right now I can't fault the decision-making. No one could have predicted Tenebris would run. He was a witness for the prosecution. It's Rigby the DA really wants."

Dirk became lost in his thoughts for a moment. Why would Tenebris break out of police custody? He was only charged with a drug count. They were holding accessory to murder out there as a carrot on a stick to get him to testify. If he helped the District Attorney, he'd be out of prison in a year, two tops. Strictly medium security stuff.

He'd essentially just traded one charge for another far more serious charge. But why? He turned to Carrie. "We've been working on this case together from the start, right?"

"Yes, I suppose so, why?"

"You know everything I do?"

"Yes, Dirk, where are you going with this?" Carrie said impatiently.

"So, you might be able to guess what I'm thinking?"

"No, dazzle me with your brilliance," Carrie said.

"Remember what Melissa said about the dolls? They were his friends. He talked to them, and he treated them as though they were human."

"Oh, I see," she said, picking up his line of reasoning. "They weren't just his friends but something more. The dolls represented something, didn't they? He was replacing something in his life he lost."

Dirk immediately dug out his notebook. "Didn't his wife die of cancer?"

"Yes, she did," Carrie said. "Could her death have been enough of a trigger to turn him into a serial killer?"

"Naturally, it could," the chief said. "Keep going, you two, I like where you're heading."

"I wonder how Rigby reacted when he saw the mess. The man was textbook OCD, with everything laid out in its proper place. His world would've been, once again, irreparably shaken." Dirk lined up imaginary surgical instruments on the table in front of him as if to illustrate his point.

"She didn't just kill the dolls," Carrie surmised. "She messed up his world pretty good, didn't she? They were replacing his wife. Melissa attacked his wife, or at least the representation of her."

"Okay, detective, so what?" the Chief asked.

"He isn't going to just give up and run away. Rigby will have to kill Melissa to make up for what she did to him and his little friends," Carrie said.

"And Tenebris has to at least attempt to stop him," Dirk finished the thought.

"Why?" the chief asked, leaning forward.

"He wants nothing more than to try to get out from under Rigby's thumb. This is his chance," Carrie answered.

"Why not just run for it?" the chief offered in counterpoint. "He's out of the van and on foot. He could keep going all the way to the tip of Florida and then take a quick trip to Cuba."

"Chief, I looked into his eyes while we were talking to him in his office." Dirk turned in his chair toward her. "He told me that Rigby would kill him, no matter what. Not only is he afraid of Rigby, but Tenebris does like those kids. He loves them, in fact. I don't think he'd be able to live with himself if he allowed Rigby to keep killing, especially now that he's had the chance to dry out from the cocaine again. As a matter of fact, I'd be willing to bet he'll give up as soon as Rigby is dead or in custody."

"So, what's our next move?" the Chief asked.

"We set up a stakeout around Melissa's home," Carrie said. "With the family out of town, the house is essentially all ours. I'll call the family for permission. Let's set up a trap and watch for either of them to show. I bet when we find one, we'll find the other."

"Do it and keep me posted," the chief said.

CHAPTER 24
INTO THE SHADOWS

Harmon Rigby stuck to the shadows as he snuck quietly through the neighborhood he'd lived in for the last two years. He knew it quite well from his frequent walks. He'd need a car if he hoped to get out of the area. The police likely believed he had escaped on foot, so the car afforded him the best chance of evasion.

Maybe he could get one from an unsuspecting neighbor. His own car was parked on the street and was undoubtedly being combed for evidence by the police by now, as he crept up an alley a few blocks from his house. One of his elderly neighbors had a car she barely used, and he could just as easily talk her into letting him have it. One way or another.

Circling back to his neighbor's house carried definite risks, but being slow and cautious by nature had served him well in these situations. Her home was across the street and four doors away. A visit to check on her welfare was not unusual for him, and he normally used the back door instead of the front. It offered him seclusion against the prying eyes of any officer passing on the sidewalk.

Myrtle was the proverbial sweet old lady that lived across the street. Neighborhood kids called her Grandma, and she loved playing the part. Rigby felt a little responsible for her in her old age, and she occasionally asked him to help her bring in items from outside too heavy for her to lift. He didn't mind doing it, and she kept him up on the local gossip to include anything that could concern him.

He knocked on the door, knowing he'd have to be cautious. Her vision and hearing had deteriorated over the years, but Myrtle's mind was as sharp as a tack. She might have seen something on the news or heard something on the radio.

After twenty seconds, there was still no answer. He rang the doorbell, fearing his knocking would attract attention. Soon, a diminutive silver-haired woman answered the door. She was wearing a house dress and a pair of heavy glasses. "Yes, who is it?" she asked from the other side of the door.

"It is me, Myrtle, Doctor Rigby."

"Oh my, Doctor, and I'm wearing nothing but my housecoat! Come in anyway, Harmon. Can you stay a minute?" The old lady opened the door to let him in. "I'll put a pot on." Rigby knew there was no way he'd get out of there without drinking a cup of her coffee.

"I suppose one cup wouldn't hurt," Rigby said, playing the role of perfect guest. "Please don't make any just for me, though. I'm in a bit of a hurry."

"Oh, don't worry yourself, dear. What can I do for you this evening?" she said as she filled a filter with scoops of coffee.

"Well, you see, I feel strange having to ask you this, but I wanted to know if I could borrow your car for a few hours. I'll bring it back with a full tank of gas, I promise."

"Absolutely, what are neighbors for? Is there something the matter with your car?" Myrtle nodded in satisfaction as the coffee maker sputtered to life, and brown liquid sizzled at the bottom of the pot.

"Oh, you know how temperamental cars can be. This part or another goes bad, and they needed to keep it for a while." Rigby accepted a cookie from the plate she offered to him. "Thank you."

"The keys are on the hook on the wall. But, in return, I need a little favor. Tomorrow, can you run me up to the store? You see, even with my new spectacles, I really still shouldn't be driving," she said. "Mean old Doctor Patrick said so."

"Isn't your daughter around to drive you?"

"She has to take my grandkids to the pediatrician. They all have the sniffles over there."

"Well, as you can imagine, I'm a big fan of following a doctor's advice. If he's worried about you taking yourself, then maybe you shouldn't." Rigby glanced at the keys to her car, hanging on the hook in the wall near the door. A small bead of sweat formed at his temple as a sound outside brought to mind legions of police officers likely just outside the door waiting to spring on him.

Myrtle poured out two cups of coffee while hitting the red button on the remote control that was sitting on the counter in the dining room. Behind Rigby, a television came to life. Because her hearing was so bad, the volume had been turned up. The noise made Rigby wince a little as he sat in his chair.

The local news anchor was discussing the recent murders. Myrtle handed him a coffee cup and sat down across from him at the dining room table. She talked about her myriad of doctor visits as Rigby struggled to listen to the television over Myrtle's voice.

"... are now searching for a suspect in connection with the murders of the teenage girls," the news anchor said. "Another attempted killing was foiled earlier today when a recently-kidnapped girl escaped from the home of the assailant. In this undated photo, here is what the suspected killer looks like."

Half-watching the screen, Myrtle shook her head. "Shame about these girls. I sure hope they catch the person who did this." Rigby could tell she couldn't completely see the picture on the screen. The small television was too far away for Myrtle to make out the images.

"...he is considered armed and dangerous," the news anchor continued, "and is believed to be still in our viewing area. His name, once again, is Dr. Harmon Rigby. He is wanted in connection with the murder of several girls and the kidnapping and attempted murder of the victim today. If you have any information for the police, please call..."

Myrtle stopped talking mid-sentence. Her mouth fell open, and her eyes were suddenly wide with fear. She'd heard the announcer correctly. She sprung up from her chair and practically ran to the sink. She moved to place her coffee cup in it but dropped it, sending shards of broken china everywhere. "Harmon, just take the keys and go. I want no trouble."

A twinge of fear ran through him as he heard his name in connection with the murders. But what did the stupid news media know? They had no concept of what he had worked so hard to build, only to have it all destroyed by that evil little snake Melissa. He should have never brought her into his inner circle. She was the asp that bit at his heel. "Myrtle, I can explain."

"No, Harmon, just go, please." Myrtle's voice became frantic and agitated. "I won't tell anyone. I promise you."

"I'm really sorry, Myrtle." Rigby rose from his chair. "I know you better than that. I like you. I always helped you because you were a good neighbor, and those are hard to find these days. This saddens me more than you can comprehend." Rigby didn't really want it to end this way. It should have been easy.

A knife Myrtle told Harmon she had bought at a county fair many years ago sat on the table. Long with a serrated cutting blade; the man who sold it to her said it could cut anything. To demonstrate this fact, he had sliced through a tin can and then he turned it on a brick he broke into two pieces. Rigby picked it up gently from amongst a few pieces of strudel.

"Harmon, I…" Myrtle turned, and their eyes met. She gasped at the glint of steel in his hands and the point aimed right at her midsection. As they stood there, he showed no displeasure toward her. He put his left hand on her shoulder and said, "Myrtle honey, thank you so much for the coffee and cookies. They were grand."

He plunged the knife, serrated edge up, into her stomach, pulling it vertically through her chest cavity, sawing as he went. For one moment of disbelief, she tried to yell out, but the sounds never came. He saw the terror in her eyes.

The blood spurted out of her body and onto the knife. Rigby felt the warm liquid covering his hand as he pushed the knife deeper into her body. Quick and surgical, he wanted her to feel as little pain as possible. It was the humane thing to do.

"Sleep now, dear Myrtle," Rigby whispered into her ear as he watched her eyes roll back into her head. He gently laid her body on the floor into a growing crimson pool.

Rigby went into the washroom and cleaned himself up as best he could. He couldn't do anything about the stains on the front of his pants. Then he made his way back into the kitchen, poured himself a to-go cup of coffee, being careful to avoid the pool of rapidly spreading blood, and took her car keys.

He felt bad for killing Myrtle. She had been a kind and innocent soul. She'd always been good to him, friendly even. "I really am sorry, dear Myrtle," he said before walking out the back and into the garage.

He knew Myrtle's daughter lived nearby, and she'd be along at some point to find her mother dead. With a quick opening of the garage and a turn of the ignition, he directed her car into the alleyway, making sure to close the door behind him. He didn't look back as he left behind the neighborhood he'd turned into his own personal killing field.

Yet he did not worry about the police. He felt a rising sense of satisfaction as he envisioned making Melissa Barlo pay for her sins.

CHAPTER 25
BUS TICKET TO VENGEANCE

Tenebris walked for miles through the woods. Although he had no idea where he was, the lights from the city illuminated the underside of the clouds, giving him a heading. He stayed off the main roads and used animal trails as much as possible.

He thought about Rigby and what his next move likely was. He understood the man intimately, and if there was one thing for certain, it was that Harmon Rigby never left loose ends.

It shouldn't take long for him to find a bus stop. From there he'd buy a bus ticket and ride toward the center of town. He knew Melissa Barlo's address. He was familiar with her neighborhood and had seen her outside the house. If she was home, finding out if her parents were there would be simple. He needed to stay hidden though. It was not unreasonable to assume she had been informed he had escaped.

He had worked out the plan in his head. Make his way to Melissa's house and find a dark corner. He had no idea how long he'd have to wait, but it likely wouldn't be long. The more daunting problem was staying out of police custody until he could execute his plan.

Tenebris patted the gun in his pocket. Its weight was somehow reassuring. *And this time it's loaded.*

After killing Rigby, he'd simply put the gun on the ground and follow police commands. Although he relished the idea of feeling the bones in Rigby's neck crushing under his hands, he knew Rigby was physically stronger. He'd just have to shoot him and be done with it.

Tenebris understood he was likely facing a considerable prison sentence. Life on the lam for someone like Tenebris was impractical. Being behind bars would allow him to read as much as he chose to. He could direct a play. He might even be eligible for parole when they proved Rigby was the killer and Tenebris had done the world a huge favor by killing him. No, in fact, no prison time at all. Maybe he could go on the talk-show circuit. Broadway would have to take him back, this time to direct the Broadway production of his own experiences.

Tenebris understood his daydreams were far-fetched, but he found some soothing relief in playing the scenarios over and over in his head.

Stumbling out of the woods, he stepped onto a raised county road. He had a long way to go, but exactly how far was unclear. He'd have to pick up the pace to make it to the next bus stop.

Rounding a lazy curve in the road, a figure appeared in the deepening twilight. A man stood next to his mailbox, looking as if he was trying to fix it. Avoiding the man was the smart move, but Tenebris also wanted to find out if he was even going the right way.

He approached the man with a friendly smile, "Excuse me, good sir! I say, excuse me, good sir! Can you tell me if I'm heading in the direction of the nearest bus stop? I need to get back into town."

The man looked up and faced him. "Well yeah, I reckon so, but you're going to have a devil of a time reaching it though. It's about five miles from here."

"Am I at least on the right track?" Tenebris asked, a bit dismayed at how far he still had to travel. He'd anticipated a long walk, but he'd never be able to close that distance in time to make the last bus.

"Yep, but, like I said, it's gonna be a hike," the man said as he finished his repairs. "Car troubles?"

He thought fast. "No, I was out in the forest, and don't I feel the fool, I got totally lost."

"Do you want a ride? I'm not going into town, but I can take you to the nearest bus stop. Even if you ran, you'll never make it in time for the last bus."

Tenebris initially thought about turning down the man's offer. He didn't want to risk the police had already put out information on him to the local populace. He knew the police were looking for him, but he had to believe the search for Rigby took precedence. Besides, his booted feet were starting to blister.

"I'd be most appreciative." Tenebris smiled at the man, genuinely thankful for Southern manners. *No one in New York would have given me a ride, that's for certain.*

Soon Tenebris and the man sat in a large pickup truck, on their way to the nearest bus stop. As the man snapped on the radio, a feeling of panic washed over Tenebris. Thankfully, only music issued from the speakers.

"Name's Wyatt, by the way, Wyatt Edgerton."

"Nice to meet you, Wyatt, I'm Phil Branson," Tenebris said. Many years of studying theater had given him a chameleon-like ability to invent a personality with little or no warning.

"It's a pleasure, Phil. So, out for a hike in the woods, you say?" Wyatt asked nonchalantly. "Great place to hike. I've gotten a little lost in there myself while deer hunting."

"It's easy to do. But I'm used to long walks, and today was no exception. You know how it is, have a day off, and you do the best you can to use up the time."

The music was interrupted with a news update on the radio. "Police are on the lookout for a man wanted in connection with multiple murders, kidnapping, and attempted murder. The man's name is Dr. Harmon Rigby. He's presumed to be armed and dangerous. If anyone has any information on the whereabouts of Dr. Rigby, you are to call 911 immediately. Do not approach this man. He's approximately six foot-two inches, slender, and bald."

Wyatt shook his head, grimacing. "Not sure what's wrong with this world. Crazy people everywhere. This guy murders a bunch of teens and kidnaps another, and he gets away from the police."

"I know this Dr. Rigby. He's a vet not too far from my house. I brought him my sick cat once." Tenebris offered up this little lie to assuage his own growing fear the man would think he was Rigby. "I missed the story, what did he do?"

"He supposedly kidnapped a girl and hid her in his garage. They think he was going to ritually kill her. The lass kept her wits about her, though, and escaped. She found a couple of police officers at a service station, and now they're tracking him down. Hope they find him and string him up by his balls, if you'll pardon the expression. Killin' those yunguns' is bad enough. But the way he did it… draining the blood out of them." A look of disgust appeared on his face. "Sick bastard."

Tenebris shuddered as a cold wave of remorse washed over him. The role he'd played in all of this felt like a heavy weight upon his soul. Prison was the best he could hope for, and he deserved it. He should've protected those kids.

"Do you believe in karma?" Tenebris asked the driver. "Because I do. You do enough bad things, and eventually something bad happens to you."

In his mind, he was the agent of karma. Tenebris knew, in his heart, he was justified in escaping from police custody, taking his last chance to set things right. He had to make sure Rigby never hurt anyone again. Maybe this act would count for something, perhaps atone for his misdeeds.

He managed a small smile at the thought of Melissa's escape. At least there was one person Rigby would never hurt again. These events would be Harmon Rigby's undoing.

Wyatt braked the truck to a halt. "Well, here's your stop. Bus comes at the top of every hour, so you got about seven minutes to wait. They're pretty reliable around here, so you should be okay. Good luck to you."

"Thank you so much for the ride, Wyatt," Tenebris said politely. "I'm glad to have met you." Then he opened the door and stepped out of the truck, closing the door behind him with a metallic thud.

Next to the bus stop was a small twenty-four-hour convenience store selling a variety of things. It looked out of place in the middle of rural Virginia but was truly a welcome sight. Within minutes, he'd bought a pre-packaged salami sandwich, a bag of nuts, and a bottle of apple juice. He had no idea how long the day would last, but he knew he should buy some food and bring it with him for the road.

The bus was only one minute late. With a whish of its pneumatic pump, the doors swung open, and Tenebris stepped inside. He tried to keep his head up and not look at the driver, just in case the man had seen a picture of him. However, his caution was unnecessary, as the driver largely ignored him.

Tenebris made his way to the back of the bus and took a corner seat. Another twenty-five minutes and he would be in Melissa's neighborhood. *A little time to relax before I end Rigby.*

CHAPTER 26
ONE LAST PERFORMANCE

Tenebris had watched enough police dramas to know better than to get off at the stop nearest Melissa's house. If the police were watching the house, they'd be keeping an eye on the street and the surrounding area as well. Glancing at the city map on the wall of the bus, he saw another bus stop three blocks away. He'd definitely want to avoid any possible surveillance, and the longer approach would allow him time to check for an obvious police presence. *Thankfully, Rigby and I look nothing alike.*

He exited the bus at his planned stop and walked about a half-block in the opposite direction from Melissa's house. He darted into the alleyway. The passage was dark and comforting, easy to hide in. It would make the approach and the wait for Rigby easier. He still had to cross one more street before he came to the Barlo residence.

In this neighborhood, the alleys were well-groomed paths. The way he was dressed, he'd fit right in with others strolling this time of night. His greatest concern was the people who lived in the neighborhood since they would all know each other on sight and would be suspicious of any new person wandering around in the dark.

Tenebris had gone to a lot of trouble to get this far, and he wasn't going to let himself be caught before the act was complete. However, he wasn't a trained killer, and he wouldn't have the heart to shoot anyone other than Rigby, so he had to be extra careful. His rage was reserved for Rigby alone.

Taking a seat on a park bench along the alley, he listened for the sounds of possible pursuers. While performing this quick security precaution, he considered what it would be like to kill Rigby. Saying you were going to take someone's life and actually doing it was another matter. At the same time, he felt his own crushing guilt for leading these kids to Rigby.

Some part of him had always reasoned away what he'd done. His drug-induced stupor made him believe that he wasn't hurting the kids, and Rigby was too kind a person to harm them either. That all changed when the third body showed up and then even the cocaine couldn't dim the sorrow that welled up inside of him. What was happening was too obvious for even him to ignore. But that was the past, and this was the present. And now he had to finish this.

Satisfied he wasn't being followed, Tenebris got up from the park bench and continued on toward the house. He left the alley and walked along the sidewalk, looking for a sign of Rigby. Perhaps his car, maybe even the man himself.

Trying to blend into his surroundings, he pulled out the salami sandwich from his pocket and started eating. Although he wasn't particularly hungry, he figured he would look less out of place if he was doing something rather than just walking along on the street, alone. With a half-block to go, he saw the pitch of the girl's house in the distance. He'd be there in about forty seconds if he kept moving.

A glint of light caught his eye as he approached. Something metallic in the distance, like a car. He slunk under the night shade of a large oak tree along the sidewalk.

It struck him as odd how a car parked along the side of a street didn't look out of place, but a car with someone just sitting inside was suspicious. In the front seat, he could see a slight glow from the dashboard. Tenebris slunk behind a clump of bushes and watched the lone car. The model of car was hard to see completely, but the car looked like it could be an official city sedan.

After a few minutes, the person inside stepped out into the night air. In the dim light from the partly cloudy sky, he saw the figure of a woman. She glanced furtively around. The female figure stretched, as if she had been sitting in the car for a long time. Her shirt came up from her pants, and he could clearly see, attached to her belt, a holster and a gun.

Why would the police be keeping an eye on the house? Why waste the resources if he was on the run? His mind flooded with possibilities. *This doesn't make any sense, unless they too figured out that my dear Dr. Rigby would feel compelled to return and kill Melissa.*

This changed the dynamics and upped the ante for Tenebris. One little mistake and he could find himself on the losing side of a police pistol. This looked like a trap had been set, but who was it for, him or Rigby?

CHAPTER 27
MOVEMENT IN THE ALLEY

Dirk and Carrie sat in a car outside the police perimeter. The sting was simple. A stand-in for Melissa was inside her bedroom, laying in the bed. That part was being played by police officer, Gretchen Seigel. Slim and short, she was a perfect substitute for the girl. In addition to being the almost the exact same size as Melissa, one would have to be within about twenty feet to suspect it wasn't her. By the time Rigby got that close, it would be too late.

At 9:30, Officer Seigel went through the motions of getting ready to go to bed. Because they couldn't cover all angles of the house as well as they liked, she had to put on a convincing show. She even dressed in Melissa's nightgown, lay down in her bed, and pretended to read the book *Watership Down* she'd found on the nightstand. Under the pillow next to her, her pistol and her handcuffs remained out of sight.

Dirk and Carrie talked for a little while about nothing in particular. Dirk's sister had a birthday party at her house they were invited to, and they tossed around ideas of what to get her while they waited for any sight of Rigby or possibly Tenebris.

He thought about the absurdity of their lives as they were discussing the mundane while simultaneously waiting for a wanted murderer to play his hand. *It all could end*, Dirk thought. *In a moment something goes terribly wrong, one of us could just no longer exist.* Yet they sat there talking over gift ideas and what to do for dinner the rest of the week.

Dirk suddenly found he couldn't take his mind off Carrie. She was such an important part of his world, and he could never imagine living without her. He just needed to get up the courage to tell her. She was his everything. Something about seeing Rigby's surgery room made him realize how fleeting life could be. He'd been close to many an unsavory character before but never one so evil. It made him wonder about their professions. *What would it mean to Carrie if I were to be killed? What if she were?*

"Carrie?"

"Yes. And if you are going to revisit your idea of getting your sister a bouncy castle for the birthday party, forget it. She already texted me you were considering it." She continued to pick at a bag of cashews she typically brought with her on every stakeout.

Dirk had a habit of being satirical when he was nervous. Now a different sensation hit at the pit of his stomach. There was a desperation there he had not felt before. For the first time in his life, everything made sense to him. "I love you. I wish I knew why it was that I couldn't have said that before because you know it is true. You are the most important person in my life, and I just needed to make sure you heard that before anything else happen in our lives."

"Wait, what?" Carrie's mouth was suddenly agape.

"I love you, Carrie," Dirk said softly, taking her hand. "I worry sometimes about you and me."

"Shut up, Dirk," Carrie said, moving in closer. "I love you too." They leaned into each other, closing their eyes in anticipation.

"1274." Carrie's radio came to life, causing both of them to jump back a little from the crackling of the handheld. Their tender moment would have to wait.

"1274, go ahead."

"Detective, you better get up here. We've got activity in the alley behind the house," the radio replied.

"1274, acknowledged. On my way," Carrie responded with a frown. Turning to Dirk, "We'll talk later. Right now, it sounds like we need to catch a bad guy. Stay here, please." She knew full well he wouldn't, but it made her feel better to say it.

* * * *

Rigby advanced along the street behind Melissa's house. From his hiding spot, he could see a squad car lurking in the shadows. He moved with purpose, thinking through his every step. He briefly considered whether killing the officer was worth the risk but decided it could raise more problems than the potential good it would do him. He only had one syringe, and he wanted to keep it for Melissa. It would be best to just avoid the police entirely and deal with them later.

He continued along a fence and into the protective shadow of a large oak tree. The moon hung like a spotlight on stage and shone down upon him. He'd need to be careful.

Rigby dropped to the ground and crawled along the well-manicured grass, staying behind trees and a freshly-painted bird feeder. Whoever lived here definitely took great care of their lawn. Thankfully, they were more an expert at gardening than at security. They'd left a nicely-trimmed hedge along the side of the house, which would hide his advance into the backyard.

Edging toward the back of the yard, the heft of the bag weighed heavy in his hands. He could almost feel the completion of his task.

Myrtle's death was unfortunate, but halting her life was necessary, and she'd be rewarded in heaven for the assistance she rendered to him. But Melissa's end would be different. Calculated and cold-blooded.

Maybe he'd try to reason with her. Perhaps she could be made to see her error and come with him. It'd be gracious of her and redeem her in his eyes. She'd so carelessly thrown away the opportunity he gave her, and maybe she'd had a change of heart.

But no, she ran from him. She'd murdered his friends. She hadn't appreciated what Rigby had to offer. *The little bitch.*

As he came to the end of the hedge, he could see the back of the house. The facade and porch sat mostly dark, with the exception of a flicker of light from the living room. The windows were closed, and he could hear the hum of the air conditioner.

* * * *

Tenebris watched the police officer for a long time. He wanted to be sure she was going to stay near the car. It wouldn't do for her to find him lurking in the bushes.

He knew he had to get into the house or at least close enough to see what was going on. Carefully avoiding the moon's prying gaze, he slunk into a neighbor's yard, which was surrounded by a wooden picket fence. As he lay there on the ground, watching the street, he became aware of other cars parked on the street. There were quite a few, and at least half of them looked like they could be police cars. He'd been so focused on the officer; he hadn't noticed them until now.

He could always backtrack and go around, yet that would not only take a long time, but it also increased the risk of him being seen. He needed a plan, some cover to let him get close. But in this neighborhood, at this time of night, there were few options.

As he lay on the ground, thinking about his current predicament, he heard movement to his side. He instantly froze. Something or someone shuffled in the grass nearby, much too light to be a human being. He carefully turned his head to the left, and a small tongue licked his face.

Looking at him with a curious expression was a small brown Pekingese. "Go away," he whispered. The dog, apparently not understanding him, sat and let out a little bark.

From inside the house, Tenebris heard someone shout, "Shut up, you noisy mutt!"

A spectacular idea flashed through his mind. There were few things more normal in suburbia than a guy taking his dog for a walk. One last chance to urinate on the world was exactly what every canine needed. Surely, no one would question that? He looked at the dog, which stupidly bounced on its haunches as if anticipating playtime.

As quietly as possible, he got from the ground. He made his way behind the tree and then up to the porch. He felt along the wall, his hand finding exactly what he was looking for; a thin leather leash hanging from a nail.

From the moment Tenebris touched the leash, the dog seemed to lose its mind. The little ball of fluff let out several more barks. Tenebris put his hand on the dog to keep it quiet. He knew the noise could have alerted the dog's owner or the police. Right on cue, the owner yelled, "I'm going to have you made into a hat if you don't shut up!" Apparently, the police were the only ones he needed to worry about, but a quick inspection of the block showed none of them were stirring.

Tenebris thought about his next move for a few seconds and decided upon a bold strategy. The next step had to be. He could have covertly moved back through the night and hidden from the police, but that wouldn't get him where he needed to go. The time had come to cast off his cloak and hide in plain sight.

Grabbing a hat from the porch, he put together a quick disguise. Anyone who knew what he looked like would instantly see though it, but he trusted that most of the police wouldn't have any more than a basic description of him. All they would see was some guy walking his dog. He could easily slip past the row of squad cars.

Digging deep into his repertoire of acting skills, he boldly clicked the leash onto the dog's collar and stepped through the gate onto the sidewalk. He kept thinking to himself, *No one to see here. Just a man walking a dog.* He turned right out of the gate and closed it as silently as he could.

He made his way past two squad cars and across the street. Fifty feet away from the alleyway, he heard a stern voice behind demanding, "Hey, what are you doing?"

Tenebris turned around slowly, startled by the voice. What if the disguise had failed? How should he respond? Should he run? What then? Maybe it would be best to play the confused homeowner. "What? Who's there?"

"This is Officer Robins," said a voice coming from his right side. "What do you think you're doing?"

He exhaled. "Oh, officer, I'm sorry. I didn't see you there. You startled me. I'm taking Princess for her nightly walk." Tenebris mused the dog would likely protest the made-up name he had given it. "Is there a problem?"

Tenebris could feel the officer's eyes glaring at him. He could almost picture the man's mind deciding if this urbanite and his happy dog could possibly pose a threat.

He answered, "This is official police business. We request everyone stay inside right now."

"I certainly understand, officer. I just need to get my little precious out for some exercise before we go to bed. I only plan to walk her to the end of the block and then right back inside. Is that okay?" The remaining fifty feet to the path leading into the alley was tantalizingly close. If the officer didn't let him pass, he'd have to go with a backup plan that he had not, as yet, conceived.

"Very well, sir, just stay on the sidewalk and get inside as soon as you can. I don't want to catch you or your dog out here again tonight. Is that clear?" The way in which Officer Robins spat the word *dog* sounded almost condescending.

"Yes, officer, I certainly understand. I'll be done before you realize it," Tenebris said, a little irritated at the officer's dismissive attitude toward the dog. He whistled to the dog and headed up the street without another word.

Just before he came to the path, he dared a look back down the road to where Officer Robins had been standing. He was still outside his car, talking on his cell phone, with his back to Tenebris.

In one fluid motion, Tenebris turned left into a shrub-lined path that led the way into the dimly lit alley. So far, he was giving one of the best performances of his career.

* * * *

Sometimes Dirk thought about following directions. Even as a child, the drive to do the opposite of what someone told him to do was too tempting. It made him want to do it all the more.

Up the road from Carrie's squad car, a man and his dog appeared to be taking a walk. He even watched the man stop and talk with a police officer working the perimeter. What was lost on the young officer struck Dirk as more than a little odd. The man was dressed in slacks and a button-down dress shirt but also wore a ball cap pulled low over his face. A strange combination. Still, likely nothing to worry about. But he had to wonder why anyone would wear a hat at night?

For several tense seconds, he resisted the urge to get out of his car, but it was overwhelming. The department's concern for his safety was admirable, but the guy looked out of place, and someone needed to follow him. It could be nothing, but then again ... people were normally in bed or on their way to bed by now, maybe watching the late show.

But Carrie said the homeowners were all told to say inside. *Probably nothing.*

* * * *

Harmon Rigby skulked through the alley toward the house. He was careful to move slowly, deliberately, and methodically, avoiding attracting any attention. He could clearly see the house from where he was standing. Most of the lights were off, with the exception of the back hallway and one bedroom. He could also see a shadow inside. She was in there, waiting. Perhaps even for him.

He could almost smell her from where he was standing. In his heart, he felt as though she was beckoning to him, asking him to come and get her. Rigby imagined the syringe entering her neck. With one quick movement, he'd have her incapacitated. Then he'd carve her body into little bits. He shook with anticipation, relishing the idea.

Rigby could never remember being a violent person before, but the thought of killing her was exciting him. The trick would be to get inside and do the job before the police knew what was happening. He figured they'd be watching the house, so he'd need to rely on stealth and cover of night. He was certain of his success. After all, he was smart, and they weren't. God was watching over *him*, not them.

The alleyways in this neighborhood provided him a pathway to proceed mostly unnoticed. If someone approached him, there'd be no way for him to identify them. On the flip side, there would be no way to tell if he were walking into a deliberate trap.

As if to confirm the problem, he heard a faint noise coming from behind him. He jumped over the low fence and squatted down so his head was just below eye-level. The noise was of feet and little paws on the pavement. A man walking a dog. At the very least, Rigby now had an idea of how far off he could distinguish people approaching. He'd have to be careful.

As soon as the man with the dog passed out of Rigby's earshot, he raised his head above the fence to ensure he was alone. Just as he did, another figure weaved their way through the neighborhood. The man was carefully stepping along the alleyway, staying in the night shade cast by the trees. Rigby had to duck again to let the man pass.

To his relief, the man continued past his hiding place, apparently following the man with the dog. For a moment, this odd turn of events made him panic, but he calmed himself down. *Nothing more than random occurrences. People just out walking these paths at night.* This time, when he looked up from the fence, the coast was clear.

Hopping the fence and heading back into the alley, he surveyed both directions just to be certain no one had seen him. Scanning the neighborhood one more time for movement, he saw an outside light turn on at a house several doors down. The back door opened, and a woman wearing a robe exited the house, carrying a bag of garbage.

While he waited for the light to go out again, he peered into the backyard of Melissa's house. In the dark, a flash of something metallic caught his eye. Only the briefest of moments, but Rigby saw a clear glint on the top of a small garden shed butting up against the fence of the yard. He hadn't noticed it before. As soon as the woman went back into her house and the light went out, he trained his night vision in the direction of the shed.

On top of the shed, trying to remain as invisible as possible, lay a figure. Dressed in black against the night, he sat motionless, as if trying to become the night itself. He seemed to be holding what looked like a rifle. *One of Satan's spies*, Rigby thought.

They sent a *sniper* to keep an eye on the girl? He felt a perverse sense of satisfaction the police thought so much of him.

His sense of pride was only momentary, as he considered what the sniper would mean. It'd make it impossible to get close to the house without being observed. Any move toward the house would likely result in the sniper putting him the crosshairs.

No, I need to make a slight change to my plans.

Rigby knew he'd never make it to the house with the sniper watching. The man would have to be taken out of the picture if he was going to be successful. That just left him with one recourse: he'd have to use his one and only syringe. It would be quick and non-lethal, but it would also mean he'd have to find some other way of killing Melissa once he'd entered the house.

How long would the sedative work on the much larger officer? Rigby wondered. Based on his own personal experience, it seemed that ten minutes would be a safe estimate. He hated the idea of giving up his last syringe of tranquilizer, but better to take his chances with Melissa than a police sniper.

To Rigby, it seemed like a lifetime to get to the garden shed. He finally reached the side of the shed and breathed a sigh of relief. Slithering a little farther along the ground, his hand hit the side of something hard. Feeling around in the darkness, his hand hit the fiberglass rail of a ladder leaning up against the garden shed.

* * * *

Tenebris was patting himself on the back for his cleverness. He walked a few houses up from the Barlo home and entered the backyard. He lay on the ground for a few moments to make sure he wasn't being followed.

As he'd hoped, the dog had proved very useful. He took the dog's leash off, patted its head, and left it to wander around its new backyard.

Tenebris planned to pick his way through several backyards before finally reaching Melissa's. He needed to remain as quiet, and as hidden, as possible.

He wasn't as concerned about the police as much as he was afraid of Rigby. He knew the man was not only dangerous but also brilliant. Rigby's intelligence made it difficult to deal with him. Even now, Tenebris wasn't completely sure Rigby wasn't a few steps ahead of him. He could've sworn he heard someone behind him as he made his way along the alley, but every time he looked back, he saw nothing, even in the piercing moonlight.

* * * *

Dirk watched the man he was following as he walked along the paved path in the alley. He was trying to stay out of the light a little too hard to remain inconspicuous. *God, I hope this isn't a wild goose chase… dog chase… or whatever.*

Dirk was just about to write off his suspicion as just a product of his overactive imagination when the man stepped out into the moonlight, illuminating his face perfectly.

Tenebris.

His instincts had proven right. A twinge ran up his spine as he realized how difficult his position was. He had no way to signal the police without alerting Tenebris. And if he spooked Tenebris, he risked scaring away Rigby in the process. For now, he'd just have to keep following him and hope an opportunity would arise for him to signal the police.

Dirk was in the alley behind the property, in between Tenebris and the Barlo residence. He was still in a good position to keep an eye on him. He stayed in the shadows, watching as the shadowy figure of Tenebris slowly approached the Barlo home.

* * * *

Harmon Rigby made his way up the ladder placed against the garden shed. The fiberglass ladder was sturdy and there was almost no noise as he put his feet on each rung. With each step, he could feel sweat running down his back. Any sudden noise and the sniper would turn around. He needed to be absolutely silent.

* * * *

Deputy Smiles, veteran police sniper, laid sentinel at his location. Every once in a while, he'd shift position just to make sure his legs didn't fall asleep. As he did, the roof tiles scraped his clothes. *No way around it*, he thought, *it's just one of those things*. He'd need to buy new pants tomorrow. He was just finishing making another minor adjustment when he felt a short prick in his calf.

Oh nuts, he thought, *I must have found a nail or something. Make that a new pair of pants and a tetanus shot.* A few seconds later though, he started to feel woozy, and his vision blurred. In a half-asleep state, just before he blacked out, he thought he saw a person jumping the fence into the yard.

CHAPTER 28
AND THIS WILL ALL BE OVER

Dirk had found another spot under a tree, just in front of a garden shed. There was still about twenty feet of space between Tenebris and him. Although Tenebris was on the other side of the fence, he could make him out through the slats. He seemed to be waiting for something.

To Dirk's left, the sound of a mumble from the top of the shed caught his attention. Then something smacked the ground with a thud. Dirk froze in place, wondering if Rigby had managed to sneak up on him. Even though the darkness had covered his advance pretty well, he had no doubt in his mind that anyone watching would see him. Dirk could see Tenebris look around as if he'd heard the noise as well but dismissed it quickly. He appeared to be focused more on the Barlo home.

While watching Tenebris squat down at the fence, he felt around in the dark for whatever had startled him. His hand made contact with something he recognized instantly: a rifle. Even in the dark, he could tell the object was a SR-25 rifle with a very high-end scope on it. Glancing up at the top of the shed, he could just make out the forearm, wrist, and hand of a person.

An icy realization gripped his consciousness. The stock on this weapon was custom. He ran his hand over the top of the sights and then over the magazine. He knew the gun. His friend and occasional shooting partner, Smiley, was up on the roof. And he would never, under any circumstances, drop this rifle. His suspicion was confirmed; things had gone terribly wrong.

* * * *

As soon as the drugs hit the sniper's bloodstream, Rigby could see the tension retreat from the sniper's body. *Sweet dreams*, he thought to himself. Turning to get off the roof, he heard a scraping noise. The sniper's rifle had slid out from his grasp and had fallen to the ground. He had to get off the ladder fast as someone may have heard the noise. Worse yet, the police could ask for a status check from the sniper at any moment. A lack of response would alert them that something was wrong.

Rigby moved quickly back down the ladder, almost falling off the last rung in his haste. He made his way back behind the shed and jumped into the yard, crouching behind a bush to avoid being seen. As he observed the yard, movement caught his eye.

Rigby wondered if God himself had been watching over him. The clouds parted, and the moonlight gave him the perfect view of a man, someone he knew well. Rigby could hardly believe his eyes. *What the hell was he doing here?*

* * * *

Tenebris could have sworn he heard something behind him. A thud in the grass. *Probably just the dog knocking something over.* The wind had picked up, and the noise could have been anything from branches rubbing together to something falling to the ground. Once again, he reached into his coat pocket to feel the reassuring cold steel of the pistol.

He needed a better vantage point. A large garbage can directly behind one of the windows offered a good place to hide. He could watch the backyard while also checking the windows.

* * * *

Dirk quickly climbed the ladder and assessed his friend, lying unconscious on the roof of the shed. Quickly taking his pulse and shaking him as firmly as he dared, he confirmed the Smiley was still breathing. He patted Smiley down for a radio before realizing it must have fallen to the ground with the rifle. There was no way he could find it to call for help. Smiley would just have to sleep it off.

Below him, he could see a figure skulking through a bush along the fence. It could've been Tenebris. He hadn't seen any police officers as he made his way down the alley before. The man turned his head only slightly, and it was just enough of a profile to discern who it was. It chilled him to the bone. Although he and Rigby had never met, he recognized the profile of the man from when he saw Rigby and Tenebris arguing in Rigby's backyard.

Dirk knew he needed to get to Tenebris as quickly as possible, or this situation was going to devolve drastically.

* * * *

Tenebris was trying to find a way to pry a window loose. He hoped he could convince the girl to hide while he exacted his revenge against Rigby. That meant getting into the house first. He couldn't lose his shot at making Rigby pay for his crimes. Redemption felt close now, and he could almost taste its sweet flavor, smell its acrid smoke. He had been careful and quiet. No one had heard or followed him.

He stood back, trying to get a better sense of how to open the outer storm window when he heard a noise behind him. Somewhere in the inky black of night, a twig snapped. He turned to face the darkness of the backyard, pulling the revolver out of his pocket.

There was an instant of disbelief. "You," Tenebris said.

"Good evening, Arthur. I figured you'd be in police custody by now. Good on you for staying clear of them." Rigby spoke quietly as he emerged from the shadows.

Tenebris stood his ground. He wasn't going to let Rigby talk him down this time. "That's far enough, Harmon. I was hoping to find you here. You couldn't keep away, could you? The idea of someone slipping out of your reach was too much to bear. You'll also appreciate that I took your advice." He aimed the weapon at Rigby. "It's loaded this time."

"Bravo, Arthur," Rigby said. "I'm glad to see you're finally growing a backbone. Something you could have used before now." Tenebris could tell Rigby eyed the gun as if he were weighing whether or not Tenebris was telling the truth.

"I was clean after leaving New York. I was happy. I remembered what I loved about acting, the theater, my life. You used me to get these kids. You filled me with nonsense, you kept me high."

"I'm sorry, Arthur, I truly am," Rigby said. He stepped to his right and moved a little closer to Tenebris. "I think I like this new version of you. We could possibly work together. We're both wanted men. With your skills and my intelligence, we could keep away from the police for the rest of our lives. Maybe find an island in the Caribbean or something? What do you say?" There was only twenty feet separating them.

Tenebris couldn't believe his ears. The audacity of the man, thinking he could talk his way out of this. "You fucking bastard," he snarled. "You don't know when to quit, do you? Here we are, at the end of it all, and you're still trying to manipulate me?"

Sober now, Tenebris saw Rigby's manipulation of him. This time, it would not work. All of Rigby's motives were suddenly exposed to the light of day, and that was what Rigby didn't yet understand. Rigby would do anything to get out of this situation. But Tenebris was no longer under his control.

"Well then, it seems we're at an impasse. I'm willing to let you walk away. I just want to tie up a few loose ends and then I'll be on my way." Rigby advanced toward the house.

"Don't move a muscle, Rigby. I am warning you." Tenebris steeled his will against his old partner in crime.

* * * *

Because both men were in the backyard, none of this conversation could be heard from the front of the house. Dirk recognized that this exchange had run its course, and Tenebris looked like he was about to pull the trigger. Dirk had to act. And he had to act fast.

Stepping from cover and into the scene, Dirk said, "Alright, Tenebris, drop it. You can't win this. The police are right out front, and they've been alerted." Dirk fibbed a little, hoping he'd said it loud enough for someone to catch the sound of the conversation, even he had no way of knowing if anyone had. The windows were high-end, and Officer Seigel likely wouldn't be able to hear the conversation through the double-paned glass. The police out front still had no idea Smiley had been incapacitated. Dirk was tempted to yell for backup but figured it could cause Tenebris to shoot. "Let's just all be real cool about this, boys."

"Mr. Bentley, you aren't going to stop me." Tenebris's voice was shaky but determined. "I came here to end Harmon Rigby, and I will. You don't understand, no one can. he'll kill again. Just like in the Pacific Northwest. The kids, he needs more of them." Tears began to stream down his face.

"Ahh, Mister Bentley," Rigby said, smiling in the faint glow from the house. "I've read all about you in the papers. Some sort of ... detective agency, right? Congrats to you, sir. As you can see, I'm unarmed, and this man is threatening my life. Perhaps even yours."

"You know, Rigby," Dirk responded, not a trace of humor on his face, "if I didn't want to see you face the death penalty, I would likely shoot you myself. So, if I were you, I would shut the fuck up right now."

Tenebris spoke again, a steely edge to his voice that Dirk hadn't heard before. "Look, Bentley, I I'm going to do time for conspiracy. Let me just add murder to the charges. Rigby must go down, and you know it's true. I'm going to kill him, andthen I'll drop the gun down. This will all be over."

Dirk could see sweat on Tenebris's brow. He wasn't sure how long it would be until he pulled the trigger, but he figured time was growing short. "Arthur, you can't make yourself the judge, jury, and executioner. He needs to face justice."

"Hmm, perhaps I'm looking at this the wrong way," Rigby interjected. "Tenebris, you're not such a bad partner. Let's just agree to a truce, and maybe we can work something out. You understand I —"

"Harmon, I loved those kids," Tenebris cut him off mid-sentence. "I enjoyed working with them. I was clean and sober and doing what I loved. Imparting what I had learned. Then you destroyed all of it. You ruined my life. I was clean, and you crushed me." He was shaking uncontrollably, and now he was crying.

"Mr. Bentley, he's going to shoot me," Rigby said, a trace of panic creeping into his voice. "You need to protect me. Protect me, please. Damn it, do something, Bentley!"

Dirk inwardly chuckled at the irony. It appeared Rigby had seriously overestimated how weak Tenebris really was. For the first time ever, Tenebris had power over his tormenter. However, the theater arts teacher was becoming increasingly unstable.

"You stole it all from me," Tenebris was shouting now. "You took everything. You hurt those girls. You murdered them. You snuffed out their young lives … you killed my legacy." A flash of light, smoke, and an explosion erupted from the barrel of the gun. Dirk was unprepared for it. He knew Tenebris might pull the trigger, but he hadn't thought the man truly had it in him. Dirk instinctively fired in response, trying to hit Tenebris in his leg in the hopes of only wounding him. Normally he'd have aimed for the chest, but for some reason, he couldn't bring himself to kill him.

Rigby spun around, as if he'd had been hit in the shoulder with a baseball bat. He ran to the back fence with surprising speed. Dirk took a few steps toward where Tenebris now lay on the ground and quickly kicked his gun away from him.

Dirk looked up just in time to see Rigby jump the fence into the alley. Dirk kept his gun trained on Rigby, but his efforts came too late. Harmon Rigby had escaped into the darkness of night.

A moment later, the whole scene erupted into chaos. Police appeared from seemingly every direction. Several police officers in uniform fell through the back door and took up positions on the patio. Three other officers, including Carrie, ran around the side of the home and lowered their weapons as soon as they saw Tenebris on the ground and Dirk kneeling next to him.

Dirk knew the protocol, keeping his weapon on Tenebris until the police arrived and had taken custody of the suspect before handing his gun to one of the officers.

Dirk told the police about Rigby's escape, pointing at the spot where he'd jumped the fence. He also sent them over to check on the sniper asleep in the shadows. The fence was white, but in the light of the police flashlights, he could see the blood spatters Rigby had left behind. Tenebris had struck Rigby, and judging by the amount of blood, the hit was good. If they didn't find him fast, Rigby would likely bleed out.

An ambulance crew, already stationed on scene, was in the backyard as soon as the weapons were secured. Tenebris was placed on a stretcher and cuffed to the rail Before they loaded him up to take him to the hospital, he grabbed Dirk by the arm. "Did I get him?" he asked.

"Yeah, Arthur, you got him."

"You know why, Mr. Bentley, don't you?" Tenebris asked as the paramedics treated his gunshot wound.

Dirk leaned against a brick wall at the end of the patio as he spoke. "You wanted to make sure he never had the chance to do this again."

"Good, I'm glad you understand." Tenebris let out a heavy sigh as he spoke. "He took everything away from me. The best I could do was to make sure he never ruined anyone else's life. He'd have just set up someplace else. I believe it was Jesus who said 'It is finished' is it not?"

"Yeah, but I'm pretty sure Jesus never shot anyone," Dirk said. He suddenly wished he was anywhere else in the world.

"True, very true," Tenebris said. "Take care of yourself, Mr. Bentley."

"You too, Arthur." Dirk watched the paramedics roll the stretcher out of the backyard.

Carrie walked over to Dirk and gave him his gun back. "Here you go. The chief is clearing you for now. However, in her words, 'you have a lot of explaining to do tomorrow.' She wants a full statement after we find Rigby. She is worried that Rigby may have some fight left in him. You can surrender your weapon when you get to the station in the morning."

Dirk stared at the ground for a few seconds. He was tired and sore. Suddenly, he felt like just taking the rest of the night off. "Why don't we just sneak away for a burger and a couple of beers? Let the regular uniform guys have all the glory this time around."

"Yeah, like you'd ever sit this out."

"I suppose you're right."

Carrie nudged his shoulder. "C'mon, lover boy, let's go stop a fugitive."

CHAPTER 29
BLOOD ON THE PAVEMENT

Rigby knew he'd been wounded. As he jumped the fence, his hand slipped because of the blood. Crimson fluid was everywhere. He could possibly stop the bleeding but not while running from the police. Adrenaline was pushing his heart harder than if he'd had completed a marathon, and all that blood was leaking out his abdomen. Using his skills as a veterinarian, he quickly did some mental math on increased heart rate from the exertion and blood loss. He needed to be treated, and now.

As he careened down the alley, he could hear the police clambering over the fence behind him, but he had a good head start on them.

He ran a couple of blocks and ducked into another alley behind a row of old buildings. They were mostly abandoned and had been for years. Peering into the window of one building, he could see a box bearing a large green cross hanging on the wall. A first aid kit.

Judging from the condition of the building, he reasoned it likely wouldn't have a security system. One of the windows had been smashed, and a board loosely covered the window opening. It easily gave with a quick push.

Climbing over the window and falling into an old storeroom, he briefly caught a glimpse of himself in the mirror. His hair was a mess, and his clothes were torn and blood-soaked. There was no way he could go to a hospital like this. They would immediately call the police.

Throwing open the box, he was disappointed to find there wasn't much inside. There were only three rolls of gauze. Not perfect, but it would slow the bleeding.

As his adrenaline wore off, he began to sweat, and then the nausea kicked in. He knew he was likely starting to suffer from hypovolemic shock, but he had to work through it. As he tried to treat the gunshot wound, his mind raced back to the moment Tenebris pulled the trigger.

"I can't believe he did it," he said to himself as he tied off a piece of the gauze dressing. Drops of blood formed a growing pool below him. He couldn't help but respect the man for taking the shot. Tenebris had always been such a weak soul. He'd caved to drugs on more than one occasion. He'd let Rigby control him with the addiction. A sign of weakness, pure and simple.

Rigby lowered himself out of the window into the alley below. His entire body hurt now. Pain shot through his joints and muscles. He was still losing blood but not as fast as before.

He turned right as he exited the window and suddenly felt a wave of confusion hit him. Which way had he come from?

Seeing the streaks of blood on the pavement, he turned the opposite direction and continued to run down the alley.

He had to get away. His friends needed him. They'd been smashed by the infernal girl, but they could be fixed or replaced. He'd find others, start with fresh souls. They would be his privileged ones, and giving their lives to his dear friends would be his greatest achievement yet. *But where?*

He'd once lived out west, but the police there had started to piece his operation together. Rigby knew he had to keep them away until they could see for themselves. Someday they would all comprehend his genius.

His brain thought of a myriad of other places he could start again. He could move to Texas, but he hated the heat, so maybe Montana. He could establish another church. A church filled with people who would understand, people who would willingly give up their sons and daughters to his friends. Surely they would.

Rigby plunged into the middle of the street and stopped to get his bearings. A split second to consider where to head next. The pause was just long enough for his brain to realize the lights and the sound of brakes he was hearing were from the big rig that was bearing down on him. In the back of his mind, he heard the voice of his mother, who said, "Now, Harmon, always check both ways before crossing the street."

* * * *

The wheels of the rig screeched as soon as the driver saw Rigby. The veteran driver, on his way home for the night, did everything he could to stop the vehicle. The overwhelming mass of the rig struck the underwhelming mass of Rigby, making a noise like a grape being squished underfoot. The driver grimaced, unaware of the role he'd played in delivering karmic retribution.

Rigby's body rolled several times under the engine block of the rig and then under the rear tires. The crushed remains of his head were found ground into the pavement, courtesy of the big rig's tires.

Harmon Rigby was profoundly dead.

CHAPTER 30
RESOLUTION

Carrie stood from examining the front end of the rig. "Well, don't need to be a trained detective to solve this one. Poor guy."

"Poor guy?" Dirk looked at her quizzically. "You mean the serial killer?"

"Ah no, I meant the truck driver. He feels awful about it. He's retiring next month. I'm guessing he doesn't realize he just saved the state a lot of trouble." She pointed to the marks on the ground where the driver tried to stop. The truck wasn't going particularly fast at the time of impact, but even so, there was no way the driver could have done anything to save Rigby. An accident, pure and simple. A very fortunate accident.

"Kind of makes me wonder though why Rigby was so obsessed with the girl. I mean, he could've just as easily set up shop in another state by now," Carrie said, still looking at the grisly sight.

"Why do people let themselves be controlled by drugs, alcohol, porn, or the internet? Why do drug addicts leave their little kids in the car while they go do the unthinkable for their next hit? Honestly, why do people do anything?" Dirk responded to himself as much as Carrie. Making sense out of the nonsensical was hard, even on the easiest of days.

"I suppose that explanation is as good as any. Still, the whole thing is tragic. I wonder if we will ever really know the depths of his crazed mind. Likely not anymore." Carrie turned from the scene and opened her squad car door.

"Should we see if Keith can meet us for a beer after we're done here? Nothing better than to wrap this up with a beer, right?"

"Naw, I think it's been a long enough night. How about some Chinese takeout, showers, and sleep?"

Putting his arm around her, he said with a grin, "Yeah, I suppose I am pretty worn-out myself. I love you, Carrie."

"Damn straight." Carrie said to him with a smile as they walked back to her squad car.

Carrie and Dirk reported to the station the next morning as instructed. Dirk turned over his firearm for ballistics testing, and one of the sergeants took his statement for record. Although at this point, Dirk's statement was moot as the Tenebris chose not to contest the charges against him. Dirk already knew there would be no charges levied against him for shooting Tenebris. He'd acted, somewhat ironically, in defense of Rigby, which was allowable under state's law. Tenebris had a gun, Rigby didn't. The shooting was justified.

During the investigation of Rigby's home, the police found a scrapbook of sorts. A serial killer expert would refer to it eerily as a trophy case. A photo taken of each victim as they were either near death or freshly dead. On a little piece of paper next to the photo he had a swipe of blood from each girl. On the facing page of each victim's photo was a picture of one of the dolls.

Rigby's home also contained several large packages of cocaine. None of them had been opened, but Tenebris would testify that they were essentially to keep him high so Rigby could control him.

Although they already knew about the murders of the girls in the area, the trophy book contained two dozen victims. Most were girls, six of them were boys. The police would eventually run the rest of the

DNA and find the kids matched cases of missing persons or unsolved murders out west. Rigby had been at this for a while and left a long trail of tears.

Tenebris turned out to be the perfect state's witness against Rigby. Although the case was essentially closed as there was no one left to prosecute, there was still his own involvement in the matter. He never denied anything; he never even entered in a non-guilty plea. Through most of the trial, the courtroom only contained the judge, the prosecutor, the court-appointed defense attorney, the court stenographer, Dirk, Keith, and the officers who worked the case.

In the end, the judge gave him ten years in a medium-security prison with a possibility for parole in five, provided the parole included a continued drug treatment program. Tenebris had simply been a pawn in Rigby's scheme. Neither the prosecuting attorney nor the defense gave any objections to the sentencing. The trial was over and done with in the span of two days, with little fanfare. Which was just how Tenebris wanted it.

CHAPTER 31
THE REVERENT DEAD

Two weeks later, Carrie, Dirk, and Keith sat around the office of the motorcycle shop, drinking coffee, eating doughnuts, and generally enjoying each other's company.

A loud knock at the office door pulled the group out of their chat. Keith, being the closest, leaned over and opened it. No one was there. Out of curiosity, Keith stepped out into the garage area. As soon as he did, Victor materialized behind him, rising up from the floor as if on an elevator. He simply floated behind him and waited, a mischievous smile on his ghostly face.

Carrie had to work hard to stifle a giggle.

"Stupid Victor playing games again," Keith said. "You'd think after being dead for so long, you'd come up with some new tricks." Keith turned on his heels to come face to face with the specter himself. Keith jumped back as if someone had kicked him. He let out a frightened yelp.

Dirk was beside himself with laughter. "See, Victor, it's like I'm always saying, less is more!"

"You stupid ghost, why don't you go back to the afterlife where you belong!" Keith yelled. He was angry, but even he had to admit a newfound respect for Victor after he and Heather saved Melissa. Had they not been successful, Rigby likely would have moved on to another victim. "You know what, Victor?" Keith said after regaining his composure, "I'm actually glad to see you."

Dirk furrowed his brow and looked at Victor. "So, Vic, what happens to Rigby now? I mean, he's your problem, in a manner of speaking."

"Oh no, not *my* problem," Victor said, shaking his head. "The afterlife has a special place for people like him. Some people call it purgatory, some call it hell, but I just call it a place I'd really would rather not visit. The guy in charge took a personal interest in Harmon Rigby's disposition. I guess if you believe in Dante's nine rings of hell, this could constitute as number ten."

"Funny, I never thought of the afterlife as being so regimented," Carrie said.

"Well, it's not, if you behave yourself when you're among the living."

With little warning, or more likely because they'd been talking and enjoying the moment too much to notice, there was another loud knock on the shop door. Dirk motioned to Victor, who promptly retreated through a back wall, but Dirk knew he was still listening. Carrie opened the door, and inside the room stepped a five-foot-four-inch nun who looked like she had to be in her mid-seventies.

"Good morning," the small woman said while walking through the door. She scanned the room and gave it a disapproving frown.

Dirk was the first to answer. "Good morning, Sister. I'm Dirk, and this is Keith and Carrie."

From the back of the shop there was a clang. Victor always made some noise when he knew Dirk had failed to introduce him as part of the team. Victor hated being treated like a second-class ghost.

"I'm guessing you're not here with a faulty motorcycle," Dirk added.

"No, my child." She pushed her simple wire-rimmed glasses up on her nose, making her look more like a librarian than a nun for a moment. "I'm most definitely not here about a motorcycle. My name is Sister Mary Sophia, and someone at the police department suggested you could assist me. I'd like your help with a delicate matter." She reached inside her habit, produced a well-worn photograph, and put it on his desk.

The photograph was of four women with their arms around each other. He instantly recognized one of them as Sister Mary Sophia. They were all dressed in shorts and T-shirts with the words "San Miguel Retreat Center" written on the front. Dirk admittedly didn't know much about Catholic nuns but found it odd to see them wearing something other than their habits.

"Are these friends of yours? Sisters from your… group… nunnery… convent?" he asked.

"A group of nuns is an order," Keith offered. "Well, technically it's a superfluity, but no one says that anymore."

"Well, yes they are," she said, leaning in closer to have a better look at Keith. "Don't I know you from somewhere?"

"Yes, Sister. I'm Pastor Keith from the Methodist Church."

Sister Mary Sophia scowled at him from over her glasses. "Figures."

Carrie broke in to save Keith. "So, what seems to be the problem, Sister? Are they dead?"

"Hardly," she said. "I saw them a month ago. They were in as good a health as anyone can expect for women our age."

"Well, then, why do you think you need a private detective?" Dirk asked.

"Because, young man, they're all missing."

Dirk pondered this curious bit of information for a moment. "The police won't help?"

"They checked it out, but the bishop claims he'd never heard of them."

Dirk pushed back from his desk and said, "Well, Sister, I guess you just hired yourself an investigator."

THE END

A Short Story: The Making of Harmon Rigby

It'd been ten torturous months for Doctor Harmon Rigby. By all accounts, they should have been his happiest. He was married and had a thriving practice. At least, he was thinking it should've been perfect as he sat by Juliana's bedside, watching her being eaten up by cancer.

Even holding her hand, he could still see the beautiful woman who was his sweetheart and soul mate. The cold, frail hand he cupped still had the mark from her wedding ring, which she now wore around her neck. Her finger was too thin for a ring. Her face, sunken and jaundiced, was still the image of his high school sweetheart.

She was in terrible pain, so much so that the morphine they gave her made her incoherent at times. He savored her lucid moments where they talked. He tried to be gentle and soothing, telling her lies about what they would do what she got out of the hospital. He wove elaborate tales of walks on the beach, vacations up the coast, and the family they would never have as her life span had slipped from months to days to hours

He recounted tales, often to the unconscious skeleton he loved, of the wonderful times they'd had. Her hair flying in the wind as their thirty-three-foot sailboat plied the waters off the west coast. They lived on their boat during the summers as much as possible and in the winter planned out their next great sea adventures.

Now his lovely, sexual soulmate lay there, waiting for the end. Juliana was down to a frail eighty pounds and had lost the ability to move. She moaned on occasion, reacting to unseen pain welling up inside of her as it overtook the morphine. His love remained as strong as ever.

Harmon thought about their plans. They were going to sail the seven seas. They wanted to have a few kids and raise them in the good Christian faith they both held dear. So many of their schemes were first put on hold due to her temporary sickness and then squashed like rotten fruit under the foot of cancer.

Forty-three minutes after the doctor made his final visit, Mrs. Juliana Rigby breathed her last.

At that moment, only Harmon and the corpse of his newly deceased wife remained in the room. He supported her hand in the quiet solitude that was the hospice ward.

Nurses finally came around to move the body and encouraged him to leave them to their work. He released her hand, kissed her lips, and exited the room. Not knowing what to do, Harmon drove for hours around town. No idea where he was going, he just drove through streets endlessly. The constant movement kept some part of his brain grounded in reality as the rest of his mind entertained terrifying thoughts of a world without his beloved. Even more dark considerations about what he might do now that his reason for living was no more.

Knowing your own death was imminent was both a blessing and a curse. Juliana had been able to help make the arrangements. She picked out the flowers, selected a simple viewing casket, and chose the musical for the funeral. The whole affair was to take place a week from the day she died. Harmon had little to do except wait for the wheels of her final wishes to take traction.

At three in the morning, Harmon pulled into the only place he could think to go. He wasn't ready to go home to his empty house. The walls and rooms were so vibrant and full of life. Everything was likely to remind him of her. He parked his car into the parking lot with a sign over it that read "Reserved for Dr. Harmon Rigby".

Minutes later, he was in his office. He switched on a small light on his desk. Harmon reached into his desk drawer and pulled out a bottle of scotch he'd been given at a birthday party. He never liked the stuff, but it would help him take his mind off the corpse of his wife lying flat on a table somewhere in the hospice morgue. The idea of them sliding her body into a refrigerator like a bell pepper or a piece of cheese was too much for him to bear. And still there was a part of him that would crawl into that space with her if only to feel her skin on his for a few more precious moments.

Although the liquor numbed the pain, it lingered under the hazy layer of scotch. Being that he didn't normally drink, the liquor went straight to his head. He poured another and was about to take a drink when he could have sworn he heard something move.

The noise sounded like shuffling, coming from the corner of the room. He glared around, expecting to find the source of the noise. At this hour there was no one else in the building but him. He felt foolish for his paranoia.

"Harmon, don't do that," a male voice implored. "No, not good at all. You are going to hurt yourself."

Harmon jumped up from the desk and went to his office door. He looked out into an empty hallway. "Anyone there?" he yelled.

Not a whisper returned in response. His voice echoed across the hallways and into the spaces of his veterinary hospital. He returned to his desk and fell back into his chair, picking up the glass as he did. Examining the world through the liquid, he could see, hanging from the coat rack, a marionette he'd bought from a street vendor in one of the border towns in Mexico.

The puppet was a silly-looking thing. It had molded plastic pistols in its hands and was dressed like a member of a mariachi band. It even had a ridiculous sombrero with the word Mexico stitched into it. It had made his wife laugh so hard that he bought it. He was continually reminded of her effervescent laugh.

He put the glass to his lips.

"Wait, Harmon, if you drink too much, you'll wake up with a headache, and I'd really much rather talk to you." The voice came again from somewhere and nowhere.

"Okay, what the hell is going on here?" Harmon slurred. "Is this some kind of joke, because I'm really not in the mood for fucking jokes." He gave the room another once-over, convinced whoever was speaking to him was inside the space with him.

He stood up and paced the office, examining his bookshelves and file drawers, spilling scotch on the floor as he walked. He looked for wires, speakers, anything someone could be using to talk to him. He'd been in this office for years, and he'd know if even a dust bunny was out of place.

"I promise you, this is no joke, Harmon," the voice repeated pleadingly. "I understand your pain."

Harmon fell back into his chair and took a big drink of the scotch. "Oh yeah, what do you know about my fucking pain?"

"Losing your wife was hard. She is a light and wonderful person, is she not?" the voice continued. "A being of pure energy. Divine in many ways, she's nothing short of an angel."

"You mean, she was a wonderful person." Tears streamed down his face anew.

"You are so sure of yourself, aren't you? Sitting there with the glass in your hand, convinced it'll take away your pain or maybe dull it enough so you can go on. Convinced your wife has passed on into the great beyond. You don't understand the great currency of the human soul. Yes, she is gone, but it doesn't mean you have to give up on her life. You need something more— a task. But not now, Harmon. Time enough after you have slept."

As the voice said this, Harmon's eyelids dropped over the convex of his eyes. He succumbed to the scotch, emotional exhaustion, and the sheer physical outlay grief required of those left to live. He dreamed of his wife, their world, of fire and pain, of suffering and redemption. In a dream, he saw himself pulling the souls of others across a great divide into an unknown world.

"Doctor Rigby?" a voice said. "Doctor Rigby, are you alright?"

Harmon's eyes opened to a woman dressed in scrubs standing in front of him. His faithful tech Mia placed a cool hand on his skin as she tried to shake him awake.

"I'm up … I'm up … Mia … I'm okay," Harmon wiped the drool from his face, and he sat up in his chair. He looked for the bottle of scotch, but the noxious liquid was strangely missing from the desk where he left it the night before. The glass was empty however, reminding him how he'd gotten his terrific headache.

"Oh sweetie, I heard about Juliana last night," Mia said, leaning on the desk. "I tried to call you afterward, but your phone went to voice mail."

"Yeah, I turned the phone off," Harmon said, straightening himself up. "I wasn't really in a talking mood last night. I drove, I ended up here and then I had a drink."

"Or five, by the looks of you," Mia added. "Not judging, I would've done the same thing, I'm sure."

He rubbed his aching head. "Hey Mia, can you cancel my appointments for today and have every priority sent over to Dr. Ridgeway?"

Dear, sweet Mia. Juliana called her his "work wife". She was indispensable to him and the clinic. The practice ran on her schedule as she was the lab tech, file clerk, accountant, and a bunch of other things Harmon was only partially aware of. She had become a fixture in their home over the years they had known her. Juliana always said Mia was a soul of pure light. Harmon was so thankful for her.

"Already done, honey," Mia said, still holding Harmon's hand. "I'll take you home. You don't need to be here."

"Mia, we don't have an intercom in this building or anything, do we?"

"No, none I'm aware of. Why?"

"Forget it, I had a weird dream last night," Harmon said as he shut off the light. The rush of wind from the closing door made the feet and hands of the dangling marionette swing back and forth, as if dancing.

Harmon stayed home one day to rest and recuperate. He called Juliana's family to give them the details. They offered to come stay with him, but he said he was fine. He returned to work four days after her death, convinced the routine would help him center himself. He needed some structure, some normalcy.

In the afternoon, after Mia had gone home for the day, he sat in his office transcribing some notes to his records.

"Harmon, I'm so glad to see you're not drinking scotch," a voice said.

The sound gave Harmon a start. He shot up from his chair and ran to look into the hallway. "What the hell?" He walked down the hallway, convinced someone was playing a sick joke on him. He had written off the events of the other night as a combination of scotch, stress, and exhaustion. "I must be losing my mind."

"No, you're not, Harmon," the voice continued. "I know this is a little upsetting to you. Why don't you sit down and let me explain?" The voice seemed as if it were right there in the room with him.

He wanted to run. There was a part of him screaming, "Don't listen." But there was another part longing to understand what the voice knew of his wife. The fear of watching his wife die and the grief of actually losing her overwhelmed him. At the moment, he found it impossible to resist the voice. He was too tired for rational thought. He'd given too much for too long to too many.

"Harmon, do you love your wife?" the voice asked.

"Love?" Harmon responded. "I think you mean loved. She died. I was there. I felt her slip away from me, and I watched her decay right in front of my eyes."

The voice let out a heavy sigh. "I think you will find that, when you look into it, you have a stunted idea of death. The body is merely a vessel for the soul, isn't it? Think back to your schooling. God puts the soul in the body, and you can give it away, can't you?"

Harmon was a veterinarian but also was a part-time pastor at his church. Raised in the Presbyterian tradition, he knew the Bible well. He'd been ordained and served as a supply minister in several churches when called upon. "But the soul belongs to God and only God."

"Well then," the voice retorted. "People give their souls to the devil, which would suggest your Christian teaching has lied to you in a sense. Think about it. Did any amount of praying save your wife? How about when an overtaxed, depressed mother drives her car full of her kids into a lake? Did God save them? How about the terrorist attack outside the cathedral last year? Where was God then, Harmon?"

"God doesn't prevent evil." Harmon resisted the voice's idea.

"My poor deluded friend. You're not seeing the point here. God could've done something, He could've intervened, but He chose not to. Why is it that an all-powerful, omnipotent God can create a world but can't save one child, one wife, from cancer?"

"But it was his will... her death was..." Harmon tried to think through what the voice was telling him. Every time he latched onto a clear thought or precept he'd been taught, he lost it. The voice asked good questions. Why was it God took his wife? Why was it he was made to suffer?

As if kicked, he got up from his desk and ran out the door, down the stairs, and into the early evening air. He needed some space to think, some fresh air to clear his head. He slowed himself to a brisk walk and after ten minutes, found his way into a small playground. A few some kids played as the streetlights snapped to life.

An older boy and girl, Harmon guessed they were twins, and a little girl, who was likely their sister, giggled on the swings and slides. The way the two older kids watched after their charge was touching. They were perfect siblings, loving even. The three enjoyed each other's company, even if they did occasionally tease or yell at each other the way siblings do.

The boy glanced at his watch and told the others they had to go home. The three walked away holding hands. Something about it made Harmon angry. He wasn't bothered by their happiness, but he was bothered because he realized this kind of joy he'd never taste. His wife had died, and with her had died his chances of having children like these. God had robbed him of that. The anger grew inside of him.

"Now you're getting it, Harmon, God robbed you of your shot," the voice suddenly said. "But it's not too late. You have the chance to feel that kind of joy, but it's going to take some work on your part."

"But what do I do?" Harmon asked.

"Don't speak, just listen," the voice commanded. "You don't want people to see you sitting on a park bench talking to yourself, do you? They'll think you're crazy. You're a smart man, a veterinarian and a reverend, and those things take brains. And now, you have me. Unlike others, Harmon, God can't take me away. I will always be with you.

"Go back to your office. I want to show you something. I need to make sure you understand what comes next for you, Harmon. I can bring you happiness, but you must do a few things for me. And when we're done, we'll create something divine and incorruptible. God himself wouldn't destroy our plans because he would see how perfect they really are."

"But mortals aren't supposed to build the divine. We are to strive to be like the divine even though we are incapable of getting there," Harmon said, covering his mouth to keep from looking like he was actually talking to himself.

"They want you to think that so you won't try. Regular churches don't appreciate that kind of competition. I'll bet Jesus himself gets lonely talking to no one as his equal. Let's raise you up, and at your right hand will sit your wife in her glory. You two together, forever."

Harmon walked back to his office. Thoughts of one day possibly being with his wife again propelled him. Something about what the voice said had soothed his troubled spirit. In his grief, he feared being alone and was beginning to see that maybe it didn't have to be that way.

On the one hand, it sounded completely irrational to think he could see the face of his wife again, not the cold sunken face of a stage four cancer victim but as she had been, alive and vibrant.

Walking into this office, he fell into the couch sitting along the wall. He sat there in total silence, waiting for something to happen. He began to doubt his own sanity as the minutes ticked by. He was about to get up when the silence was violated.

"Alright, Harmon, first off, I want you to know I'm your friend." The voice spoke kindly in a soothing tone. "I've watched you from afar for a while now. Your feelings, your heart, your mind, and needs. I see everything you do. Come with me, and we can take our journey together."

"I don't understand," Harmon pleaded. "Where are we going?"

"We're not physically *going* anywhere. This is a journey of the mind and soul. I promise you this: once we begin this trip together, we'll never be alone again. Once we have done the work, we will find your wife's soul and bring her into our collective. A collective we will build and all be together. Doesn't that sound lovely?"

"But who are you? I can't even see you," Harmon said, glancing around the room.

"Oh, but Harmon, you can. Look with your heart, not your eyes. Forget what you think is reality," the voice instructed.

Harmon got up and walked around the bookshelves and walls. He examined every corner of the room. Everything looked like it had always been. Books, the chair, the couch, the marionette all appeared the same to him as before. That was when he saw it. The marionette had moved. The stirring was slight. Julianna's marionette, hanging from its strings, was stretching one pistol-holding hand toward him. It'd been there, all along, a friend, just watching, perhaps waiting, for the perfect moment to reveal itself.

"You," Harmon said, grabbing the marionette from where it hung. "You've been watching me all this time. But what is your name? Please tell me."

"That's right, Harmon," the doll said. "I'm called Mr. Sanchez, and I'm here to tell you that you've been ordained by God for greatness. You'll help bring about a change in the way the world looks at God. In the process, you'll be reunited with your wife. It's a mission, a calling if you will. To start, we need a soul. One that is pure of heart and sanctified, perfect in every way. I'll show you what to do. You shall bring the first soul to me."

"I'll do it," Harmon said, holding the doll in his lap. It felt like a sudden weight was lifted off his shoulders. He realized what Jonah must have felt like when he accepted his orders to go to the doomed city of Nineveh. He knew his wife was not dead, merely asleep and waiting for him to bring her back. And Mr. Sanchez, his angel from on high, was handing him the secret to make it happen. "I'll accept this mission from God. Just tell me what to do. I'll do anything you command to see my Juliana again."

"Good, I'm glad to hear that. It won't be easy, but we'll make the world a better place. We need to start simple, with someone pure of heart. Someone you already know."

Harmon instinctively reached for his desk phone and dialed a number, "Hello, it's Harmon … no, nothing's wrong. I was wondering if you can help me this weekend. I've something I need to do, and you're the perfect soul to lend a hand. Can you come over about two o'clock on Saturday? Yes, oh fantastic. Great, see you then. Thanks, Mia."

THE END

ACKNOWLEDGEMENTS

Once again, I have to thank tons of people for their love and support during this process. Of course, *The Dramatic Dead,* would have not even seen the first keystroke if it were not for my wife for her love and understanding as I type away furiously, night after night, and talk about the project until I'm sure she's wanted to beat me to death with an old shoe or a whiffle ball bat. I also have to thank my children for putting up with the odd author's life I lead. They are my family and come with me on this journey, sometimes reluctantly.

As you may or may not know, this is a re-write of the original book. I am normally completely against re-writing novels, but this one was personal for me since there were always things I really wanted to smooth out and shine up. A special thanks to all who have read the original work.

I need to thank my editor, who beats me about the head and shoulders (metaphorically of course) to make me a better writer. Honestly, she is amazing to work with and I consider myself super lucky.

And finally, I need to thank *Charles* and *Jim,* of my Patreon crew! You guys are the best and your support made this all happen!

Did you Enjoy This Book? Please leave a review!
Also by author Bryan Nowak

Horror:
Riapoke
Crimson Tassels
Code Name: Formula 12 (also available on Audible)
The App

Mystery:
The Dramatic Dead (Book 1)
The Reverent Dead (Book 2)
*The Nameless Dead **Fall/Winter 2023** (Book 3)*

Dean Cordaine: The Diamond Studded Legs Matter
Dean Cordaine: The Fallen Oath Matter

Science Fiction:
The Bagorian Chronicles (Book 1)
Usurper's Throne (Book 2)

Made in the USA
Middletown, DE
02 June 2023

31671317R00176